The Fruit of Stone

ALSO BY MARK SPRAGG

Where Rivers Change Direction

The Fruit of Stone

Mark Spragg

Riverhead Books *a member of Penguin Putnam Inc.* New York 2002

Riverhead Books
a member of
Penguin Putnam Inc.
375 Hudson Street
New York, NY 10014

Epigraph on page ix from *The Branch Will Not Break,*
© 1983 by James Wright and reprinted by kind permission
of Wesleyan University Press.

Library of Congress Cataloging-in-Publication Data

Spragg, Mark, date.
    The fruit of stone / Mark Spragg.
        p.   cm.
    ISBN 1-57322-223-2
        I. Title
PS3619.P73F78   2002   2002016941
813'.6—dc21

Printed in the United States of America
10   9   8   7   6   5   4   3   2   1

This book is printed on acid-free paper. ∞

Book design by Marysarah Quinn

For Virginia,

because of Virginia,

always,

and

for my brother,

Richard,

and

for Dorothy Banks,

who gave a boy a gift of words,

my love

I feel the seasons changing beneath me,
Under the floor.
She is braiding the waters of air into the plaited manes
Of happy colts.
They canter, without making a sound, along the shores
Of melting snow.

—James Wright, from "Mary Bly"

The Fruit of Stone

Chapter One

✳

Birdsong strikes up and musters in the first soft press of dawn. Starlings, sparrows, magpies, meadowlarks, blackbirds. There is the flush and shuffle of feathers. Throat tunings. The hollowing chitter of beaks. Bursts of flight. Wrens, flycatchers, cowbirds, crows. Complaint. Exultation. They work the meadow grass, the cottonwoods along the creek, the open barnloft, alive in tilting sweeps of hand-size shadows. The raptors float silently a thousand feet above, turning, spiraling atop the early-morning thermals, hunting the edge of the ebbing night.

A downdraft masses cool and heavy against the escarpment of the Front Range and totters and slides from the warming sky. It thrums against the sides of the stocktank, the outbuildings, the house; ripples the surface of the pond below the barn. It swings the pasture grasses east, lifts the boughs of a Douglas fir beside the house, scatters in bursts of cottonwood and aspen leaf. It smells of dew, juniper, sage, pine, horseshit, and stone. It chills McEban's exposed shoulders, his arms; pricks him away from sleep. He turns in his bed. He drifts. He is, for this brief moment, without memory, without longing. Simply one of God's naked creatures, accepting of the seasons.

The wasp-yellow curtains quake at the window, reflect as light beige. The bedroom furniture stands in subdued angles of gray and darker grays. Gretchen's dress, cornflower blue, draped over the ladder-back of an oak chair, catches in a predawn shade of snow-shadow. Her plain cotton bra and panties lie wadded on the seat of the chair, dull as weathered vertebra.

McEban doubles a pillow under the side of his head and relaxes into it, and hooks the hem of the sheet with a forefinger, and draws it gently back from her. He feels the flash of her body's heat against his own and lies blinking in the half-light, remembering that he has known this woman all of her life. Forty years and change, he thinks. He remembers they were children together, and that he loved her when she was a girl, and later, and that he loves her now.

He looks into a corner of the room, at their reflections caught in the freestanding mirror. There is the curve of her spine, lambent; flawless as a small burl of cumulus. She flexes and turns, and her reflection turns onto its back, its legs and arms splayed, settling. McEban looks away from the mirror. He looks again at the woman beside him.

Her arms are sun-stained to her shoulders, and her legs to her knees, and her face flecked with freckles. The rest of her runs milky, gone translucent in places, and at those places puzzled faintly with bluish veins—at her throat, the sides of her breasts, the smooth slope of flesh that draws low across her hips into the nappy wedge of auburn hair.

She moans lowly and moves her head from side to side and her long hair pools to the sides of her neck, spills across her shoulders, across the pillow, across the sheet, appears artesian. He cups a palmful of the hair to his nose and inhales. He has prayed to have this woman in his arms, and feels full of the power of his prayers. Her hair smells sweet as blood.

He is afraid to look again into the mirror. He is afraid of what he might see. It is his belief that his family's ghosts watch and record his transgressions. He imagines them as judgmental, with notebooks—as scouts for a prudish God. And then he thinks of Bennett. He thinks of the three of them—Gretchen and Bennett, and himself.

He thinks that Bennett does not believe in an afterlife, in witnesses, doesn't give a shit for the quick or the dead. He thinks he has never heard Bennett speak of his dreams. He has, in fact, heard the man state aloud that dreams are for the unfocused. He knows Bennett's trust lies in a world he can kick. A world that kicks back. And Bennett is his best friend, and Gretchen is Bennett's wife. He thinks there is no way for that not to be a blow. In the real world, for a focused man.

He looks again at Gretchen, to the woman who is his best friend's wife, lying here, beside him, in this house where he was a boy.

He'd heard her park in the drive and recognized the sound of the truck and did not believe it. He'd wondered if he was dreaming. It was after midnight, and there was just a paring of moon, Venus unclouded and lamping, fallen to the west of the moon, fallen down the vault of blue-black sky.

He heard her in the hallway, recognized her steps, heard her undressing at the foot of his bed, the sound of her breath, and still did not believe it. Even when she was beside him in his bed he did not trust the scent of her, the feel of her skin against his own.

"Who is this?" he asked.

"It's me."

"I don't believe you," he said. "This is just a dream."

She pressed herself harder against the length of him. She kissed him. She cupped his hand over her breast. "Does this feel like a dream?"

"Yes," he said. "It feels like my dream."

He reaches out in the soft morning light and rests his hand gently on her abdomen. Just his hand. The hand rises and falls. She fidgets slightly against its weight. Her eyes flick under their lids. Her lips part as if to speak.

He remembers her younger. Before the gray got a start in her hair. Before gravity pulled half a lifetime of living through her flesh. He can't help himself. She bends her left leg at its knee and settles the foot against the inside of her right calf, her thighs opening, and he remembers her at seventeen, in his arms. He feels the weight of wanting her all the time between. Twenty-three years, he thinks. The bulk of his life.

He remembers her standing in a falling light, spring light, unsteady on her bare feet. He remembers her kneeling on the uneven ground. She knelt on a blanket. He remembers her raking her hands back through her thick hair, drawing it into a ponytail. There was the sound of the creek. There was a hatch of mayflies. The air was gauzy with pollen and insect wings, the sun halved by the horizon, nearly set. Her breasts rose with her arms, cast cups of shadow, and her red hair ignited. That is what the slant of sunlight did in her red hair. He wondered that her hands did not burn.

He concentrates on their breathing, and the effort allows him a sense of fragile union. He concentrates on his breath, and hers, and doesn't wonder if he is wrong in the world. He doesn't worry that the walls are shelved with the eyes of the curious and judgmental dead. He feels boyish, sweet-natured, innocent, even lucky. That is the way he's feeling when she comes awake.

She smiles and looks at his hand, where it rests on her belly. She lifts his hand and turns it and kisses its palm. She swings her legs over the side of the bed and sits. She shakes her head, and her hair lifts and falls at her shoulders. She still holds his hand.

"Did you sleep?" she asks.

He nods.

She turns to see him nodding and smiles again. "I didn't plan this."

He stares at her.

"Honestly," she says.

"I wish you had."

"But I didn't. It just happened."

The sun breaks the horizon and slaps the room alive and stark. The reds, greens, blues, yellows throb. She stands in the glaring light, and he reaches out to her. He looks up the length of his mottled arm, to the soiled fingers, the broken nails, the stubble of worn hairs spiking the lengths of the fingers. He means to ask some question, something hopeful, but his mind is struck blank by a plain and primitive gratitude.

He pulls in his arm and bends his knees. He rolls against his hip and sits on the opposite side of the bed.

Insect chorus spikes through the morning birdsong, and he knows the nightchill has settled in the trees along the creek, in the ditches, and, thinly, where the ground falls low.

He watches her stand from the bed and step her long legs into her underpants, hook her bra at her waist, turn it, shrug into its cool lace, run her thumbs under its straps. She drops her dress over her head and pulls it away from her belly and hips, and it settles and hangs in the morning light. She takes up her canvas bookbag from the back of the chair and ducks through its single strap and adjusts the strap between her breasts.

He knows the bookbag holds field guides for flowers, birds, trees. At least one novel. No doubt two, perhaps three, books of poetry. And Milton. She doesn't go out of the house without Milton.

Woody yips and bounces on his front legs, and they look at him. He blocks the bedroom doorway and is anxious for his day's labor. His tongue lolls from his muzzle, his brindled body bleeding out of definition in the still-dark hallway.

Gretchen squats at the dog's head and rubs his shoulders, works the length of his ribs. His eyes go soft with pleasure. He forgets he is ugly and common and owned to work cows.

"I love you," she says. Her hands are deep in the dog's ruff, and she muscles him back and forth over his shoulders, and he mouths at her wrists.

"I love you more," McEban says. He has not stood from the edge of the bed.

She looks over her shoulder. "It's not a contest," she says.

"It feels like it is."

She stands away from the dog. She leans into the doorjamb. "You love me more than I love you, or more than Bennett loves me?"

"Both," he says. He knows he is capable of saying anything. He knows a prayer has been answered and a vacancy made in his desires. He has no control over what may be sucked into the void.

"You remember what it was like before?" he asks.

"Before what?"

"The time before last night. When we were kids."

"That was a lifetime ago," she says.

"It doesn't seem that way to me."

She adjusts the bookbag against her hip.

"I remember the light," he says. He looks up at her.

She squares herself in the doorway. She doesn't look away. "I can't remember whether it was day or night. Not even the time of year." She still doesn't look away. She means to hold him there, in front of her, without the escape of memory.

He nods and looks down to where his hands cap his knees. "You want me to pick you up for the auction?" he asks.

"Yes, I do."

"Tomorrow?"

"Yes."

"I thought you might've changed your mind."

"How would Bennett get home?" she asks. "If I changed my mind?"

She turns away and he hears her in the shaded hallway and the dog's toenails on the floorboards at her heels. He hears the screendoor slam, and the dog barking once from the kitchen, and then again.

He walks to the window and squints into the glare. He watches her drive across the plank bridge, the boards thumping against their loose spikes. He watches her on the dirt section road, the rise of the red talc behind her. The wind has hushed, and the dust swells to the roadside and powders the borrow ditches rusty.

"It was the first of June," he says. "It was the very last part of the day."

He sat at the kitchen table with his mother and grandmother. His heels were hooked on the front rung of his chair, and his knees pressed against the underside of the table. He was eight. It was 1968. He does not remember that they spoke. There was the tinny clink of silverware. The burble of the electric coffeepot on the counter. He was waiting for the day to happen to him. He was working his way to the bottom of a bowl of creamed wheat.

He heard his father in the hallway and looked up from his breakfast and smiled at the man. His father was in a hurry. He didn't smile back. He moved to them, and passed without so much as a nod. He held a pistol at his side, low against his thigh. He kicked through the screendoor and marched to the center of the yard and stopped. He gripped the gun in both hands. He raised it slightly away from his waist and took a deep breath and emptied all six chambers into the ground between his feet. Boom, boom, boom. Boom, boom, boom. Just like that.

The boy's mother and grandmother winced at each round's report but did not move from the table. They put down their silverware and stared into their plates. The world stood quieter than it had. For a single long moment he could remember no sound at all.

He unhooked his heels and slid from the chair and stood at the screendoor.

The red-and-white Hereford cows along the fence had bolted away into the irrigated pasture. Sprays of hoofstruck water rose and hung in the air about them. They bunched at the pasture's north corner, milling, their calves bawling and nuzzling their mothers' bags. A row of red-winged blackbirds lifted from an electrical line and flapped in the air, then settled farther downwind in a stand of cottonwood.

"Your father cannot tolerate crabgrass," his mother said.

He looked over his shoulder to his mother. He still stood at the screendoor. She began to giggle and couldn't stop.

His grandmother scowled and pushed her glasses up the bridge of her nose. "Crabgrass?" she asked.

"Gardening," his mother said. She had stopped laughing. She stood and carried her dishes to the sink, and pressed her fingers to her temples and turned. Her pupils had come large in her eyes. "Migraine," she announced. She could as well have said, "Sunrise."

His grandmother snorted and took up her spoon and scraped at the rind of her truck-ripened grapefruit. They heard the back door open and close and his mother settle into her chair on the back porch.

"My ancient ass," his grandmother whispered, but she wasn't trying to be quiet.

It was as though there had been an argument, and now the argument was done.

His father stood on the lawn. He stared at the ground. He was dressed in his single suit. A wool serge, dark blue, the trousers worn pale at the knees and seat, the jacket at the elbows. The suit had been McEban's grandfather's. It had come with the ranch. Handed down like work and debt and weather. He'd seen his father wear the thing to funerals, and weddings, and on these occasional acts of emotional disobedience.

His father took a step toward the barn, shook his head, and thrust the pistol into the waistband of his trousers. He blinked into the cloudless sky and turned and looked back at the house.

McEban stepped away from the screen to let him in and the man poured a mug of coffee and leaned against the counter and sipped the coffee. His hat was tipped back from his face. The face appeared drawn. It was unshaven. The belly of his shirt bunched above the pistol's wooden grip.

"You about done with your breakfast?" he asked.

"Yes, sir," McEban told him.

"You get all the way done I'll want your help. We need to move those bulls in with the cows."

"He's helping me today," his grandmother said.

His father turned and stared plainly at her.

"For how long?" he asked.

"For as long as I need him," she said. "There's a garden to put up. And I bought flats of fruit at the IGA. They'll spoil."

His father nodded and sucked at his teeth.

"I better get out of these clothes," he said.

He paused by her as he passed. He kissed the top of her head, and when he was out of the room the old woman said, "He gets his good manners from your grandfather."

She crimped the halved grapefruit rind in her fist, held it above her upturned face, squeezed the last of its sour juice into her open mouth.

She gripped the sides of her chair and stepped it back from the table. Right side, left side, right, hefting and releasing separately the weight of each considerable buttock. She stacked their breakfast dishes and carried them to the sink. McEban stood by his chair. His bladder ached and his ears rang.

"You learn anything useful this morning?" she asked.

He looked up at her, pinched his nose, and blew hard to clear his ears. "I learned to stay out of the yard when Dad's dressed up."

His grandmother smiled and then began to chuckle. The sleeves of her housecoat were pushed past her elbows. Her forearms and hands were shiny with dishwater. Her cheeks were flushed.

"That suit's going to fit you someday, too," she said.

McEban's bad foot throbs and his gut rumbles, and he thinks he might suffer the shits. He feels hungry, but not ready for his breakfast.

He bends at the kitchen sink and sucks water from his cupped hands and straightens and stretches both arms above his head. The water runs back along his forearms, and there is the soft staccato pop of the cartilage in his shoulders and lower back. His shirt hangs open, unsnapped, and he grips at the slight roll of fat that rides over a kidney, and fingers the glazed line of scar tissue that loops high across the hip.

He works his thumb against the fingerpads of a hand and counts. Eight broken ribs. A split pelvis, twice. Both knees shot. Five teeth knocked out. A broken collarbone. Right wrist. Left arm. An ankle. A clubbed foot. He doesn't count the stitches. He knows he's taken enough stitches to make a quilt.

He tries to remember any single horse wreck, and only one comes clear. He can recall a tractor wreck, and a goring. He remembers the half-blind bull that got him down in the loading ramp, and he remembers that his father turned the bull into hamburger. The revenge of carnivores, he thinks.

He runs his tongue against the capped teeth at the front of his mouth and thinks about replacement parts. "Jesus Christ," he says aloud. He looks down at the dog. "It's no goddamn wonder I live alone. I'm either working or in intensive care."

He turns on the radio over the sink and leans into the counter and listens to the ag report, and then the local birthday and anniversary club, and when he turns the radio off imagines he hears footsteps in the hallway. He looks into it and there is no one, and he knows that he wants someone there. Or on the porch. Flushing a toilet. Coughing. An old woman would do, he thinks. A boy would do nicely. He thinks of the sound of a boy in the house, and he thinks of the half-dozen women he's dated in the last twenty years. He thinks that none of them was Gretchen.

He pictures the women standing together, grouped for a photograph. Phyllis, Gwen, and Rachel he puts to the front. They are short, stout women, their hips and thighs stuccoed with cellulite. Arlene, Dolly, and Joyce stand behind them. Thinner, quick-tempered. Arlene has pale, thyroid-enlarged eyes. All six present themselves hunched, their shoulders dropped down and over their breasts. "Heart-shrunken," he says aloud, but thinks they could have given him children. Any one of them. He looks down at Woody. "What about that?" he asks, and the dog cocks his head. "We're probably both too old to start now," he says, but knows he is only making conversation with a neutered dog.

He spreads honey and peanut butter on separate slices of white bread and presses them into a sandwich. He carries the sandwich to the mudroom and sits on a plank bench. He bites into the bread to free his hands and pulls on a pair of calf-high irrigation boots over his leather workboots. He stares out at the brown and overgrown square of front yard and reminds himself, as he does each morning, to buy a length of garden hose and a sprinkler when he's next in town. He stands and lets Woody out through the screen and steps back into the kitchen and takes the receiver from the wallphone. He dials Wyoming Information.

When the operator comes on he asks for the number of the Holiday Inn in Cody, and while the number is ringing he sits at the kitchen table.

"Holiday Inn," a voice answers. It is a young woman's voice.

"Bennett Reilly," he says, but he can hardly hear himself say the name.

"Excuse me, sir?"

He clears his throat. He lays his breakfast sandwich on the table. "Mr. Bennett Reilly," he repeats. Louder this time.

He listens to the buzz on the line, the patter of the receptionist's fingers on her keyboard.

"There is no Mr. Reilly," she says.

McEban spells out the name. First name and last. "He's a real-estate broker," he says. "He's there for a convention. You have a convention of real-estate brokers, don't you?"

"Yes, sir."

"Would you have another look?"

"There's nothing under Reilly."

He thumbs his sandwich open and pats it shut. "Try Alan Patrick," he says.

"Patrick?"

"They work together. Alan drove them over."

"There's a Mr. Patrick," she tells him. "I'll put you through."

He listens to the phone ring and looks at the wall clock, and it reads 6:12, and Bennett comes on the line after four rings and coughs and sucks at a noseful of snot and says, "Excuse me," and blows his nose, and then, "Hello," and then again, "Hello."

McEban listens to each word and after a pause realizes he's holding his breath.

"You're a prick, whoever you are," Bennett says, and the line goes dead, and McEban stands and hangs up the receiver and leans against the wall and stares into the grayed mesh of the screen.

When the dog whines he steps through the mudroom, swings the door open, hears it slap at his back. He stands unsteadily in the yard.

A gust of water-cooled breeze bursts up from the stockpond, and he leans forward and rests his palms against his thighs and inhales deeply through his nose. His gut fills and paunches with the damp morning air. He exhales the breath in a guttural cough, snapping his belly up tight. Air in, air out. Ten rounds of breath and he has completed nine months, and now one day, of this ritual huffing. Nine months and two days without a cigarette. He straightens, breathes evenly, totters forward a step. His eyes water. His skull feels brittle, nearly weightless.

Woody strikes out across the drive, snuffling in arcs, and McEban follows. They work through the yarrow, paintbrush, and sage and top a low rise opposite the house. The sun is hard and new. It deepens the red in the iron soil under their feet.

It is on this hill, in this red soil, that the bones of his family lie: the bodies of his father, his brother, his grandmother and his grandfather. He looks down at his hands. He flexes his hands. He thinks of his family's hands. He's been told he has his father's hands. The hands of Jock McEban. He sees his father standing behind those hands. A big man, sledge-muscled, blond and watery-eyed. A man of duty. A man who put his shoulder against the life God gave him and went to work. A man who should not have looked up from his work.

McEban turns and sits back against his father's marker and stretches his legs out straight. He flicks a woodtick from his thigh. He raises his hands before his face. The hands are long-fingered, thick, yellowed in callus, cracked, and now sunstruck. Hands meant for the land, he thinks, for animals. A waste on women, no doubt, short or tall.

He drops his right hand to the smallest stone marker. He traces the name chiseled there. He doesn't have to look. Bailey McEban is the name his fingers read. He closes his eyes and searches for some memory of his brother. His twin. They must have looked alike, but there are no photographs, and now he is all that's left. He thinks of Bailey; of the infant boy found dead at just fourteen months. He wonders if he was there, in the crib beside his brother, perhaps asleep when the body was found. He has never thought to ask.

He wonders about his brother's voice. He cocks his head. He listens. He believes his brother has told him something he cannot remember. He pictures Bailey's round mouth forming its first soft words. Perhaps his brother's ghost means to say it again, he thinks. Aloud. He listens harder.

The Bighorns rise beyond the ranch to the west. Their palisades of limestone and granite shimmer, opalescent in the dawn, reflective as thousand-foot stands of pearled glare. The mountains entire—rolling north and south—shouldered into patches of apple-jade meadow, their expanse come morning-bright, descending in waves of green pine, green fir, green aspen, gone to tar and emerald in the deep collapse of their separate drainages. Owl Creek to the south. Trail Creek farther south. Cabin Creek just north. And behind the ranch, the north and south forks of Horse Creek.

He shifts against his father's tombstone and wishes he'd thought to bring his grandfather's binoculars. They hang from a peg in the mudroom and weigh nearly as much as a hand sledge, but they bring the mountains up close in hazy circles.

McEban likes to scan the high meadows for the copper-colored smudges he knows to be his Hereford cows and calves grazing down their summer pasture. They are the evidence of his family's history. Red meat. Animals. New calves sprung from the semen of bulls that are themselves the big, rust-and-white-splotched children of bulls McEban's father had raised.

This is my place in the world, he thinks. Horse Creek. The hay meadows that it irrigates. Two sections of deeded wildgrass and sage and rock. Forest Service grazing leases. Timber and stone drawn up and fashioned into homestead, barn, springhouse: the dozen buildings it's taken for a family to winter and summer against the Wyoming sun, the seasonal choirs of wind.

He drops his head back and blinks into the blue wash of sky. He tries to imagine himself a different man. It is a game he played against the long days of his boyhood. As a boy he could imagine himself anywhere. McEban of Paris, London, Lima. McEban of the Outback, the pampas. But now the game serves to remind him that Wyoming is the only place he truly knows, that Wyoming is the place he didn't leave.

He rights his head and stares into the morning lightscape. He searches for the souls of his father, and grandfather, and brother, ready for work. He feels their hands held out to him. It is their grip that holds him steady on this land. That's what he thinks. He thinks there is a duty to the land, and he thinks he has not had a son, and that the land will lie naked at his passing. He wonders if a wife could have made a difference. He wonders about the difference Gretchen would have made.

He turns and presses the heels of his hands onto the top of his father's stone. He reads the name from the marker. Reads aloud, "John McEban." He looks at his grandfather's and grandmother's markers and reads aloud their names as well. "Angus and Cleva."

He looks to the east. There are pads of cloud, their edges windtorn to scallop, a handful of them thrown up before the sun. They blossom orange, purple, trail skirts of scarlet—a raft of lilies caught at the shore of sky.

✳

The Romans feared us," his grandmother said. "Feared us like they feared their deaths."

He leaned into the sink skinning carrots and beets, trimming broccoli heads, snapping the ends from beans, shelling peas. His grandmother stood at the stove, over the tubs of boiling water, and lifted the jars from the tubs with tongs and stood them to cool. The countertops were lined with pint jars, quart jars; the condensation dripped from the walls.

The window sashes were propped open, but there was no breeze in the late–August heat.

"We are Picts," she announced. The pride shone on her face.

She turned to him, plump and sweat-soaked in her housecoat and apron.

"In the night our men stripped naked and rolled in the ashes of their fires," she said. She turned and bent at her waist. She held the steaming tongs in her hand. "They took up bits of charcoal," she said, "and drew pictures of the killing they'd do. They drew the pictures on their naked bodies."

His grandmother gripped the tongs more tightly and traced the outlines of the dead and dying Romans against her belly and her breasts.

"And they made the pictures of our gods," she added, and made those tracings too.

She filled the jars with blanched beans and beets and broccoli and peas, with scalded tomatoes, and screwed the lids down to seat. The lids popped, snug against their rubber gaskets, and his head swam in the heat.

"Are you faint, boyo?" his grandmother asked.

He nodded and she took him by a shoulder and steered him into a chair.

"Our women, too," she said. "Naked. Naked as the day they were born. They fought naked with their men. They died at their men's sides."

She stood in front of him and flapped her apron to cool his face and laughed, and when she laughed her body ran heavier with sweat. Her gray hair came undone from where she'd gathered it at the back of her head, and it hung about her shoulders, and matted to her forehead and at her temples.

"The women whose time it was to bleed smeared the blood on their bellies and on their thighs." She leaned into him. She gripped her breasts and her voice rose. "Imagine it, boyo," she said. "We ran naked in the night. In the forests. We howled. We threw ourselves against the Romans' wall. That's who you are. That's the blood that's come up strong in your head."

She held her face close to his. She whispered, "Do you know what happened then?"

He shook his head. She smiled and straightened.

"The Romans pissed down their legs and ran like children." She pressed her hands to her hips. "That's what happened then."

She walked to the living room and returned with the framed photograph of her wedding day and held it beside her face, the photograph facing out. The picture glass flashed cool and began to cloud in the steam.

"This was a day," she said.

She pulled a wooden chair in front of his and sat with the photograph in her lap. She leaned back and pursed her lips, and they listened to the pots boil on the stove.

"Two years after this photograph was made your grandfather and I were on Ellis Island. 1917," she said, "and both of us only twenty-two. We brought a trunk of clothes, a Bible, a bar of soap, a box of buttons, our burrs, and this picture wrapped in a woolen vest. Think of it, boyo."

She propped the picture against the bulge of her gut. Her wet thumbs worked along the frame-edge.

"It was ungodly hot in the receiving hall," his grandmother said, "and we stunk from the weeks of passage, but we were in love and we kept our eyes sharp. We stood on line. I stood behind the man, and he reached behind and took my hand. We never stepped away."

She leaned forward, the wedding picture still in her lap.

"Your grandfather was an even-spoken man. Even then. He didn't say what he didn't mean. When we got to the front of the line, I stepped to his side. He told the immigration officer that we were from a farm east of Coldstream. Southwest of Edinburgh. That our farm was sold. He told the man that we had some savings. He said we'd save more. He said we'd come for a new life. He told the man we were moving west. He told it all twice. I heard it both times."

His grandmother righted herself in the chair and turned the photograph and pressed it to her heart. She closed her eyes.

"We told them all we'd come to take up this new country. We told them our arms were young and our backs were strong. We told them we'd hold America to our hearts."

She opened her eyes and looked to her sides and lowered her voice.

"We didn't tell them we'd kill them," she said. "Kill every last mother's son of them if we were turned away."

She stood all at once and steadied herself against the chair and walked the wedding photo back to the mantel in the living room, and returned. She stood the chair under the table.

"Get up," she said. "We've had our rest."

He got up and leaned into the double sink and took up a paring knife and cut the stalks and leaves to length for the compost bin.

"When did Ansel come?" he asked.

"Later," she said. "Almost thirty years. 1947. It was after the second war and your father was just old enough to be of use."

He nodded and scooped the rootcrop peelings out of the sink basin and sacked them.

She spooned whole plums from their flats and eased them into the boiling water and set a timer to know when they were blanched.

"Ansel hitchhiked down from Red Lodge, Montana," she said. "He carried his saddle and a GI duffel. He said his health was good and he was single. He said he planned for both to stay that way."

She ladled the plums into quart jars and poured boiling water and sugared syrup and a dose of Fruit-Fresh in after them and seated the lids.

"He claimed he'd killed enough perfectly good folks in the war to lose the right to raise any of his own. He told your grandfather he wasn't the type of man to require a vacation. He said two Saturday nights in town each month would get him by. He said he sipped his whiskey and only laid down with unmarried women."

His grandmother stood back from the stove.

"Can you imagine?" she asked. "That rail-thin boy stood there in front of your grandfather and made those claims for all the world to hear?"

"What did my grandfather say?"

"He said he guessed we'd find out whether the man was accurate, or just dull."

"Am I related?"

"To Ansel?" she asked.

He nodded.

"By work you are," she said. "It's the next step down from blood."

McEban comes off the ridge at an angle that brings him to the corner of the corrals. A barrel-chested bay, a roan, and a paint circle at the rails and nicker. The paint is belly-pinched and anxious. The barn, posts, poles, and sage cast hollows of purple-black shadow to the west. The barn-shadow cuts a clean edge through the corrals, and the bay stops in the shadow's border, halved light and dark, and stands spraddle-legged. He balances on the toes of his back hooves and pisses onto the manure-caked earth. The earth is nightcool and the kidney-warm piss steams. The smell of it rises sharply in the air.

He bends and slides between two poles and straightens and reaches the bay as the horse steps forward from its toilet. He grips a fist of mane at the horse's withers and catches what spring he can from his left leg and swings up and sits the big gelding. The bloodred horse steps forward and stands and steps again. McEban feels the familiar spread in his hips. The warmth of the animal rises into his trunk and holds there, in his body, like some accustomed odor. He slides his heels along its ribs, and the horse walks into the barn, and McEban ducks along its neck. He rides the horse into a stall, and when it noses at the feedbox he slides to his feet.

The roan and the paint enter the barn and nicker and bob their heads, and step, one after the other along the walkway, and stand in their stalls, stamping in anticipation. Their hoofstrikes on the barnboards rise against the loft and gather there and drop.

He pours half a coffee-can of grain into their separate feedboxes. The bay lips McEban's shoulder and yawns its yellow teeth bare and noses into the oats.

He returns to the corrals and fills the castiron bathtub he uses for a watering trough and squeezes between the south-facing rails. He wades through the barnweed grown along the side of the building, and when a thistle pricks his thigh he hops into the air, backpedaling into the dirt yard at the front of the barn. He'd been thinking about snakes.

He skirts the stockpond below the barn and walks the edge of the near alfalfa field and steps up on the concrete bulwark of the first big headgate. He sits on the wheel-valve and squints into the acreage directly east. The weather has been right this summer—hot early, the nights warm—and he and Ansel had taken a second-cutting from this pasture before the end of August. Both cuttings are stacked in a paling block at the fence corner where the land is slightly risen, standing dry, away from the sweep of irrigation.

It has frosted hard for two nights but now warmed, and they will irrigate until it starts to freeze regularly and then run a dozen horses and some breed cows in from the sage and wildgrass hills, and put them on this overgreened land. There is this pasture and the one below it, and the one farther down, on both sides of the creek.

When the pastures are eaten short, and winter-blanched, and drifted with snow, they'll feed the hay and some feedstore cake until the grazeland starts back green in May and they can begin the cycle of their farming once again.

McEban hears a door slam and turns to the sound and watches Ansel stand out on his cabin's porch. The cabin is two hundred yards down the creek. It is the original homestead and is tucked to the back of a stand of old-growth cottonwood. Its corners are dovetailed and snug, and its sides weathered gray as the cottonwoods' bark, in places gone white as Ansel's hair. The tops of the big trees are all trained prairiewise, curved eastward by a hundred years of pruning winds.

McEban wishes he could have seen the building of the thing. He wishes he could conjure the homesteader, Barhaug, at work with his broadax and slick and adz. Hear the sounds of the mules skidding the lengths of lodgepole in. But when he thinks of the cabin it is only Ansel he imagines.

He tries to remember any part of his life without Ansel and cannot, and now the old man is what's left. Just him and the old man.

On the third Wednesday of every month Ansel walks up to the big house and sits on a kitchen chair with a dish towel safety-pinned at his neck. McEban clips his ivory-white hair back to an inch-long bristle, leveled flat on the top. The old man leaves a dollar bill on the counter when they're done. McEban cuts his hair for twelve dollars a year.

When he drives to town for groceries Ansel rides with him, and when they're in the store the old man pushes a separate cart. He puts his tobacco, and sardines, and Tabasco in the cart. A loaf of rye bread, a *Western Horseman* magazine, or a *Time,* a tin of psyllium husk powder, and on holidays they stop at a liquor store for a bottle of schnapps. Ansel won't put the groceries or the booze on the ranch account, and McEban doesn't argue with him. If the old man couldn't buy his haircut and a few groceries he wouldn't care to draw his pay, and if he didn't work for money he would believe himself done.

McEban prays that the old man is a long way from done, but has recently imagined him dead; sees him in daydreams held upright by his shovel, or a strand of wire, or the squeeze chute, in a stall, sometimes leaning against a patient horse. McEban doesn't know what he will do then—when he discovers the old man dead.

He watches Ansel shoulder a dozen canvas irrigation dams, three at a time, away from where they stand rolled against his porchrail. He tilts them down into the bed of his truck. He throws a shovel on top of the dams and idles the two-track that runs the south side of the pasture and stops at the headgate and steps out of the truck. He draws a cloth sack of tobacco and cigarette papers from a shirt pocket and rolls a smoke. "Can I make you one?" he asks.

"I quit," McEban tells him.

Ansel nods and strikes a wooden match with his thumbnail. He lights the cigarette and spits a flake of tobacco from his tongue.

"Just allowing for backslide," he says. He leans against the fender, smoking, looking east. "I thought maybe you might've broke down and done something else last night you're going to regret."

McEban stands from the wheel-valve, and his shadow stands with him, and holds steady at his back. "What is it you think you know about what kind of night I had?"

The morning has come still, and the smoke rises and curls from under Ansel's hatbrim and slides into the open air above the hat's crown. He doesn't turn. "If you want your company to stay a secret," he says, "tell her to turn off her headlights when she drives past my place. I haven't lost my eyesight." He hooks a bootheel up against the tire's tread and looks back at McEban. "Or my imagination, either."

McEban turns full against the sun. "I'll tell her about the head-lights," he says. "If it looks like it might happen again I'll tell her."

Ansel squints up through the smoke. "I thought it'd be better if I said something. I didn't want you to worry about what I knew."

"I wasn't worried."

"And you don't have to worry about what I might say."

"I'm not worried about that either."

Ansel shifts against the fender and turns away. "I'd be worried," he says.

He stubs his cigarette in the wheelwell and pulls his irrigation boots from behind the truckseat and steps them on. He shoulders his shovel. "Let's get this water spread," he says. "I've got other things I want to do today."

McEban opens the wheel-valve, and the water turns into the top ditch, pollen-thick, twisting out of the gate in a stained froth, and then smoothly luteous. Woody chases along the ditchbank, biting at the wet swell, barking, sitting to sneeze and snarl, snapping his muzzle in delight.

Ansel shovels his first dam tight where it seeps and works back along the ditch and levels the bank with his shovel. He brings the flood out evenly over the field. McEban carries two dams to the ditch below and drops them where they'll be needed. On these pastures, under this sun, these two men have spent their lives spreading water. They don't wonder what must be done next.

A flash of metal catches, turning in the sun, and McEban looks to Ansel's cabin and watches the sheriff's four-wheel drive nose in at the porch and park.

He hears Ansel walking toward him, the old man's feet sticking in the spread of water-darkened earth. Ansel stops by McEban's side and spits.

The sheriff is far enough away to present just a turd-size lump of county-brown uniform. He stands beside his outfit. They watch him reach back through its window and bring out his Stetson and seat it on his head.

Ansel stabs his shovel into the ditchbank. "Until I see the man I always forget what a fat bastard he is. Why do you suppose that is?"

"You still shooting out our neighbors' yardlights?"

"Course I am." Ansel snorts and turns toward his truck. The spread of water sends up a glare around him. "They aren't my neighbors."

"Their land borders ours."

"It didn't five years ago."

"Things change."

Ansel turns and squints toward McEban. "Then the ranchette-owning, mercury-light-installing sons of bitches ought to get used to it changing from day to night."

"You want me to walk down there with you?"

"I want you to creep up behind him and slap him on the ear with your spade, but you won't."

"You think about what it might be like to spend time in jail?"

"Probably no more than you."

"I'm not shooting out anyone's lights."

"And I'm not sleeping with my neighbor's wife."

Ansel turns with his eyes wide for emphasis and steps into the truck's cab with his boots shining wet. He idles toward the cabin and stops the truck and leans out its window.

"There aren't supposed to be lights at night," he yells, and after just a moment of thought, his head and shoulders still thrust out the window, "It bothers the goddamn wildlife."

McEban waves to the fat sheriff and the man waves back. He sets his dams and walks a hundred yards along the ditch toward the house. He bends through the fencewires and weaves into a windbreak of cotton-wood, Russian olive, brush willow, and caragana. He skirts the olives, careful of their thorns, stomps down a stand of thistle, and squats at the northernmost end of the windbreak, looking back at the house.

Woody digs and snaps at a sage gnarl, and McEban hooks his armpits over his kneecaps and settles his butt against his boot tops. He searches the porch for movement. He wonders what it would be like to see Gretchen on the porch, sipping her morning coffee, tucked up safely in the throw of mild shadow.

When his grandmother had the store-bought fruit canned and the kitchen cleaned and they'd had a sandwich, she told him she was done with him.

"Go find your father," she said. "He might still want your help with those bulls."

It was just early afternoon, and he walked to the corrals and couldn't find the man. He walked up to the cemetery rise and shaded his eyes and couldn't see him in the pastures along the creek.

He circled the house and stood at the screened back porch and peered in at his mother in her rocker where she napped.

When the stepboards creaked she opened her eyes.

"Who's there?" she asked.

"It's me," he said.

"It's just the headpain," she said. "If you mean to walk there, take your boots off."

He stepped into the yard and pulled his boots off and tiptoed up through the screendoor and eased it shut and sat down cross-legged at her feet.

"Did you take your medicine?" he asked.

"For all the good it does," she said. "My mind just feels smeared." She blinked at him. "Maybe a glass of cool water would help."

He went into the house and came back with the water and stood by her while she drank. She handed him the glass when she was done.

"How bad is it?" he asked.

"How bad have you ever been hurt?"

"In the head?"

"Anywhere."

"This spring," he told her, "at branding time. When I got kicked by the all-red cow." He shifted in his stocking feet. "When the cow kicked me between my legs."

"That's how bad," his mother whispered. "If the Lord packed my skull tight with boy testicles and had it kicked by a mother cow. That's how bad."

He nodded in appreciation and sat on a bench and hunched over where he sat and felt his mother's pain low, and spreading, in his body.

When her rocker settled away from its creak and stood quiet, he watched her while she slept. She slept with her eyes open, and when he stood and took up his boots her eyes followed him. He could see his reflection, wholly, in the dark mirrors of his mother's eyes.

W oody growls and McEban turns to the sound and finds a bull snake come out of the coolness of the windbreak for the early-morning sun.

"Sit," he says, and the dog sits and they eye the snake.

It lies motionless, shining yellow and brown, wrist-thick at its center, four feet in length, its unlidded eyes reflecting man, dog, horizon, and the white islands of cloud that have come loose against the dome of sky. It tastes the air and the dog whines, and the black forked tongue quivers.

"Stop now," says McEban and Woody swallows his whine, and McEban lifts himself away from the ache in his legs.

The bull snake raises the front foot of itself up stiffly and exhales the air of its single lung in one long rush of guttural threat. It is an unsnakelike sound, and the dog steps back and looks at McEban and sits again, but nervously.

"Isn't that something," says McEban.

An ancient sense of unease pricks across his shoulders, his neck, at the base of his skull. The snake sucks full of air and issues the same rasping threat. There is no hissing. It is the sound a large lizard might make. McEban looks along the snake's body, searching for legs, some vestigial reminder of legs. There is only the smooth overlap of scales.

"Enough of this shit," he says and stands completely and kicks a spray of dirt and gravel at the thing.

The snake coils in bends of slender muscle and turns and ropes away, flashing in the overgrowth of damp grasses. McEban sits again, his legs stretched before him. He shakes the tension from his trunk. Woody sits against him, leaning along his ribs, nuzzling at his armpit. A pair of ravens glide in low over the windbreak and circle, cawing. It is a lonesome and piercing and familiar sound. McEban drops his head back to watch. Above the pair, high on the morning thermals, a mob of half a thousand ravens lift and joust, swirling in the air. At this distance they look to be just chips of obsidian against the sun. McEban wonders if it is God who's littered the sky. He imagines a god squatted at work in his heavens, knapping black bolts of lightning from a bedrock of volcanic glass. He imagines his god to have working-man's hands.

He loops an arm over Woody's shoulders and shuts his eyes and thinks of the refuse God must make in his industry, and it is his father's voice he hears.

"B. McEban," Jock would shout into the air. "Come here, lad. My world needs you." And louder, "B. McEban."

In the dream he sits naked on a plain wooden chair. He breathes evenly. His breath enters, spreads, bubbles in his blood. There is moonlight in the room and the ambers and shadows that it brings. The windows stand open and the night is warm and deep and green, and it has rained but the rain has quit and the sky is clear. He can hear the collect and release of water through the open windows. It falls from the palms of leaves, to broader palms of leaves, pooling on the night-dark ground.

She stands before him. She knows desire is what has brought him to her room. She smiles and begins to turn. And then faster, and there is the sound of her turning in the air.

Her arms and legs lift and fall away as she spins, head back, hair black, as thickened with the night as a dark shuck of succulent. The hair falls to her waist and arcs and slaps at her back, at her shoulders, and her body rotates, glistening brown and terra-cotta in the moonlight. Sweat drips from her knees, breasts, elbows, fingertips, and soaks the smooth board floor.

He hears the horses outside stamping in their sleep. Dark horses. Bay, sorrel, black-brown, gray horses. Horses with hides as pale as his own.

Chapter Two

※

McEban backs the truck and a horse trailer to the open-faced shed along the east side of the barn and brings the yardlight on below the barn. The glare strikes the work-bared ground, slanting in angles under the eaves, against the tin roofing, in the cat-faced spiders' webs. Miller moths circle against the big bulb. Woody chuffs through the loose hay littering the shed's floor, worrying the mice, and McEban bends over the smaller of two Deere tractors. He starts the tractor and tests its hydraulics. It has a front bucket and a power takeoff rigged for a tiller.

He backs the tractor into the horse trailer and the noise of the engine in the steel-sided trailer pounds into his skeleton, and he settles the bucket and the tiller-tines against the trailer's floor and shuts the tractor down. He stands out of the trailer and wags his head from side to side, trying to pop the ringing from his ears, from the base of his skull. He walks to the yardlight and turns it off at the pole. He leans against the pole, waiting for his eyes to adjust. His ears still ring.

It has stayed warm through the night and the moon is set, and it is now wholly dark. His legs and arms tingle, itch where the bones have been broken and knit back together, and his bad foot seems made of jagged parts.

When he can make out the truck's cab, he limps to its side and opens the door and whistles through his front teeth. Woody jumps onto the seat and settles against the far doorpanel. McEban steps in after him.

"You want the window down?" he asks.

The dog looks at him, smiling, and McEban lies along the seat and cranks the window down.

That is the way they sit, in the darkness, in the silence with the windows down, with the trailer hitched behind them, the tractor loaded, until the night is nearly done, until there is enough light to make out the pale twin ruts of the two-track before them.

McEban drives to the highway, never out of second gear, and up the gravelled road to Gretchen and Bennett's.

The house and barn stand unlit, and he parks below the house, by the creek, and backs the tractor out of the trailer and idles to the far corner of Gretchen's acre of garden plot.

In mid-September it frosted hard, and then less hard for the two nights after, and her tomato plants and peppers and beans stand wilted and bent. Even the broccoli did not survive. He works the tiller into the ground. He watches the rubbery plants turn under. It is warm again now, and their stalks ooze a greenish juice.

When he looks up from his work Gretchen stands on the steps of the sheep wagon. It is parked between the garden and the creek. It is where she stores her tools and a folding chair and white-gas lamp. She has kept the wagon by her garden for years, as an encampment, a convenience for the anchoritic side of her nature.

He knows it's where she comes to read on summer evenings. On certain evenings he has watched from the darkness. He's watched her set up the chair under the hiss of the gas light and read, and wave the insects away from her face, and get up from her reading and carry the lantern into her garden and stand it to her side while she changes the irrigation. He's watched her return to the wagon's steps and sit just out of the light and listen to the music the water makes. Just that: with her head tilted on her neck, and her eyes closed. He's watched from a distance in the dark, quietly, careful with his breath.

She knuckles her eyes and yawns, and McEban throttles off the tiller and lets the tractor cough and die.

"You don't have to do that," she says.

He looks down at his hands where they grip the steering wheel. "I do it every fall," he says. "After a frost."

She rocks away from her right hip, stretching. "You could have stayed at home if you're going to pout."

"I'm not pouting. I'm just trying to get my work done."

"Your voice sounds pouty."

"I'll watch how I sound," he says.

She walks to the edge of the broken ground and steps down a tomato stalk. It's frost-blackened and limp, and she stands along its length. "I should have got these covered," she says. "Or pulled up and hung in the cellar. It's a waste."

"Nobody saw that coldsnap coming. Not even the guy that does the weather."

"I saw it," she says. "I checked the temperature every half hour. All night long. When it got cold I didn't do anything but watch it get colder."

She points her chin to a heap of fireplace ash and household compost and horseshit mounded at the south corner of the plot. "You'll till that compost in?"

"Yes, I will," he tells her. He spits over the tractor's fender. The ruined garden spreads around him, to his sides. There is the slick, sugary smell of decay. "You think this is the way we'll all go?"

There's just enough light to see her wince. "I think all flesh is grass," she says. She stands up straighter.

"That Milton?"

"Isaiah," she says. She clasps her hands behind her back and raises them to stretch the sleep from her shoulders. She lets her arms drop to her sides. "Leave the north end alone," she says. "There's still potatoes in the ground."

"It's your garden."

"Could you eat some breakfast?"

"How long have you been sleeping down here?" He nods toward the sheep wagon and knows he doesn't have to.

"For a while."

"How long's a while?"

"Since spring."

He looks back to her. "I didn't know that."

"You wouldn't know it because you're not here when I get in and out of bed." She turns away and stops and turns back. "It doesn't feel like I belong up at the house anymore. I don't deserve it."

"I guess you'd be the best judge of where you should sleep."

She sucks her cheeks in between her teeth and bites into them, and stares blinking at the newly broken earth. "I'll make us something to eat," is all she says.

He watches her wind through the white aspen trunks, moving away from him. He has always, his whole life, thought of her in the way he thinks of aspen: cleanly fragrant, solid, magical in sunlight. He listens to the clicking of the aspen leaves over his head. It is a crisp sound, a brittle purring, and he knows, without looking up, that the leaves have started to flush gold, in beauty, briefly, before they darken and fall.

It only takes him a half hour to spread and till the compost under and he parks the tractor out of the garden, under the bright leaves, and walks to the house.

The kitchen's built into the northwest corner, cool and shadowed until evening, and a three-bulbed fixture hums above the dining table. McEban sets his hat on the floor by his chair and nods at Gretchen and hunches over his meal.

She stands at the sink, leaning back against the counter. She holds her plate in front of her.

His egg yolk spreads and he mops it with his toast, and he mops the grease the potatoes were fried in with the toast, just a smear of it, and straightens away from his plate. He brings his coffee mug to his chin and holds it there while he chews.

"You want anything else?" she asks.

"I guess I'm done."

She nods and he sips his coffee and watches her eat. When she's finished she sets her plate on the counter.

"I feel torn up about Bennett," he says.

"I always have." She's looking down, tracing a pattern in the linoleum with her heel.

He sets his coffee on the table and turns sideways on his chair. He crosses his left foot up and pulls his boot off. He sets the boot on the floor and works at the foot with both hands. He doesn't look up at her.

She watches him squeezing and pulling at the foot. "Do you know when it'll hurt, or does it just hurt when it wants to?"

"Sometimes the weather sets it off," he says. He looks up to her. "Mostly it hurts when it wants to."

She sits across from him at the table. She leans on her arms, toward him. "The other night wasn't the start of anything," she says.

"What was it?"

"It was just the night before last night."

He looks down at his hands. He watches them work at the socked foot. "I've loved you my whole life."

She leans back in her chair. "You should quit."

"I can't. I've tried." He still stares down at the foot.

"Then you should have said something a long time ago."

He looks up at her, across the table. The tabletop holds a soft glow from the overhead light, and the glow rises into their faces, muting their features, allowing them to appear younger to one another. "I'm saying it now."

"It's too late," she tells him. "Loving me now is too late."

She takes his plate up from the table and carries it to the sink and stacks hers on top of it and turns the water on them.

"You better get that boot on," she says. "Unless you plan on driving to Cody barefoot."

He was a long and awkward boy, mostly bone and pale skin. He burned red in the summers, and he peeled. The beads of his spine, his collarbones and shoulders and elbows, rose against the fabric of his workshirts, the winged bones of his hips, his knees, in knobs against the denim of his jeans. When he moved, when he walked or ran, his arms and legs flailed away from his thin trunk and knifed at the air.

At the supper table his grandmother gripped a fistful of his white-blond hair and turned his face to hers and smiled down into his blue eyes.

"It's like having a colt underfoot," she said.

He smiled back the best he could and bent to his meal. He asked for a second helping and longed for the thickness of a man. For his father's strength, and Ansel's. At night he prayed he would someday be useful in a man's world.

He saved his allowance. When it seemed like it would take forever he begged his grandmother for an advance against the allowance, and when she gave it to him and didn't ask why, he sent away for a Charles Atlas course.

He had it delivered to Bennett's, and when it arrived, he brought it home under his shirt. He excused himself to his room and sat alone, studying its promises of strength.

It took him a week, but when he had the light-blue sheets of instruction memorized he wrapped them in a winter coat and hid the coat at the back of his closet. He did not want his family to know he was dissatisfied with the boy they'd made, and fed, and watered.

In the middle of the summer nights he lay in his bed and flexed the separate parts of himself, according to his memory. He gripped a wrist and pinned the arm above the wrist to the mattress and strained against the grip. And then he worked the other arm. Back and forth. He worked both sides of himself. Resistance, he thought. Practice. A hard thing done, time and again, might make for a hardened man.

His plan was to walk out of his room in ninety days transformed to muscle. And he planned to act more surprised than any of them.

He imagined himself with his father at the barn. He pictured his father's face as he stepped in front of the man and squatted and hooked the anvil in the crooks of his arms.

He saw himself straightening, lifting the anvil away from the round of cottonwood on which it stood, and standing with the block of solid iron come to rest against his rippled abdomen.

"Let me get that for you," he planned to say. He could see himself standing effortlessly with the anvil, looking to his sides, as if bored. "This old thing's been in my way for months."

He thought he might cock a hip, maybe spit.

He imagined his father's face lighted with admiration. For long moments he saw himself through his father's eyes—in the future, the near future, when the exercises took hold.

When the exercising made him too warm under his bedcovers, he stepped into the moonlight before the freestanding mirror. He pushed himself harder in the night air. He thought of himself as an undiscovered Charles Atlas. As a boy of unnatural powers. He drew his arms into curves, like the curves of a ram's horns, from his shoulders to each side of his head, his fists bobbing by his ears. He stood in the ram's-horn pose, straining, grinning at himself. The moonlight shone against his knuckles, on his moon-white forehead and cheeks, flatly against the quilted long underwear he wore.

"I am in disguise," he said to the mirror. "I am a surprise." He dropped his arms and stepped closer to the mirror.

And when he heard his mother below him, at work in the kitchen—the clatter of dishware, the scrape of chairlegs and tablelegs on the linoleum floor—he ran through the exercises a second time, and a third time, silently.

When his arms became heavy with blood and his feet chilled he lay on the floor and laced his hands behind his head and curled into sit-ups. Forty sit-ups. Fifty. Sixty. Until his gut burned and cramped.

And then he stretched his arms above his head and straightened his legs and held his breath and listened for the wind. Most nights the house flexed and groaned against the sweep of the west and north-westerly winds—nightcooled and constant and thick with the wind-stirred topsoils. The branches of the cottonwoods and lilacs scratched against the board siding, clicking, whispering, busy. It was the same sound his mother made below him in the kitchen. Just sounds in the night.

"I am like my mother," he said aloud. He thought that he and his mother both worked at night, secretly unlocking their magic.

Gretchen shifts on the truckseat and slides the floor vent open with the side of her heel. The air is hot off the asphalt and smells of tar blisters, road grit, exhaust, faintly of sage.

They top the Bighorns and start their descent.

She lifts the hem of her skirt to catch the draft, and the skirtcloth lofts and stands quivering to her waist. She rolls her head to the side, against the seatback, to have a look at McEban. He drives with his arms straight away from his shoulders. He drives into the shadow the truck throws onto the highway ahead of them. She rocks her knees to cool the tops and insides of her thighs, and raises her legs and presses her soles against the dash to let the air work at the backs of her thighs. She pushes up in the seat.

"I'm sorry," she says.

It is still early morning and the sun stands behind them, on their necks and shoulders, at the back of McEban's head. The windows are down and he sits hatless, and his straw-colored hair lifts and thrashes in feathers of yellow light. His face is cast in shadow, expressionless as a stone. He turns and stares at the flapping skirtcloth.

"About Bennett?"

"About all of us," she says.

The morning sun halves his face. Fans of lighter skin spoke away from the corner of the sunstruck eye and shelve in a half-dozen rounded curves under it. He downshifts into the first of the steep switchbacks that drop them, by degree, into the Bighorn Basin. The engine whines against the pull of momentum and gravity.

"We could leave," he says. "We could go through Cody and just keep going."

"Today?"

"Right now," he says. "Today."

The air is dry. There is just the swirl of hot wind in the cab, just the sigh of the tires on the highway. She tucks her chin and levels her gaze. She breathes in deeply and holds her breath and stares into the windshield's glare. It's daubed orange, yellow, rust, and milk, unevenly smudged by the shattered bodies of insects.

"How far do you think we'd have to go to leave Bennett behind?" she asks.

"He wouldn't know where we were. Not if we didn't tell him."

"And we'd forget where he was? Just like that?"

Below them the basinscape stretches for fifty miles to the west. Reefs of sandstone and hardpack rise into fractured ridges. Between the ridges lie broad embayments of sage, prickly pear, yucca, wind-stunted scrub brush. There are dull, plantless smears of bentonite and alkali.

"You think you could do that to Bennett?" she asks.

"I think I could. Right now I think I could."

She squints, and the scene below them blurs to sweeps of aqua, lavender, slate, chalk: a large and broken bowl of insubstantial graze-land, coaxed into irrigated strips of alfalfa along its waterways, and emerald tracts of beanleaf and beet top.

On the far horizon the Absarokas stand sun-slapped and jagged against the sky, shouldering out of the pastel plain in dark-green folds of fir and pine, patched above timberline with the ragged remains of last winter's snowfields.

She thinks that on this side the continent's water drains to the Gulf of Mexico, on the Absarokas' west slope, to the Pacific.

"I don't think you could leave here. Whether I was married to Bennett or not," she says. "I don't think you should kid yourself about that."

He hasn't slept well for two nights. "I could leave for you. Early on I could have," he says. "And that's not something I think you can kid yourself about."

She closes her eyes. Her body rocks slightly on the seat. She sips at the air and drops her head forward. She can feel the tears start, and she squeezes her eyes tighter and presses the flats of her hands against her abdomen. She promises herself to remember the feel of McEban's hands upon her flesh, and vows that he will never know. She promises herself the luxury of the memory, and when she opens her eyes they are out on the basin and the air is hotter, come hazy with the heat; a flood of heat.

He pushes into the steering wheel and arches his back and turns to her. Her skirt still slaps against her legs, and her red hair blows across her face, snaking in the sunlight.

"I need to know why," he says. "After so long."

Heat waves rise and quaver upon the asphalt, and Woody works the back of the pickup bed, from wheelwell to wheelwell, his ears and lips flapping in the hot airstream. They can hear the scrape of his nails on the metal.

"Because I could," she says, and because her answer startles her she sits up straighter on the seat.

"Just because you could?" he asks. "Just that?"

"Do you know why you do everything you do?"

"Mostly I do."

"Well, I don't."

She draws her knees under her and resettles and smoothes her dress over her knees. Her back is very straight.

"I did it because I wanted to know what it was like," she says. "I wanted to make sure I knew what it felt like."

A strand of hair catches in the corner of her mouth, and she pulls it free.

"You didn't think about how I'd feel?"

"No," she says. "I didn't think about that a lot."

"What about now?"

She looks away at the horizon. "It was for me." Her voice has gone soft and she is hard to hear over the tires. "It wasn't for you."

Her eyes are wet, but she's not crying. Her nose runs, and she wipes it with the back of her hand. She curls down on the seat with her cheek against his thigh, and he puts a hand in her hair. She closes her eyes and her head rocks against his thigh.

"It was the first of June," she whispers. "Just at sunset. I remember the mayflies."

He feels vaguely nauseous and opens his mouth to speak, and closes it without speaking. He doesn't look down at her. He drives the flat, straight stretch of two-lane before them. He keeps the truck centered on the highway, between the soft shoulders that fall away to the drainage ditches. He doesn't look to his sides. He knows that past the ditches the land stands blanched, wind-scoured, and poor.

He lets her sleep through Cody and turns off the Yellowstone highway west of Cody and into the rodeo grounds. He still doesn't wake her.

There's a twenty-foot banner draped over the sign that advertises the nightly rodeo. The banner announces a wild-horse-and-burro adoption.

It's late morning, the last of September, but Fourth-of-July hot. He idles along the east side of the macadam parking lot and skirts the pen that gathers the team-roping steers. To the west the roofed bleachers rise up unnaturally angled against the rounded horizon. The empty runs of aluminum seating flash in bands of reflection across the truck's windshield. Flash, flash, flash. And then again. Like a series of soundless explosions.

He drops the truck off the lip of pavement and onto the pale and gravel-scattered earth. Gretchen still sleeps curled on the truckseat, her head on the top of his thigh, her hands clasped under her chin.

There's a motor home parked past the gate that opens into the labyrinth of catchpens and alleyways, and he noses the truck in beside it and cuts the engine. In red, white, and blue lettering, printed on the sheetmetal of the motor home's side, he reads, AMERICAN DREAM. Gretchen sits up straight, stretches, and yawns.

"What time is it?" she asks.

"It's eleven-thirty."

"Do we have water?" Her mouth feels woolen. She sucks at her tongue in an effort to work up enough spit to swallow.

"Woody has a jug in the back," he tells her. "It'll've gotten hot but it's there. They'll have Coke and coffee once the auction starts. They might have it now."

She searches the horizons, looking for cloud cover, but there is just the blue and moistureless sky. Cedar Mountain and Rattlesnake are snapped up sharply against the western curve of sky, tan and green, and brought so close in the clear air the arena appears tucked against the swell of their foothills.

She turns on the seat. Her left cheek is reddened and creased where it rested against his leg. "It shouldn't be this hot."

He means to agree but they hear a scream they recognize as Bennett's, and McEban stands out of the truck. He steps up onto the lowest rail of the catchpen's fencing and finds Bennett in the middle of the big pen, on his back. Curtis Hanson is on top of him with his left hand locked on Bennett's throat, beating him rhythmically with his right fist. Bennett's thrown both forearms across his face and bleats for help.

"Hey," shouts McEban. He steps up on the next rail and swings a leg over the top of the fencing.

Curtis pauses and squints into the sun. Curtis usually wears glasses but doesn't have them on. His right arm is cocked shoulder-high, the fist made and ready to come down again on Bennett.

"Hey yourself. Is that McEban?"

"Yes, it is. Here in front of you." McEban waves. "Up on this fence."

He steps down into the pen and walks to Curtis. He tries not to seem in a hurry. He tries to appear as though they're just neighbors leaned against opposite sides of a fence they share. He knows Curtis as a dull man, and tasky; as good help. He knows if Curtis doesn't feel all the way done with a chore he doesn't come in for lunch. McEban stops a yard from Bennett's head. Curtis's face is red and beaded with sweat. The veins stand discolored on his forehead. His hat has rolled off to the side, come to rest on its crown.

"It's hot," says McEban.

"Worst I've seen this time of year."

They both look down at Bennett. Bennett holds his hands over his face and stares up through his fingers. His eyes are wide. Curtis's arm is still cocked, the fist still made.

McEban finds a toothpick in his shirt pocket and works it into his mouth. "I probably couldn't get you to take a break from that, could I?"

"I'm not sure I need a break." Curtis opens his fist into a hand and wipes at his face with the hand and closes it back into a fist. He looks up at McEban. "The man's a prick."

McEban says, "Say you're a prick, Bennett."

Bennett agrees he's a prick but doesn't take his hands away from his face.

"That do anything for you?" McEban asks.

"Do you think he means it?" Curtis stares hard down at Bennett.

McEban puts the toothpick back in his pocket. "I guess that's enough," he says.

Curtis squints up into the sun. Sweat drips from his chin onto the backs of Bennett's hands. "Enough of what?"

"It doesn't matter whether he means it. Come off him."

"What if I won't?"

"Then I'll drag you off him."

Curtis is squaring his shoulders to McEban when Gretchen steps out of the sunglare and up close to him. He's thrown in the pole of her slender shadow and just recognizes her and is starting to smile when she catches him high in the temple with a length of lumber, and he sits back against Bennett's thighs and exhales all at once.

"Shit," he says. He presses a hand to his head, and when he brings the hand away the palm is glossy with blood. He sniffs at the blood.

"Get off my husband," she says.

Curtis slumps to the side and crawls a little away and sits heavily. He doesn't take his eyes from Gretchen. She's brought the board up again, leveling it like a bat.

"Shit," he says again. The left side of his face has come slick. The blood runs under his shirtcollar, and the shirtcloth at his shoulder is damped red. "I can't believe you hit me that hard."

Gretchen widens her stance. "I'm ready to hit you again."

"I believe you." He holds the heel of his left hand against his temple. He spits and struggles into a crouch. "I'm done with it," he says. He shrugs and picks up his hat. He grimaces when he seats the hat. "I probably ought to go over and have a look at these sale horses." He stands all the way up. "Everybody okay about this?"

"I'm okay," says McEban.

Bennett's arms have fallen to his sides, but he's made no effort to get to his feet. His face is blotched red and purple, his left eye's gone weepy, and he bleeds from the nose.

"You okay, Bennett?" Curtis asks.

Bennett nods but doesn't lift his head away from the ground.

"We're all okay," Gretchen says.

Curtis backs away toward the bleacherseats. "I'm sorry I had to be hit," he says.

Bennett rolls to his side and draws his knees to his gut and pushes himself upright. His back sucks at the wet manure and mud when he comes away from the ground. He sits cross-legged and spits a gob of blood to his side. "How do you think they got this pen so wet?"

"Probably with a water truck," says McEban. "Probably didn't want to work up so much dust the bidders'd go home hoarse."

"That's got to be it. Is he gone?"

"He's going," Gretchen tells him. She lays the board down in front of him and kneels on it and takes a cotton scarf from her bookbag. She spits on the scarf and dabs at the blood that's run from his nose.

"Did you miss me?" he asks.

"I did until I saw you. You know what this was about?"

She spits on the scarf again and tilts Bennett's head back and cleans the blood from his chin.

"He's pissed I sold his uncle Jimmy's place to that dude from New Jersey."

"I don't think there's anybody who's happy about it," says McEban.

"The New Jersey guy is."

"He as big as Curtis?" Gretchen asks.

Bennett looks toward the pens, making sure Curtis isn't on his way back. "About half," he admits. He catches the lashes of the damaged eye between his thumb and forefinger and pulls the lid away from the eyeball and over the lower lashes and releases it. McEban extends a hand and pulls him to his feet and he stands blinking. "You got a clean shirt with you?" he asks.

"There's one in the truck. It's not clean but it's better than yours."

Gretchen spits on the scarf again and rubs at the blood and horse-shit on his cheek until she's got a bare spot to kiss. "I'm going over to get something to drink," she tells him.

"I love you," Bennett says.

"I love you too."

He eased his bedroom door open and stepped into the hallway and stood in the darkness and stared into the moon-sliced bedroom his parents used. He listened to the rhythms of his father's sleep. The man's turnings, his steady breaths. He stared at the lighted triangle of sheet next to his father, where his mother should be, the bedspread and quilts turned back doubly.

He skated silently in his socks in the hallway, and stood in the doorway to the kitchen. He blinked against the light. He studied his mother's bursts of voiceless exercise. Counted the repetitions. Heard the squeal of her bare feet on the floor.

He watched her pull a chair to the counter and stand on the chair and empty the cupboards. The light over the kitchen sink brought her body into silhouette. Her slim body turned and flexed and stretched beneath the shabby material of her summer sleeping gown.

She washed each plate, bowl, platter, glass, and cup. She scrubbed the empty shelves with a stiff brush and wiped them dry. She reshelved the dishes and glassware. The odor of ammonia made his eyes water. The kitchen light made them ache.

He stepped through the doorway and backed into the foot-and-a-half slice of space between the refrigerator and the wall. He rounded his shoulders and backed right in and lowered his butt onto his heels. He hooked his arms over his kneecaps and leveled his chin, and felt safe in his watching.

She turned the chairs onto their seats atop the table and filled a bucket with hot water and cleanser and got on her hands and knees and scoured the floor. She paused near him and threw her head back, and her black hair fell along her back, across her shoulders. Her face and the muscles in her forearms twitched. She tried to mouth his name, and when she couldn't she dropped her head and continued her work.

His chest got tight and he lowered his forehead to the caps of his knees and closed his eyes. He listened. He thought of her as some large, featherless bird. That was the picture that came clear in his mind, with his eyes closed, listening. He saw his mother as a bird trapped in a cage of light, working its borders, anxious for flight. And finally he slept.

It was the sound of his body moving, not the feel of it, but the sound of its friction against the wall and the refrigerator box that woke him.

He looked up the length of his father's arm, and down to where his father's fist clutched the front of his quilted undershirt. He felt himself being pulled upright and moved to the side and leaned against the wall. He watched his father return to the stove. It was just dawn and the kitchen surfaces were dull and the shadows weak.

His legs and arms and shoulders tingled. He shook his arms and stomped his feet on the spotless linoleum and wagged his head. His father stood away from the stove. He held a castiron skillet in his hand. His face was rested and he was smiling. He was dressed for work.

"You hungry?" his father asked. The kitchen smelled of meat and grease and coffee, and, still, the tang of ammonia.

He nodded and moved to the table and pulled out a chair. His mother slept at the table. Her arms were folded in front of her, and her head was turned and laid against the side of a forearm. Her mouth was open and the light caught in a thin stream of spittle at the corner of her mouth. She hiccuped in her sleep.

His father fried bacon, and sliced cornmeal mush into the grease, and fried it too. He buttered toast and stacked the toast onto a platter with the meat and mush and put the platter in the oven. He set a glass of milk on the table in front of his son.

"You keep your mother company last night?"

He told his father he hadn't meant to. He said it had just happened that way.

His father nodded and smiled and knelt beside his sleeping wife. He lifted her feet away from the front rung of the chair and settled their soles gently on the floor. He worked an arm behind her knees and circled his other arm across her back, at the bottom of her ribs, and stood all at once.

Her nightgown fell loose from the backs of her legs, and there was the pale run of her thighs, and the boy remembered the flesh belonged to his mother, and looked away, and back again when his father caught up the fabric in the crook of his arm.

She murmured and turned into her husband's chest, and he smiled and bent his head and rubbed his cheek against her cheek to clear the stain of spittle that ran toward her ear.

He stared down at his wife's sleeping face. He breathed in deeply and asked, "You ever notice how good your mother smells?" He looked at his son, lost for a moment. "I guess that's just something I'd notice."

He carried her from the room. He settled her on their bed and she reached out in her sleep and clutched at the air, and he caught her hands and held them until she quieted. He folded her arms on her chest and covered her with the quilt and smoothed her hair and kissed her forehead and knelt by the bed and bowed his head and prayed. Silently. His lips moving. His eyes closed.

McEban stood in the hallway, ready for his breakfast, and when his mother was quiet in her sleep he followed his father back to the kitchen. His father bent at the oven and pulled the warmed platter out and set it on the table. They sat across from one another, the platter between them.

"You want syrup on your mush?" his father asked.

"Just salt."

"It's there beside you." His father sat at the table with his coffee and took up a single slice of bacon from the platter. "How's your breakfast?"

"It's good."

"I might yet make a cook." He sipped his coffee. "What do you think of that?"

McEban smiled and nodded and stood away from the table. He got a jar of jelly from the refrigerator and sat back down. He scooped the jelly onto a slice of toast and leveled it with a knife. He licked the knife clean and balanced it on the rim of his plate.

His father walked his cup to the sink and looked down into the cup.

"She does the best she can." He spoke softly, turned away from his son. "That's not something you should forget."

McEban nodded, chewing at the jellied toast.

His father rinsed the cup and walked to the mudroom. He pulled on his overalls and gloves and from the mudroom told his son to put what he wouldn't eat back in the oven for his grandmother's breakfast. He told him to wash his dishes and leave them to drain by the sink.

"Wash that jelly knife twice," he said.

McEban climbs into the pickup bed and opens the toolbox and pulls out a blue denim workshirt. The shirt's oilstained at the cuffs and chest, and Woody sniffs at it and circles and curls in the thin block of shade the tailgate casts and yawns until he squeaks, and lies panting. McEban drapes the denim shirt over the side panel and takes a battered tin dish and water-filled plastic milk jug from the toolbox. He fills the dish and when Woody laps it empty he fills it again.

Bennett strips off his shirt and throws it in the cab. His chest and belly are hairless as the top of his head, and slack, and white as supermarket eggshell. His chest has grown soft and fallen into tits, and his shoulders wing up thinly out of the surrounding flab. His gut covers his belt buckle. He hooks the sides of his pants with his thumbs and tugs at the waistband, and his stomach, from belt to sternum, balloons and falls. His navel's prolapsed into what appears merely a squiggle of blunted pigtail.

"That thing as hard as your liver?" McEban asks.

Bennett pats the sides of his belly and looks down to what he's got in his hands. "Handsome, isn't it?"

"Looks to me like a heart attack."

"Women love it."

"What women?"

"Women who prefer successful men."

"I didn't know you were that successful." McEban sets the milk jug back in the toolbox and slams the lid.

"Well, my wife just loves the hell out of it," says Bennett. He tries to tuck the workshirt and can't and arranges his belt to comfortably sling his gut. "Did you see her swing that board?"

"I saw her."

"She caught him with the edge of it," he says. "That's a woman in love. If she didn't love me she'd've just slapped him with the flat of it."

McEban steps over the sidewall, onto the top of the tire, and swings the other leg down.

"That's what I would've done," he says.

He tells Woody to stay and walks with Bennett in the apron of sun-stunted pigweed along the outside of the chainlink fence, and they enter the rodeo grounds at a gate in the north side of the fencing. It's where the trucks and horse trailers turn in to park, and a chalky dust is risen in the air, and the dusty air falls upon them, and upon the row of portable red toilets standing to one side of the gate. An oil-field supply company's logo is raised on the toilets' sides. On the opposite side of the gate there is a cinder-block building.

Bennett steps into a toilet and McEban stands shuffling in the sun. In the mid-distance Heart Mountain rises out of the plain to the north, seared olive and elk-colored, its rock summits collared with dwarfed pine. He stares into the sky just above the mountain and listens to the squeals and laughter of the kids at his back, the stamping of hooves from the stockpens, the rev of engines, the clang of metal gates, a dog-fight. All this and the constant drone of flies.

"Was that you who called me yesterday morning?" Bennett asks from inside the red plastic toilet, or that is what McEban thinks he hears. He looks up at the vent at the top of the thing.

"What?"

"Did you call me?" Bennett shouts, and the toilet door rocks open, and he steps out gasping, tugging at his zipper.

"How was that?" McEban asks.

Bennett grips the smooth, molded corner of the toilet. "I'd guess a lot like pissing in a sauna." He stands for a moment panting and then staggers to a galvanized pipe strapped against the side of the cinderblock building and unhooks the hose from its bibcock and turns the water on and cups his hands under the flow. He straddles the overflow and splashes the water against his face and over his neck. "It's warm."

"They just ditch in these lines a foot down," McEban tells him. "They drain the water out when it starts to freeze."

Bennett turns off the spigot and straightens and runs his hands back through the fringe of hair at the sides of his head. "I know why the water's warm." He leans back against the shaded blocks. "Yesterday morning," he says. "Did you call me at the Holiday Inn?"

McEban looks to the pens. "I wanted to hear your voice." For a long minute he watches the birds lift and settle and squabble and strut through the litter of fresh horseshit, and then he looks back at Bennett and shrugs. "I thought I had something to say, but then I called and found out I didn't."

The water drips from Bennett's jawline to the collar of his borrowed shirt. "You know that's strange even for you?"

McEban nods. "It won't happen again."

Bennett drops his head and stares at the water-dampened ground. He looks back up at McEban. "It was a long-distance call."

"It won't happen again." McEban turns toward the stockpens. They're tucked against the bucking chutes and spread away to the north in a puzzle of alleyways and gated rectangles. The bottom bleacherseats stairstep skyward from the tops of the chutes in an angled tier, casting slats of brown-black shadow over the pens directly under them. Everything else falls out under the sun.

"You coming?" McEban doesn't turn.

"Soon as I cool off," Bennett says. "I'm right behind you."

McEban nods and walks to the edge of the pens and shoulders into a crowded alleyway. The lane is choked with adolescent boys, secretaries, shop owners, and here and there an early-morning drunk. There are oilfield workers, carpenters, truckers, plumbers, car salesmen, janitors, mechanics, electricians, welders; fat and lean, long-haired, towering and bent, tattooed, purposeful, idle. The men's faces are hardened against the limit of their wages, tight with the dislocation of shiftwork and overtime.

Almost everyone wears a T-shirt. The shirts advertise professional sports teams, breweries, bars, riding clubs, biases. A muscled-up young man grips a penrail and pushes back against the tension of his hamstrings. A foreman's wallet extends from the back pocket of his jeans, and a chain curves down from the wallet's corner and fastens to a beltloop. He wears a tight black T-shirt tucked at the waist. McEban leans into the penrails at the man's side, and the man looks at him and back into the pen. They stand side by side, blinking into the pen of ten weanling fillies: four bays, two sorrels, three pintos, a buckskin.

The horses are snub-headed and short-coupled, already grown out in guard hairs, and nervous as deer. There is a strip of shaved hair up high on their necks, next to their manes. In the strip a four-digit number has been freeze-branded on their skins. There is a red nylon noose snugged at their throats. A black plastic tag wags from the red cord. The same four-digit number can be read in raised white lettering on the tag.

All ten horses huddle together at the far corner of the pen, between the corner and a hundred-gallon watering tub. They pace, and stand,

and pace again. Their heads and tails are up, and their hides twitch against the persistence of the flies. They cock their hindlegs. They bare their teeth and swing their heads. The little buckskin's mane is bitten into bristle. Her withers and sides and ass are pocked with dozens of crescent-shaped scabs. She squares her front shoulders and paws at the ground. The floor of the pen is broken and uneven and risen up past her hocks in a soiled spread of uneaten hay.

McEban turns and steps away from the man with the foreman's wallet. The air seems suddenly thin, and he folds his arms behind his neck to better fill his lungs.

"Are you alright?" the man asks.

McEban feels a steady tug at his waist, at the sides of his thighs, and looks down to see what has him, and there is nothing. Only the rise of the boot-stirred dust.

He looks into the crowd for Bennett and cannot find him. He searches the faces that move past, and there is still the feeling that he is being pulled into the earth.

"I was with a friend," he says.

"What's he look like?"

"He looks beat up."

"Welcome to the club," the man says and laughs, and McEban continues to squint into the passing faces.

He thinks he should know these people but cannot remember any single person's name. He can picture the little Japanese pickups they drive. He can see himself pulling those trucks from snowbanks and the mud-sloppy borrow ditches where they've slid and become bogged to the hubs. He sees the chainsaws and tractors he's lent, hears the advice he's offered about seasons and antibiotics and the births of animals. He sees their dogs, and the dogs he's shot and buried, when they've packed and run his calves.

He knows he's visited their five- and ten-acre tracts of fenced land. Taken coffee in the kitchens of their aluminum-sided homes, and looked out on their corrals and the open sheds they've built against the weather. He knows the sheds house lawnmowers and rototillers and irrigation-canal pumps and the sheep, calves, and pigs their kids nurse into 4H projects. He knows the men to be over-worked and as honest as their bank accounts allow.

There are a few late-season tourists. They're geared out in two-hundred-dollar hiking boots and high-tech tunics that wick the sweat from their bodies. They shake hands with one another and stand together and whisper. Their fingers are smooth and unmuscled and beautiful. A gray-haired man in a button-down shirt and pressed khaki trousers shyly sweeps the crowd with a video camera.

Everyone carries a Styrofoam cup of coffee, a canned soft drink, a bottle of spring water, an energy bar, a doughnut. Everyone carries an orange bid card—in a back pocket, a shirt pocket, cupped in a palm, stuck in a hatband.

There is an occasional cowboy, and a less-than-occasional cowboy's wife. They stand alone, or in pairs. When they catch McEban's eye, they nod, and he nods back.

McEban looks up to where the sun is stamped upon the sky and pulls his feet free from where he stands, and moves along the fencing to the pens next to the bucking chutes. He stands breathing easier in the shade.

No one stands to study an old black stud. He's in a pen by himself. The pen is tucked under the bleachers, and the horse is quartered with planks of black shadow. He doesn't pace, or shift, or stamp, or flex against the flies. He's scarred, and battle-bitten, swaybacked, and stout as a shrunken draft horse. There is a thumbprint of white on his fore-head and nowhere else. His tail hangs to the ground. His tail and mane are tangled with hayleaf and broken weedstalk. He carries his head low, and when he snorts, the pendust puffs high as his eyes. His eyes are tar-black and wet, and they scan the world for threat.

McEban leans at the black stud's pen. He folds his arms on a shoulder-high rail and rests his chin on the back of a hand. "Hello, old man," he whispers, and the stud moves a single ear to better hear the roundness of the man's voice, and that's all he does.

Bennett leans in against the fencing at McEban's side. "He isn't going to make much of a pet."

"No, he's not," McEban allows.

"You step in there and I'll bet he could bite a fist-size chunk out of you about anywhere he wanted."

McEban whistles a single low note through his teeth, and the stud vectors his other ear to catch the sound. His mane is parted at his fore-lock and hangs past his eyes and over his eyes. He blows and the pendust rises and settles.

McEban shifts his weight from one hip to the other. He whistles again. The black stud blinks, and both ears twitch, and McEban pushes back from the rail and turns to the alleyway. He levels his gaze. He looks hard into the crowd. There are laughter and conversation and several dozen dark holes that hadn't been there a moment ago. They are circular and stand waist-high to the men, and whole children have fallen into them. When he tries to focus on the holes they pulse and shift to the peripheries. He shakes his head.

To his left, in the middle distance, there's a pen of bay and black and brown studs. Two- and three- and four-year-olds. Nine of them. They pace the limits of their pen. Their necks and chests are lathered, and they're lathered from their balls to their hocks. McEban can smell them. They smell of salted molasses. He knows it to be the odor of fear. The horses circle and snort and duck and circle some more. Their necks are swollen and their nutsacks sucked up tight. A woman's voice comes loose from the crowd. "Buy 'em all," she shouts. "Buy 'em all, and turn 'em loose." The young studs pace.

McEban turns to Bennett. "I thought I lost you," he says.

"I was right behind you." Bennett's weepy eye is swollen shut, and it lifts his face into an unusual cant. "Are you alright?"

"I'm fine."

"You look pale as me."

McEban smiles and slobbers at the edges of the smile and wipes his mouth with the back of a hand. He can taste a sour mix of shortening and egg yolk. He smacks his lips and swallows and turns away and bends at his waist and pukes just once. He grips the penrail and spits to clear his mouth and straightens. The black stud steps back a pace. He watches with his wet eyes. McEban grips harder on a steel pipe of the fencing.

"I guess breakfast didn't set right," he says.

He spits again and scuffs at the stain he's made in the dust with the side of his boot and squares himself to Bennett. Bennett's eyes have come active in his face. He looks like he did when they were boys, McEban thinks—just a boy excited by some accident. McEban smiles again and turns loose of the penrail.

"Why don't you walk over and find your wife?" he asks.

"You going to puke again?"

"It's probably just the sun. I'll come over in a minute. My head's already clearing."

"I'll get us something to eat," Bennett says. "Eating hardly ever hurts."

McEban watches Bennett work into the crowd, turning his shoulders to the left and right to slant his way through. Dust hangs in the alleyway and the people appear to have wobbled loose from their outlines, become blurred, but the dark circles have cleared. Bennett stops at the end of the alleyway and turns. He raises a hand above his head and waves and smiles and lets the hand drop to his side. McEban waves back. He leans against the black stud's pen and closes his eyes.

H is grandmother had her breakfast of fried mush and bacon, and McEban was just done with the breakfast dishes when Bennett walked onto the porch and stood against the screendoor and stared through the mesh. He had a bath towel draped around his neck. He watched McEban drying his hands.

"What are you doing?" Bennett asked.

"The dishes. You walk over here?"

"I came with my dad."

Bennett stepped back to allow McEban out through the door, and they stood together on the porch and watched his father and Brian Reilly where they leaned into the side panels of Mr. Reilly's pickup. They talked across the bed of the truck and his father pointed toward the Bighorns, and they turned and stared to the west.

"Where's your mom?" McEban asked.

"At church. It's Sunday. You want to go swimming?"

Beads of sweat stood across Bennett's forehead and his upper lip, and at the thickened wattles of his neck. His lowest shirtsnap was broken and his belly-fat rolled out and over the waist of his jeans.

"It isn't even hot yet."

"It's hot enough for me," Bennett said. "My mom says my furnace is set on high. She says if I wasn't a good sweater I'd probably burst into flames."

McEban looked back to where his father stood at the pickup. "I better ask."

"I asked for you."

"You asked if I could go swimming?"

"He saw me when I got out of the truck. He looked right at this towel, so, I asked him."

"What'd he say?"

"He said, 'Good morning.'"

"Was that all he said?"

"He said, 'I'll bet you're glad not to be in church.'"

Bennett waited for McEban to get a towel of his own and they skirted the pasture away from their fathers and struck the waist-high bottom grass and followed the creek upstream. The grasshoppers clung to their legs, and they picked them off as they walked. The sun warmed the mosquitoes to their daybeds and the flies came to work, and white-and-orange butterflies dipped and guttered in the morning light.

They stopped above the headgate, at the big bend in Horse Creek, where the creek curved back against an ell of stiffer ground, and stared down into the turning green water.

"You wish Bailey had lived?" Bennett asked.

"Of course I do."

"Every day?"

"I'm wishing it now."

Bennett took a fist of yellow baling twine from his back pocket, and they sat in the grass and pulled off their boots and socks and stripped out of their jeans and shirts and underpants. They waded out onto the sandbar that led into the head of the long, curving pool. They stood thigh-deep in the water, and the light off the water made them squint and bow their heads.

They waded chest-deep into the pool, where the brush willows lined the bank, and gripped down the willow stalks and tied them into bundles with lengths of twine. The cool water made them gasp, and they stood still until their breathing quieted.

"I guess I'll have to do," Bennett said. The water eased the weight away from his bones, and he felt lighter in the world. "For a brother."

"For Bailey?"

"I don't think your mom's going to have any more."

"I guess you've done fine," McEban said.

They smiled and still squinted into the glare, and the water rolled against their young skins, smooth as jade, and sweet.

They bent the willow bundles back and tied them in loops and tied their wrists to the loops, helping each other with the knots, and nodded at once, their faces stamped with smiles, and lifted their feet away from the shifting creek bottom and let the current sweep them out into the pool.

They hung by their wrists, their arms pulled back to the sides of their heads, their bodies trailing, bobbing, the slow current stretching them taut.

They shut their eyes against the sun and didn't speak and settled against the suck and pull of the fish-thick stream. Only their faces and hands broke the water's surface, and their dreams rose to the surface of their minds.

They spent the morning hours that way, drained of concern, quieted, and the speckled trout forgot they were boys, thought of them only as unexpected spars, as shapes that cast new shadows, and moved in and held themselves against the curves of the boys' backs.

And that is how they drifted. As just lengths of idle and faultless flesh. Boys lost from the industry of their lives.

The auctioneer paces the length of a flatbed trailer parked at the west side of the pens. In the middle of the trailer stands a cafeteria-issue metal table. A battery-operated speaker is set on the table's end. The auctioneer holds a microphone to his mouth and repeats: "One, two, three. Testing, one, two, three."

A pinch-faced woman sits on a folding chair behind the table and fans through the sheets of paper that sort the horses by pen number and freeze-brand. She pushes her glasses higher on the bridge of her nose and weights the papers with small gray stones in case of a wind.

There are twenty-four feet of four-high aluminum bleacherseats dragged into a half-circle in front of the flatbed. The bidders stack themselves on the sun-heated seats and shift for position and visit and laugh. The auctioneer tells the crowd they have the BLM and the Cody Stampede Board to thank for today's auction. He tells them that cowboys gathered 315 wild horses out of the McCullough Peaks, held these 188 for adoption, turned the rest back for seed.

"There's only so much grass," he says.

Spotters pace in the area between the flatbed and the bidders. They are tall, loud-voiced, and shameless men. They study the crowd, gauging who will buy and who will not.

The auctioneer steps to the limit of the microphone's cord. "One-hundred-and-twenty-five-dollar minimum," he announces. "Two-fifty for a mare-foal pair. Horses go to the highest bidder."

McEban stands to the side of the bleachers and finds Bennett in the front row between Gretchen and Gretchen's cousin Holly. Holly wears a ballcap and a pair of black batwing chaps and spurs. She balances her infant daughter and an insulated Conoco coffee mug on separate knees, and Gretchen lies across Bennett's lap and speaks to her and they both laugh, and Holly works a pint of rum out of her diaper bag and hands it to Bennett. Gretchen holds their waxed cups of soda, and Holly's mug, low between her legs, and Bennett tops them off and slips the rum bottle back into the diaper bag. They toast the smiling child, and the child wriggles and coos and grips fistfuls of the dense sunlight from in front of its mother's face.

"These animals will make horses," sings the auctioneer. "You bet they will. All they need's a chance."

McEban moves to the rear of the bleacherseats. A moonfaced Northern Cheyenne man sits at the end, on the top row. He looks down at McEban and nods and turns back to the auctioneer. A long black braid falls from the back of his black hat and lies along the length of his spine. His blond girlfriend sits squeezed against his side. She wears a fringed buckskin jacket with the print of a chief on its back. The chief wears a headdress. The young Cheyenne and the blond woman hold hands and lean into each other, from knee to shoulder.

Curtis sits just below them. He has cleaned the blood from his face, and his hat is pushed back, and there is only a lump at his hairline. The lump is yellowed and dark. He drinks a beer and leans back to say something to the couple behind him and sees McEban and lifts his beer and smiles. McEban smiles back.

Over the adult conversation and the laughter of children and the sounds of frightened horses and the drone of flies there is the squeal and sharp clang of metal gates and the snap of stockwhips.

The auctioneer tells the crowd the horses will be run into the roundpen three at a time. That the highest bidder will be offered first choice.

"One time through. One look. Take one, take two, take three," he sings.

McEban skirts the concession stand and climbs the stairs to a catwalk that feeds and empties the seats over the bucking chutes. A sign reads BUZZARD'S ROOST. He stands on the catwalk and bends over the railing and looks down into the pens of milling horses and over the crowd and the parking lot and the canyon beyond that the Shoshone River has worn out of the plain.

There's a second flatbed trailer parked beyond the auctioneer, stacked with steel-tubed fence sections meant to be stood into alleyways for the loading after the sale. Directly below him stands a dun-colored filly. Her tail is tucked and her head held so low McEban cannot see her ears past her narrow withers. She's tight through the waist, and from above holds the outline of an athletic woman, sitting, leaned forward, resolute.

The auctioneer tells the crowd that all out-of-county buyers will need a brand inspection and a health certificate for the horses they buy. He tells them a veterinarian stands ready for that purpose and that there's no charge for the paperwork. He tells them that buyers are required to fill out a private-maintenance-and-care agreement. And that there are cowboys, men who have had their hands on these wild horses, who will help with the loading. He tells them today will cost them no skin. Only money.

McEban watches a stockman step into a pen, and he watches the horses come up high on their feet. The man waves his arms and shouts and whistles and snaps his whip, and when he's shaved off three animals a second man swings the gate open and the horses are allowed to escape into the alleyway.

In the alleyway there is a third man with a whip. He snaps his whip in the dust-dulled air and turns the horses north, and follows, blocking their escape, and turns them west into a second alleyway and closes a gate at the turn.

The alleyway narrows into a long, curved chute, and the horses are worked along the chute, in front of a series of whipsnaps, the gates clanging behind them. They try to turn and cannot and they rear. They shake their heads and chomp their tongues. Their eyes and nostrils come wild for a better look at this new world, and the smell of it. They're held up tight, chest to ass, in the squeezeway, and the second horse wears the smear of his brother's or sister's shit on his chest, as does the last. They are packed that tightly. They paw the dust up in the squeezeway, and it holds against them like a curse.

The auctioneer announces the horses by sex and color and age and number, and they are released into the roundpen. There is another man in the roundpen. The ringman. He also carries a whip. He turns them, and they kick up gravel and gravel-clotted horseshit in their turn. And he turns them again, and then again, shortening their efforts at escape, keeping them displayed against the white metal fencing in front of the bleacherseats. They grow wet and dark with sweat. And they slaver and swing ribbons of drool into the air. The bidders stand and crane forward and shade their eyes.

The paints bid out high, and the soil-colored colts go low. "Here," a spotter calls. "And here," calls another.

And the auctioneer sings: "There's two, and now a quarter. I've got my quarter. And now a half. Half. Half. Half. Who's going to give me a half for this spotted little filly? Now, I've got the two and a half. You bet. And now three."

"Here," calls a spotter and raises one arm and points to the bidder, and the bidder nods.

A filly weanling sticks her tail in the air the way an antelope would and shits in an arc, and quivers, and her nervous gut sucks in against her ribs, and the bidders laugh and raise their orange cards and stand and wave the cards.

"Here. Here. Here," the spotters call.

The buyers are identified and a gate opens at the far side of the roundpen, and the ringman turns the bought horses into an alleyway that leads back into the puzzle of pens. They run stiffly. They hold their noses inches above the ground, snorting, searching for a stretch of earth that is free from the scent of men.

"Loadslips," the auctioneer tells the crowd. "You get them when you pay. Everybody loads at the end of the sale."

Women stand and fan their faces with their bid cards and pull their sweaty T-shirts away from their bellies and backs and breasts.

A bald man backs his truck to the bleachers and props the lid of his toolbox open. The toolbox is bolted against the cab. He's filled it with ice and beer and sells the cans of beer for three dollars each. The auctioneer calls a boy from the crowd and sends him to fetch a can and tips the boy a dollar. Lines form at the portable toilets. Mothers smear their children's faces with sunscreen, and the horses are run through in knots of three and sold. A woman stands and slaps the face of the man seated at her back and then she slaps him again.

The black stud is brought in alone. He stands with his chest pressed against the penrails, facing the crowd, snorting, and holding his breath when he's not. His body is bunched up tight. The ringman steps away from him and raises his whip and looks over his shoulder to find the fencing he thinks he might have to climb. A white-haired old woman totters up with the help of a cane and bids a beer-drunk man down and buys the stud. She sets off, wobbling on the uneven parking lot, to find her sons.

Three at a time. Sometimes four. The dust is in the air and will not settle, and smells of hoof-beaten minerals and urine and fry-grease and beer. The sun stands high. Shadows fall close, or not at all.

A little bay stud weanling is the last run through.

"Who's going to give me twenty-five, just twenty-five dollars to start?" asks the auctioneer. "We're not here to make money, we're here to make cowboys. I'm not lying to anyone when I tell you this fine little man's got a one-hundred-dollar vet bill in his future."

The buyers bend low for the evidence. There's a peach-size hernia high on the weanling's gut, against a bottom rib. He turns clumsily, with his weight over his forequarters, and probably always has. The ringman keeps the little stud whipped up against the fencing.

"Twenty-five," sings the auctioneer. "A little patchwork and he'll make a good horse. Who's going to give me the twenty-five?"

"I will," calls Gretchen. She sets her waxed cup on the ground and stands and steadies herself against Bennett. She waves her bid card in the air.

"Sold," says the auctioneer, and the spotters smile, and McEban starts down the steps from the Buzzard's Roost to bring his truck and trailer around.

I n the dream her body is touched by rinds, triangles, scimitars, scallops of shadow. Light and shadow.

He wonders what his watching affects. He wonders if his eyes will wear her skin too thin. He worries over accident. He estimates the world to crackle with disaster.

What would happen to her, he wonders, if she were to lie out naked under this full moon? Dream moon. If she were to sleep under the flight of bats? Hundreds of them. Would they find her body with their voices? Would their appreciation, their curiosity, wick her echoless? Could she weather their choir? Would she wake craving a dinner of insect and nectar and fruit?

He thinks of the advantages of winged mammals. The secrets of echolocation. He wonders if every man, woman, and child is pressed finally to death by the weight of angels, by their need to witness our cowardice, our small braveries.

All this he wonders and means to ask about in his prayers. He prays to remember when he wakes.

Chapter Three

※

McEban parks in the alley behind the Miracle Bar, and Holly's the first to stand out of the truck. She still wears her cap and chaps and spurs and the swelled globe of a single breast falls from her open shirtfront. The nipple is dark and taut, and slick from her daughter's gumming, and her shirt sags wet with sweat for the length of her spine and under each arm.

Gretchen takes up the child long enough for Holly to palm the breast back into its bra-cup and snap her shirt closed. Bennett shakes the rum bottle and the last inch of liquor catches golden in the sunlight.

"No more for this mom," Holly says. She leans down into her daughter's sleeping face and sniffs, and cradles the child back into her arms. She winks at Gretchen. "I believe my milk's gone wild."

Bennett steps to the Miracle's alley door, and tips back the rum and tosses the empty bottle into an open Dumpster. "Can we buy you something to eat?"

"I'll come in for a burger," Holly says. She laughs because she's hot and drowsy, and because of the soft flex of her daughter in her arms, and because it feels good to laugh.

Gretchen sways in the glare off the trailergate, caught for a moment in the slap of afternoon light, the sweet spread of rum. "I'll be in in a minute," she says.

"Order me a cheeseburger," McEban says. He stands by the trailer's side. "And one for Woody." He lifts his hat away from his face and peers in at the weanling stud. "Woody likes catsup."

The little stud stands spraddled on the trailer's floorboards. He carries his head low and rolls his eyes at McEban. He's braced and still ready for a fight. Gretchen folds her arms against the trailerside. She looks to the fresh dents and scrapes that run along both inside panels and on the inside of the trailergate.

"What do you think of him?" she asks.

McEban shifts his weight and rubs the knot that's risen hard on the front of his leg. The horse squats lower and chatters its teeth like a cat. "I don't think I feel lucky enough to step him out and try to get him loaded again," he says. "I probably don't need to be kicked twice in the same day."

"Happy birthday."

McEban turns to her but she just squints in at the weanling. She shrugs a shoulder up against her jawline to wipe the sweat away but will not turn.

"What's that supposed to mean?" he asks.

"It means today was the first day I had to shop."

"You bought me a ruptured horse for my birthday?"

"I thought I'd get you something you could improve." She steps away from the trailer.

"He'll surprise you." He bends again at the trailer. "He's going to make a horse."

"Everything surprises me," she says, and he listens to the faint sound of her steps, the bardoor opening and falling closed.

He reaches over the trailer's side panel, talking slowly, evenly, his pocketknife open in his hand. "There, son," he whispers, "that's the man," and he pulls the blade back sharply and the weanling quivers like he's stepped on ice, and the nylon noose and numbered tag drop to the floorboards.

The horse bows his head between his legs and snorts and keeps his head that way. His ribs heave against his dark-red sides, and the pouch of ruptured gut stands tight. McEban pockets the knife and rubs his thigh.

"I'll bet you're thirsty." He straightens and limps back on the knotted leg. "I am."

When he steps inside the Miracle he catches his breath in the air-conditioned darkness and stands huffing against the chill. His eyes water and he presses the heel of a hand to his brow. He can feel the muscles across his shoulders tighten, cinching at the back of his scalp.

"You got a headache?"

He drops his hand and blinks to focus. A middle-aged woman stands before him. Her hair's been freshly permed and smells sharply of chemicals. Like dry-cleaning, McEban thinks.

"I'm Mrs. Spaulding," she says.

"I'll be fine," he says. "Somebody new buy this place?"

"I did. About a month ago. How can you tell?"

"I don't remember the air-conditioning being used this much."

Past Mrs. Spaulding a young soldier sits straight on his barstool, smoking, blowing rings at the backbar.

Bennett and Gretchen and Holly are settled in a booth. Over the booth there's an oil painting of a pair of sage grouse, and spaced away from the sage grouse, encircling the room, the unframed canvases of parrots, chickadees, flamingoes, eagles, pelicans, wood ducks, a parakeet.

"Did you change the burgers too?" McEban asks.

"I've kept the booze and the food the same." Mrs. Spaulding smoothes the front of her apron with both hands. "The paintings aren't just décor," she says. "They're for sale. Sometimes people forget to ask."

McEban nods and stares down at the salad bar at his side. A stainless-steel corner catches the dull-blue flash of a neon Hamm's sign. He stirs a finger through a tub of melting ice and iceberg lettuce.

"Can I buy this bowl of lettuce from you?" he asks.

"There's not much lettuce left."

"I'm not after the lettuce."

"I'll need the bowl back," she says.

He lifts the bowl out of the spread of ice and holds it up in both hands, careful not to slosh the water out.

"I don't know much about art."

Mrs. Spaulding shrugs. "That's too bad."

He backs out through the door and into the sunlight and sets the metal bowl in the alley-dirt by the trailer tongue. He scoops the half-dozen torn leaves of lettuce out and opens a hinged half-door high in the nose of the trailer. He lifts the bowl in through the door and levels it in the manger.

The little stud paws at the floorboards and snaps his jaws. McEban stands away from the door. He hears the horse step forward and pause and step again. He hears him suck at the icy water and stop and hold his muzzle above the bowl, the water dripping from the horse's chin whiskers.

When the horse is altogether finished McEban pulls the bowl out and sets it in the pickup's bed, and Woody laps up the last of the water. The wet stainless throws an oval of glare against the cab, and McEban leans into the truck's side and reaches an open hand in and Woody presses his chest into the hand.

There is the rise and slack of traffic on the side streets. The spiking drone of a motorcycle working through its lower gears, backing off for a stoplight. The buzz of flies at the Dumpster, the general weight of sunlight. And then the truck falls into shadow and a wind plucks at the alley-dirt.

McEban looks to the west, to a high bank of cumulus risen off the mountains. Woody lifts his nose and sniffs at the surge of ozone, and the temperature drops ten degrees all at once.

"Don't you love it here?" McEban asks.

He steps to the side mirror just as the first big drops strike and sizzle on the truck metal. He whistles Woody out of the truckbed and they sit together in the cab.

The temperature drops another ten degrees and the rain turns to hail, and they listen to the sharp snare-drum shatter of the ice pellets against the truck's hood and roof. The windows steam. Woody climbs onto McEban's lap, and McEban sets his hat crown-down on the seat and rests his head against the seatback and shuts his eyes.

"I ordered you a cheeseburger," he says.

In the early spring dawn it was his job to break the skims of ice that sealed the water troughs. He shoveled the broken shards out of the cold water, and they broke upon the frost-stiffened ground and sparkled in the weak light. The earth still held itself hard, stunned from a season of below-freezing nights.

He kicked the ice chunks away from the troughs so they wouldn't freeze into jagged drifts and hung the scoop shovel on a nail driven into the barnside. He slapped his hands together until he could feel them sting and bent through the corral rails and stood out of the wind. The wind was raw and down from Canada. It reddened his face and cracked the meat of his lower lip. He drew the bloody lip back between his teeth and held it there and looked away toward the creek.

He was looking toward the creek when his father led two saddled horses from the barn. The wings of the man's chaps caught in the wind and slapped at the sides of his legs, and he stood up onto his horse and left the second horse trailing its reins on the stonehard ground.

"You get those troughs cleared?" his father asked.

"Yes, sir. I did."

When he spoke he felt his lip split more deeply, and he sucked it back between his teeth. He caught up the reins of the second horse and stood by its shoulder, and when his father nodded he looped the off-rein around the horse's neck and shortened the near-rein so the animal would spin into him. He turned the stirrup forward and seated his foot and kicked away from the ground. He'd just gained the off-stirrup when the horse bowed its head and farted and crow-hopped sideways toward the creek.

He heard his father yell, "Pull his goddamn head up," and he sawed back on the reins, and the horse stumbled and stood and blew hard in the chilled air.

"That smacks the blood out of your ass," his father said, but he was smiling when he spoke.

"Yes, sir," he said. "It does." He was smiling too.

His father spurred his horse into the trees along the creek, and McEban reined back a pace to study him, and the horse he sat, not their parts, but the whole of them. It was what he meant to take away from his father. He meant to ride like his father rode.

The Naugahyde booth is brown, stained nearly black at the top of the seatback by years of hair-oil, and the seat is patched with lengths of gray duct tape. It crackles when McEban settles in.

Bennett rests his elbows against the tabletop and holds a bottle of Coors to his swollen eye. His cheeks are red and speckled as the Formica, and there's an empty shot glass slid to the table's edge.

"Are you drunk?" McEban asks.

"I'm getting there."

Gretchen's at work at the pool table in front of the streetside windows. She's set a beer bottle on the north and south bumpers and shoots back and forth, stopping between shots to drink and chalk her cue.

They watch the soldier push away from the bar's edge and stagger to the pool table. He circles Gretchen, watching her pocket the balls. His arms hang loosely at his sides. He clenches a cigarette in his front teeth, and his lips are pulled back from his teeth. He digs two quarters out of his pants pocket and snaps them on the bumper above the coin slot and smoothes out a twenty-dollar bill beside the quarters.

"Where's Holly?" McEban asks.

"She ate and went home. Where were you?"

"Woody and I took a nap in the truck."

The soldier's cigarette ash falls and powders the green felt. Gretchen smiles at him and starts to hum.

"How drunk's Gretchen?" McEban asks.

"She's just flushed. Rum just makes her flushed."

"She's drinking beer now."

Bennett squints toward his wife with his unswollen eye. "Beer just makes her flushed too. She'll kick his ass."

Mrs. Spaulding slides two baskets of fries onto the table. There's a cheeseburger on top of each basket.

"What do you want to drink?" she asks.

"A cup of coffee," McEban tells her. "And could I get you to take one of these cheeseburgers back? Maybe keep it warm if you could?"

"They said you wanted two."

"The second one's for my dog."

"I won't have a dog in here," she says.

"I didn't bring him in."

Mrs. Spaulding tucks her chin to have a look over the top of her glasses. "The burger won't be as good left under the warming lamp."

"My dog's not a whiner." McEban smiles because he thinks the pun's funny. Mrs. Spaulding does not.

She spreads out a paper napkin and wraps up a cheeseburger. "What about the fries?" she asks.

"I'll take care of those," Bennett says. He drags a basket of fries to his side of the table and asks her to bring him another beer and a shot when she gets the chance.

McEban watches Gretchen at the pool table, pacing, lining up the ten ball. The young soldier stands with his legs spread wide, his cue stick stabbed between his feet. He holds his head back to let the cigarette smoke rise away from his eyes.

"I saw Ansel in Ishawooa last week," Bennett says. He sips his beer and turns the bottle and presses it back against his eye. "He was buying rifle cartridges at the Army Surplus Store."

McEban snorts.

"Why is that funny?"

Gretchen sinks the ten in the southwest corner pocket and straightens, and the soldier levels his head.

"It's funny because Thorpe was over the other day and warned him off shooting out the neighbors' yardlights."

"Where's he want your neighbors to live?"

"Someplace else." McEban sucks the hamburger grease from a thumb and wipes his hands. "When he looks up at that subdivision that used to be your dad's place it ruins his whole day."

"Is that why he doesn't like me?"

"Mostly," McEban says.

Mrs. Spaulding brings the coffee and beer and a shot of bourbon and Bennett downs the shot and sets the empty glass back at the table's edge and nods for another. Mrs. Spaulding looks at McEban. "It'll be okay," McEban says. "I'm the one driving."

She turns back to the bar and Bennett scoots up higher against the tabletop. "We're all just a bunch of white immigrant sons of bitches," he says. His face is screwed up into a battered complaint. "Ansel didn't get here first. He just got here before the next guy did."

McEban holds the coffee cup under his chin, and the steam rises into his face. "He didn't like you when you were a kid either."

Bennett relaxes his face and opens his mouth and closes his mouth and sits back in the booth. "No shit?"

"No shit."

"Then I guess it can't be helped."

Mrs. Spaulding leaves a refilled shot glass on the table, and Bennett takes it up and turns it slowly between his thumb and forefinger.

"When you get a chance tell Ansel I've got to make a living whether he likes me or not. Just tell him that."

"You can tell him yourself."

Bennett nods. "I will," he says. He stares down at the shot of bourbon. "Hell, I don't especially like what I do." He looks up at McEban. His eyes have moistened. "But I'm too meek to learn anything new. Aren't the meek supposed to inherit something?"

"You aren't meek," McEban tells him. "You're just too much of a pussy to keep a ranch together."

"Well, there ought to be a prize for that too," Bennett says, and the soldier shouts "Damn it" and digs another couple of quarters from his pants pocket for a new rack of balls and unfolds a twenty from his shirt pocket.

"You think that's going to be trouble?" McEban asks.

"I think I don't know what's going to be trouble."

"Do you ever think how lucky we are not to be any older?"

Bennett throws back the bourbon, and grimaces and sips his beer. "I almost always feel lucky. If I'm not around you or Ansel."

"If we were ten years older Vietnam would've probably gotten us."

Bennett sucks in through his clenched teeth. He likes the way the cool air feels at the back of his mouth. "That's not something I think about," he says. "Do you think about it?"

"Yeah, I do."

Gretchen breaks the new rack of balls, and Bennett stops his beer just at his lips, listening for a ball to drop. When it does they both look toward the table to see whether she's shooting solids or stripes.

"Would you die for her?" McEban asks.

"What the hell kind of question is that?"

"Would you?"

Bennett brings his beer bottle up close to his good eye. Through the brown glass McEban appears dark and soft and indistinct. "It's not going to come to that," he says. "We're all too old to have it come to that." And after a moment, "I've got to piss."

He scoots to the edge of the booth and pulls himself up by the pair of chromed prongs mounted on the booth's end and stands weaving in the smoky air.

"You need some help?"

Bennett stares at him for a long moment. "I forgot why I'm up," he says, and when McEban gets up to help him to the restroom Bennett swings a big, huffing roundhouse and misses McEban by a foot, and his legs buckle and he sits all the way down on the floor. He looks up and smiles. He's still smiling when his good eye rolls back and he slumps to his side.

Gretchen strides over thumping her pool cue against the floor like a walking stick. She stares down at Bennett and when he doesn't move takes up his half-full beer and tilts it back. She wipes her mouth with the back of her hand.

Her eyes are wild and dark, and she's charged up over her string of pool victories. "You, therefore," she says, "who wish to remain free, either instantly be wise or, as soon as possible, cease to be fools." She grins and chugs the last swallow of Bennett's beer.

"That Isaiah?" McEban asks.

"Milton."

Bennett rolls over on his back and starts to snore.

"He tried to hit me," McEban says. "You think he suspects something?"

Gretchen sits on the edge of the booth. "I think he's suspected something his whole life." She stares at the floor, still gripping her cue. She shakes her head. "It's a goddamn miracle the suspense hasn't killed him."

"Can you help me get him in the truck?"

She shakes her head and says, "I don't think I can." She tries to stand and falls back unconscious, sprawled on the boothseat.

The soldier weaves at McEban's side. "I could help you," he says.

"I'll give you twenty dollars if you do."

"I wasn't asking to get hired."

"I know you weren't," McEban tells him. "How much did she win from you?"

"Sixty dollars."

"Is that all you have?"

"I have seventeen dollars left."

"Then let me give you twenty for your help. What's your name?"

Bennett holds his breath, and they both stare down at him until he starts snoring again.

"Hadley," the soldier says. He leans his cue stick against the table and strips off his tunic and bends over Gretchen. Her skirt is ridden high on her thighs, and her bookbag has fallen underneath the table. Hadley brings the bookbag up and settles it against her belly and finds both her wrists and pulls her upright on the seat. Her head lolls to her left shoulder.

"Don't let me catch you grabbing her ass or anything," McEban says.

"I'm just a bad pool player," says Hadley. "I'm not a pervert."

McEban takes up Gretchen by the ankles and Hadley grips her under the arms, and they carry her out through the alley door and prop her upright in the middle of the truckseat. McEban puts Woody in the pickup's bed.

When they come back in for Bennett, Mrs. Spaulding hands McEban his second cheeseburger, and he unsnaps the belly of his shirt and slips it inside.

"At least we didn't break anything," he says.

"You sure I can't sell you a painting?"

"Maybe next time. We already bought a horse today."

Hadley leans against the table, out of breath, staring down at the considerable rise of Bennett's belly. He pinches the cigarette from his teeth and stubs it out in an ashtray. "Was that twenty dollars apiece?" he asks.

They crossed Horse Creek and the horses drank and came out of the water blowing, their bellies dark and steaming in the cool air.

His father spurred his horse into the sage and grass foothills, and McEban followed. They curved southward, out across the belly of a hill, and struck a west-running fenceline and rode the fence west and stopped at its corner. The wind was still out of the north and hard on them. The horses' hooves raised little puffs of dust.

His father stood down from the buckskin he rode and skirted the horse's ass, his left arm laid along its rump, chanting "There, son, that's the man" to let the horse know where he was, and unsnapped the saddle scabbard and pulled the rifle free.

McEban stood by the fence, holding his horse, and his father handed him the buckskin's reins.

"Walk them down the fence," he said. "Hold them tight and watch yourself. They aren't going to like this a bit."

The man's cheeks were flushed and mottled by the wind. He looked into the fence corner and the boy looked too.

The horses pulled back steadily against their bridle reins and rolled their eyes.

A doe deer lay gray and gaunt before them, on her side, her left front shoulder dislocated, the leg drawn back and up, as though in her sleep she had reached for something above herself, just beyond her grasp. Two wires were twisted around her pastern, and her shrunken body hung down from the diamond-shaped snare. She had begun to rot and she smelled of decay.

McEban shut his eyes and stood braced against the shifting wind, against the stench of the nearly dead thing before him.

He imagined her well, sleek, welcoming the spring; with her kind. In his imagination he could see her approach the fence, settle her weight back to jump. He could feel the miscalculation. Could hear the toe of the heart-shaped black hoof click against the topwire, hear the wire sing, see her flight tip, the leg stabbing down for balance, stabbing down between the wires, top and secondmost, and the scramble and fall, the wires scissoring the leg and holding fast.

A bank of cloud-shadow moved over them and the sun broke free against the midsky and flashed his eyelids pink, and he stepped back one pace and sucked at the air. When he opened his eyes he looked away from the fence corner to the bottom of the hillside. He looked to the leafless cottonwoods that grew in against the sage. The day had warmed enough for the trees to come sweet with sap. But that was all there was. Just the scent of summer flushed up for a moment when the wind changed. Just the promise of ease.

He looked again at the doe. The ground around her was scarred with the effort of her struggle. She breathed through her mouth, and her tongue was fallen from her muzzle and dry and caked with dirt. Her cheek was busy with ants.

She watched them but did not lift her head. When she blinked she blinked slowly and only the curve of her lashes caught the light. There was no struggle left in her eyes.

"This is the harm we do," his father said.

He stepped forward and bolted a shell into the rifle's chamber, and McEban stepped back and opened his mouth. The doe still did not move.

"I can do this," he said.

His father turned to him and searched his face. He held the rifle in both hands, across his waist. The wind had eased.

"I'm not sure you can," he said.

"I can."

"And after it's done?"

"I can do that too."

"Even though you're not sure what that is?"

"Yes."

The man looked south and then down at the rifle he held. He thought of the life he was asked to live when he was a boy. When he was just twelve.

"This is faster than your mother wants you to grow," he said.

"I'm not like her," McEban said. "Not altogether."

"No, you're not."

He stepped forward and held the rifle out to his son, and the boy gripped it by the forestock and offered the braid of bridle reins he held in his hand.

"The safety's on," his father said. He walked away with the horses and stood with them at a distance.

McEban swung back to the fence corner. The doe's eyes were large and brown and stayed on him, and because it's what he'd said he would do, he seated the rifle stock into his shoulder and thumbed the safety off. He sighted along the barrel. Dozens of woodticks fed in the scallops of her ears, bloated big as thumbnails, gone bluish white, gorged with her blood.

He brought the front sight down between her eyes. He held the gun steady and he held his breath. When she blinked he squeezed the trigger, and the rifle bucked against his cheek and went still. He lowered the rifle from his shoulder. And then he lowered his eyes.

He heard the horses dance their iron shoes against a scatter of stones and his father talking to them in a low and steady voice: "There, son, that's the man, stand solid. Stand."

He heard the horses quiet and his father bring them up behind him and he stood for a moment and looked down at what he had just done. And then his father stepped up and took the rifle from him and leaned it in the fence corner and held the wires apart, and McEban straddled the new corpse and pulled its leg free. The leg dropped against the haired body and bounced and lay still. The sage and the posts were flecked with blood.

"There isn't a lot that feels like you think it's going to," his father said.

"Is that true for everything?"

"In my experience." He slid the rifle into its scabbard and stepped up on the buckskin. "What happened to your lip?"

"It split in the cold."

"Just now?"

"This morning."

The man took a pair of yellow cloth gloves from his jacket pocket and pulled them on and looked down at the dead doe. He unbuckled his catchrope and handed it to the boy. "I don't want her left out here."

"Why?" McEban's ears rang from the gunshot.

"Because I ride past here a lot," he said and turned his horse down the fenceline, riding east.

McEban stops the truck on the shoulder of the two-lane at the top of the Bighorns. He turns off the headlights and stands out to piss, and Woody jumps onto the still-warm macadam and lifts a leg against a front tire. The engine pings. The sun has set and the night sky is swelled up black and prickling with starlight. The Milky Way casts a smear of light directly overhead, and it brings the limestone scarps up pale from the dark timber and glows softly on the truck metal. The weanling steps and stamps on the trailer's floorboards. An owl hoots, and then another, and the owlsounds roll in softly and hold against the lower ground.

Bennett leans against the passenger-side window, sleeping with his mouth open, and Gretchen is curled under his shoulder. She coughs and resettles herself against her husband.

McEban pulls the cheeseburger from under his shirt and peels back the napkin and takes a bite and drops the rest to the pavement. Woody wolfs the burger and the catsup-smeared half of the bun and tosses the other half of the bun in the air and lets it fall and circles it, snapping at it.

Orion lies on its side against the uneven horizon to the southeast, and the moon breaks the earth's curve: oblong and orange and searing in the dark sky. It rises up into the constellation's chest, and shadows fall back from the truck and trailer, man and dog. A coyote yips. Nothing answers. Jupiter and Mars and the North Star bear down, and McEban wonders what his life might be like alone. He tries to imagine his life without Bennett and Gretchen, without Ansel to return home to, and cannot. He tries to imagine a life without this high rocky ground and feels vacant and useless as the constellation before him, as any man defined by just an assemblage of lighted points.

He drives slowly off the Bighorns, through drifts of moonlight, and when he's gained the rolling grazeland at their base, slows the truck for half a hundred Black Angus cows that line both sides of the borrow ditch. He worries that a calf might become alarmed and try to cross through the headlights. He thinks he should call Gene and Anna Maris when he gets home and tell them they have a fence down.

He turns off the county road and gears down on the dirt track that leads up along Horse Creek. Gretchen jostles on the seat beside him, against Bennett. Her left arm hangs off the front of the seat, and her hand bounces back against the shifting column.

The lights are on at Ansel's, and he honks as he drives by. He looks in the side mirror and sees the porchlight flick on and off, and he grinds into compound and eases the truck and trailer across a shallow irrigation ditch and through an open wiregate.

The pasture is dry and he cuts the headlights and allows the truck to idle in a wide arc that returns him to the fence. He stands out into the night and puffs his cheeks and blows. He stretches his arms wide and turns his palms to the sky. He thinks that even blind he would know he is home. He feels it in his hands.

He walks to the back of the trailer and swings the trailergate open. The hinges squeal like a rolled-on shoat, and the sound catches in his spine and he shivers. The weanling kicks one hindfoot into the night air and cocks the leg, ready to kick again.

The moon is centered in the sapphire-blue sky, and it is enough to dull the starlight. A dozen usable geldings work the fenceline along the lane. They are curious and hopeful for grain. They appear soft and round and dark as legged cattails in the moonlight. They stop along the fence and pace. They lean against the topwire for a better look and whinny and nip at one another and draw closer and stop. They approach as though a trap is laid.

A rangy bay ducks his head at the open gate. He snorts at the ground and paws and gathers his weight in his hindquarters and bursts through the opening. The others follow in twos and threes, and when they are all safely through circle the pasture bucking and playful and glad for their lives.

McEban reckons his notion of freedom to be like theirs, parceled into pasture and corral, hemmed by barbed wire.

He stands the gatepost into a bottom loop of wire and draws it tight and drops a wire loop over the top of the post, and returns to the side of the trailer. The little mustang swings his muzzle against the trailer's slats and bares his teeth. McEban thinks the weanling will not back into this new world. He thinks he will come out all at once, head first and fierce.

The cab of the truck rocks, and he watches Gretchen rise into the back window.

"Come out and have a look at this," he calls.

She steps out of the truck and stumbles and catches herself against its side. The weanling stud squeals. The older horses have gathered at the back of the trailer. They snort and nicker softly in their throats, and the weanling stamps and turns and backs against the manger. Gretchen spits to clear her mouth.

"How do you feel?" he asks.

"Is there anything to drink?"

"Up at the house."

"What time is it?"

"After midnight."

The weanling steps one foot out of the trailer and snorts at the pasture and the geldings press toward him, and he backs into the trailer once again.

"I didn't think you'd ever come back," she says.

McEban looks toward Gretchen. He can hear the weanling pace. Gretchen holds onto the truck's side panel with both hands.

"I don't know what you're talking about."

"When you went away to college," she says.

"But I did come back."

"I know you did. I'm just saying I didn't think you would. Not then."

A miller moth flutters against McEban's face, against his lips, nearly into his mouth. He waves a hand in front of his face. "Even if I hadn't come back," he says, "I thought you'd wait longer than you did."

"I thought I would too." She straightens her bookbag and pulls down her dress at the waist and breathes in deeply. The dark night air stings in her chest and she coughs, and when she stops coughing tells him that she thinks he's a fine man.

"Thank you," he says.

"I'm serious."

"I believe you."

"Just so you know."

The weanling tries to rear in the trailer and rises into a steel cross-beam and it knocks him into a crouch, and he comes out of the trailer as though it's collapsing around him. The gelded horses flush away to the east, and then fall in behind him as he runs. He runs for what he believes is his life. He hits the south fence at a run. The wires sing and stretch, and he's thrown onto his back where he kicks and shrieks and struggles to his feet. He staggers and paws into the darkness and stands finally, shaking his head.

Gretchen has taken a step toward the colt.

"How long is this going to go on?" she asks.

"Until it stops."

He knelt by the doe and lifted her ruined head from the ground. He slipped the loop of the catchrope around her neck and stood and wiped his bloodied hands on his pantlegs. He backed away, paying out the coils of his father's lariat, and when he reached the knot in the end he stopped. He stood and held on tight to the rope's end. That was as far as he could go. The wind came up hard again and thrashed at his chest, and he dropped the rope and brought his horse around.

He picked the rope out of the sage and swung into the saddle and dallied and reined the horse away. He turned in the saddle to watch the rope draw tight at the doe's throat. He held his breath.

She came along easily in the patches of open ground and then caught on a sage and pulled free and bounced up the rope after them. The horse shied and whistled but after it happened again did not even turn. McEban sat straight on the horse and didn't look back either.

That was the way he brought her out. By not looking back.

He dragged her out of the sage and onto a dirt track, and there was only the sound her body made on the hardpacked ground. Like the sound of deep water curling under a cutbank, he thought.

At the end of the track the ground was worn into the rutted circle of a turnaround, and where the turnaround quit the ground dropped away into a steep-sided ravine. The ravine was strewn with cans, bottles, weather-blanched cardboard, scraps of broken lumber, bones, wind-tattered plastic. There was a swather with no tines. A ruptured water heater. A stove. The recent litter of fresh garbage, the buzz of flies. It was his family's small patch of landfill.

He undallied the lariat and stood down from his horse.

The day was still chill and when he filled his chest he thought he could feel his heart beat against the cool sacks of his lungs. The lariat lay hard in his hands. He drew the doe's ragged body to him, hand over hand, down the length of the rope. The horse backed away, ears pricked, and rolled its eyes.

He knelt and slipped the rope from the doe's neck and grasped a hindleg with both hands and bunched the muscles in his shoulders and across his back. He stepped to the side and swung her out into the air and dropped his arms and watched her fall. The flies rose into the air and settled. He looked at his hands for fresh blood and there was none. He picked the end of the rope out of the dust and coiled it and stepped to his horse, but the horse sidestepped away. It held its chin high, careful not to walk on the bridle reins. He cursed the horse and caught up the trailing reins and stepped in close to its shoulder and spun into the saddle. He pulled his hat snug on his head and dug in his heels, but the horse just lunged and fell into a trot, and would not buck.

He reined the horse onto the two-track and closed his eyes and crossed his hands, one atop the other, on the saddle's horn and rode that way. With his eyes shut and his body filled with the cool dry air.

A tall bay leans into the little stud and nuzzles his shoulder and snorts, and the weanling turns and kicks and the other horses press in close, all of them quivering in the moonlight. And then they run.

"There's someone you don't know about," she says. "A man."

"You aren't talking about Bennett?"

"No. Not Bennett. Another man. A man I love."

The horses move fast along the fenceline. The weanling runs at their center.

"I don't believe you," he says.

"I thought you might already know."

"How would I know?"

"I don't know how you'd know. But sometimes people know. Some things just happen," she says, "and other people know about them."

He cocks his head. He listens for the stretch and snap of the wires, and when there is just the drumming of hooves on the grassed pasture he asks her how long some things have just happened.

"For a year. He came up from Denver," she says. "He's a physicist. I met him when he came to give a talk at a Nature Conservancy meeting."

McEban feels the rhythm of the horses' movement, the pulse of it in the soles of his feet. "What'd he talk about?"

"What?"

"The physicist. You said he gave a talk."

"The nature of light," she says. "He talked about light."

McEban nods. He squints into the pasture's halflight. He watches the dark forms of the horses moving against the gauzy moonscape.

"Is that why you came over the other night?" he asks. "To say goodbye?"

"That's why I came over."

He nods and looks toward the house as if he expects to see the lights come on and their silhouettes appear in a window, but the windows are dark. The glass reflects as would slabs of black jade.

"Does Bennett know?"

"If he does he hasn't said anything." She spits again to clear her mouth. "I don't think he knows."

The little stud trots the fenceline. He smells the wire as he moves along it. He rolls his eyes, searching for a place where the wire will quit. He nickers into the darkness beyond the wire. The geldings follow and flush away and are drawn back. They keep him close enough to scent. It is as though they are afraid if he is lost he will be lost from them forever. They flare their soft nostrils, drawn to his odor of wildness.

A reef of broken clouds move across the moon, and Gretchen falls dull in the shadows and flashes clear in the riffs of moonlight.

"I'm leaving," she says.

"When?"

"Tomorrow," she says, and after a moment asks, "Did you hear me?"

"I heard you." He calls Woody out of the truck and pushes the topwire down where a staple has worked free and steps over. "This is a good place to cross," he calls.

"What?"

"The fence. If you step over here, you won't snag your dress."

"I need to go home," she tells him. "I need to put Bennett to bed."

He pushes the wire down and steps back over and opens the gate and lays it back along the fence. He walks to the truck and leans in through the window to look at Bennett asleep against the far door-panel.

He hears the thudding of wings so close overhead he ducks and throws an arm over his head.

"What do you think that was?" he asks.

"I don't know. It could have been an owl." She looks into the trees at the pasture's edge. She still holds on to the side of the truck.

"I'll help you get Bennett to the house," he says. "Get him to bed."

He opens the truckdoor and the cablight falls out hard against him, and he winces and shuts the door.

She lays a hand along his forearm. "Are you alright?"

He turns to her and blinks. "I'm sorry," he says. "I wasn't listening."

"Are you alright?"

"I'm fine." He opens the door again and steps back and she slides to the middle of the seat. He gets in after her and shuts the door.

The little horse has turned against the far corner and is coming back along the fenceline but just at a trot.

"Do you think he'll hit the fence again?"

"I think he's got it out of his system," he says. "I think he'll be just fine."

In the dream she stands against the cocked rise of her left hip, her right leg spread wide to steady the drop of her ribcage and shoulders. She's winded and sucks at the air. Her breasts heave unevenly and run slick with sweat and her belly runs with sweat, and it gathers in the alluvium of the curled and coal-colored hair that tangles between her legs, and drops from the soft split of her vulva.

He thinks of the warm heart of a forest. Hot heart, he thinks, and supposes her a woman sprung from such a place; lush, a collector of dew, a vessel where hallucinations might ferment.

She steps to him and takes his head in her hands and presses the side of his face to her belly, her hands in his hair, and holds him there. He is afraid, but more afraid to struggle. He shuts his eyes. He listens. For a moment he imagines melody, an anthem, but in a language he does not own. He shuts his eyes tighter and feels more alone than he imagined possible, and when he thinks he might have to cry out she pulls him to his feet.

He is lightheaded and she steadies him where he stands. He tilts forward, unbalanced, falling—into her damp breath, against her fruit-smooth flesh.

Chapter Four

✳

McEban tries to sleep but the bed still smells of Gretchen, and he gets up and strips off the sheets and the mattress pad and walks them to the laundry room. He lies down on the bare mattress and she still seems somehow there, and he stands and shouts, "Son of a bitch," and his voice echoes in the hallway and Woody staggers to his feet, and McEban kicks the wallboard and the dog whines to be let out.

He pulls a quilt from the linen closet and curls onto the sofa in the living room. In the darkness he imagines the house constricting against him—a little tighter each time he exhales. He hears his grandmother's voice, but can't understand what she means to tell him. He walks to the mantel and turns Angus and Cleva's wedding picture facedown, and draws the quilt around his shoulders and sits propped in a corner of the room.

He naps raggedly for an hour in the midpart of the night and wakes with the sensation of falling through unlit water. He struggles up and pitches over and lies panting on the floorboards. When he can get into his clothes he finds his bedroll and carries it to the barn.

He climbs into the loft and opens the doors on each end of the loft and lays out the bedroll in the soft rush of moonlight. He listens to Horse Creek falling against its bed of rounded stones, to cricketsong, to the patter of mice, and finally sleeps for several dreamless hours in the last, and darkest, part of the night.

It is past dawn when he comes awake.

There are a half-dozen barncats curled in the loose hay along the length of the bedroll's canvas sheath. The cats sit up blinking and yawn their mouths into pink scallops and stretch and move away when he reaches a hand to them.

He kicks out of his bedding and pulls on his boots and combs his fingers back through his hair. His head feels thick and he squeezes his nose shut and blows. His ears pop and he swallows deliberately, and they pop again.

He can hear a horse shifting its weight and the sawing purr of a rasp. He stands and limps against the weakness of his bad foot to the edge of the loft and looks down into the ground-floor bay. The barndoors stand open to the east, and the bay glares in a cube of morning light. Haydust and powdered horseshit have worked up into the sunlight and hang heavy in the air.

Ansel's curled under the right hindleg of a dappled gray mare they call Lilly. The horse is haltered and tied off to a stanchion that divides one stall from another. There's a curve of slack in the leadrope, and Lilly stands sleepily blinking her white lashes. She raises her head to watch McEban descend the ladder from the loft. She does not shy or pull back against her lead. When he stands on the ground she nickers low in her throat.

Ansel doesn't look up from his work. "Good morning," he says.

"Good morning."

McEban walks into the balded circle of yard outside the barndoors and turns and faces the barnside and pisses at the foot of the shadow he throws. The sun feels warm on his back, the morning air sweet and thick with flies. He steps back into the open doorway.

"I didn't know we were in the wild-horse business," Ansel says.

He still doesn't look up. He fits a steel shoe loosely to the gray's leveled hoof and eyes for spread. He grips her hoof and lifts her leg away and stands at her flank. The gray lowers just the tip of the hoof to the ground. She holds her weight in her off hip.

"You have a look at that weanling this morning?" McEban asks.

"I had a look at the fist of gut poked out on his belly." Ansel turns and stands the heels of the shoe against the anvil. He brings a hand sledge down hard on the shoe's toe.

"He was a birthday present," says McEban.

"From who?"

"From Gretchen."

"She buy you anything bigger?"

"Just the weanling."

Ansel holds the shoe at arm's length and studies it and repositions it on the anvil and strikes again with the hammer. He holds it up in the light.

"I thought she liked you better than that."

"So did I," says McEban.

Ansel sets the shoeing box at Lilly's side and fans half a dozen shoeing nails between a thumb and forefinger and bites down on them. He steps to her flank and taps the side of his boot against her dark hoof, and she picks up the leg and he slides under it, walking it back, taking the weight on his knees, the hoof turned up, the leg extended past her ass. She sweeps her tail and it catches him full across his face. He bows his head until the sting falls out of his cheeks and eyes.

"Gretchen's in love with another man," McEban says.

Ansel looks up from under the horse. He slobbers around the nails stuck in his mouth and plucks them out and spits. "Besides you and Bennett?"

"Yeah. Besides us." There is no change in Ansel's face. "She says she's in love with a physicist."

Ansel nods and bites down again on the nails. He fits the shoe to the hoof and hammers a nail through its toe and catches the nailend in the hammer claw and works it off.

"Where'd she find a physicist?"

"At a Nature Conservancy meeting a year ago. I guess he was up from Denver. She's leaving."

Ansel nails each side of the heel and stands and stretches a cramp from his back. His chinks are worn into a hole on the left thigh, and his jeans show through. He's smiling around the remaining nails in his mouth.

"I say something funny?" McEban asks.

Ansel squints to focus. "I guess it's funnier if it's not you." His face runs with sweat from the shoeing. He drags a forearm across his eyes, and when McEban doesn't say anything else he shuffles back under the gray's hindfoot and seats the rest of the nails. "Reach me that rasp."

McEban pulls a flat rasp from the shoeing box and hands it to him. Ansel scrapes a groove under the nailends and crimps them over into the groove. He runs the rasp around the hoofedge until he's worked it flush with the shoe and steps out from under the weight.

"She tell you all this last night?"

McEban just nods.

"She tell Bennett too?"

"Bennett was drunk."

Ansel drops the rasp and hammer in the shoeing box and unsnaps his chinks. He hefts the box and walks it out of the way and sets it down.

"You turn this horse out for me?"

McEban unties the halter rope and leads Lilly through the yard to a gate that opens into the east pasture. He steps through the gate and unfastens the halter, and she bends to the grass. He walks back into the barn, looping the leadrope over the halter's headstall.

"I'm getting too old to shoe horses," Ansel says. He sits on an overturned wooden crate with his legs stretched out in the sun. He rubs his knees. "There ought to be a whole class of work I just point out for you to do."

"You don't act like you're a whole lot surprised."

Ansel curls his right hand into a loose fist and brings the fist up to have a look at the knuckles. "I'm surprised it didn't happen sooner."

He's skinned a knuckle and the blood runs across the back of his hand and drips onto his thigh and darkens the chap-leather and doesn't look like blood at all. "Are you torn up?"

"Course I'm torn up."

"Did you try to stop her?"

McEban stands back out of the light. He holds Lilly's halter at his side. "I'm not sure it would have done a bit of good if I had."

"What about going after her?"

McEban stares at the pale mare alone in the near pasture. Lilly looks up into the trees along the creek, and McEban looks too, and there is nothing. "That's probably something I should've done a long time ago," he says.

The big storm fell against the ranch in the late spring of 1972. It was after midnight. The storm broke upon the Bighorns and gathered itself against their east slope and dropped like a faulted slab of continent. McEban was twelve.

The house heaved and shrieked and shuddered, and he thought there were horses on the roof and sat up in his bed. He listened as the shingles flapped loose and skittered into the wind. He stood at his bedroom window. He watched the lightning shatter the cloud-blackened sky. The pines thrashed and groaned. There was only twenty minutes of heavy rain, but it came in through the damaged roof, and flashed Horse Creek into a wall of flood. The thunder throbbed in his bones and rolled south and west and onto the plains, and he wondered if it carried parts of him with it.

He raised the bottom window sash fully to the night. His ears still hummed from the thunderclaps but he could hear the rush of the creek. There was the tang of stone in the air, chipped from the Bighorns by a dozen close lightning strikes, and the perfume of alfalfa and lilac.

He breathed in deeply and returned to his bed feeling wild and predatory, and after a while he slept. In his sleep he dreamed of antelope. Seven does with their young. He sat on a vast plain of thick, flesh-colored grasses. He sat with his brother, side by side, quietly, unmoving, watching. A breeze lifted their hair, and it flapped in white wings against their foreheads. That was all. Just the slightest of winds. The antelope approached. A step. A long pause of gathered curiosity. A step. Like that. And then they came closer. The lead doe's fawn stood back against its mother's hip and licked its nose, and its black nose shone darkly in its pale face.

He woke because he thought he'd heard his brother laugh, and he found his mother sitting on the edge of his bed. Her eyes were fixed on him and he didn't recognize her at first, and his breath caught high in his chest.

"Hush now," she whispered.

The window was still open and the room was chilled. She reached into the collar of her robe and lifted a Saint Christopher medal over her head. It caught in the moonlight. She lowered its chain over his head and her hands brushed his ears, and the medal settled upon his chest. She held her open hand over the medal and pressed the disc against his skin.

"Now this belongs to you," she said and kissed his forehead and slipped under the covers with him.

He turned and lay facing the wall, and she wriggled the length of her body against his. Her knees pressed the backs of his knees. Her left arm squeezed him to her.

His head rested under her chin, at her throat. When she spoke he could feel the vibrations of her speech in his skull.

She spoke of the protection Saint Christopher would bring him. No matter his need. No matter his crimes. No matter where he traveled. She spoke into the cup of his ear. Her breath smelled tart and woody and familiar, like freshly split stovewood, like the clean healthy meat of a tree.

She told him that Christopher had gathered a child in his arms at a river crossing. As a kindness, a service. That the river would have swept the child away. She didn't know the river's name.

She said that Christopher was in midstream when he began to buckle under the weight of the child. "It was the baby Jesus," she whispered. "The child carried the weight of the world in his hands. Christopher carried them both," she said. "I don't think he was a young man, either."

She told him that the saint doubted he could continue; that he thought he would stagger and fall into the water and drown, and drown the infant Savior with him. "He straightened under that weight." She was still whispering. "He groaned to God, and he cried to God of his pain, and then he put just one foot ahead of the next and bore them both out. Weight of the world and all." And then she rose on an elbow and kissed his cheek and slipped from the bed.

He heard her moving in the hallway. He put his hand to his cheek and it came away damp, and he held his palm to his nose and it smelled like his mother's voice. He felt the medal shift against his chest, and he curled down tightly in his bed and began to cry and couldn't stop.

McEban backs the pickup to a dozen treated corral posts. There's a fifty-five-gallon drum that's been torched in half and buried in the ground and filled with creosote and ten years of motor oil they've drained from the oil pans of their trucks and tractors. The posts are stood in the drum and their butt-ends absorb the coal tar and oil and take a long time to rot when set in the ground.

He works a post out of the drum and skids it onto the pickup bed and drives to the toolshed and throws a shovel and tamping bar in next to the post. He finds a handful of ring-shanked spikes, a framing hammer, and a pry bar and gets in the cab and lays them on the seat. He wants simple work he doesn't have to watch himself do; something hard and rote. He wants work that won't kick him or bite him or get him on the ground and step on him.

He parks by where the corrals narrow into a lane to the creek. At the corner, where the corrals squeeze into the lane, there's a post broken off level with the ground.

He hooks the pry bar behind each rail at the bad post and loosens the rails and pulls them away. Their far ends are still attached to solid posts, and the nails squeal when he pulls the rails back. He lets the near ends fall together, and the rails fan up to his right and left. He kneels on the rails' ends and drives the spikes through and hooks the hammer claw under the spikeheads and pulls the spikes free. The ones he can't pound straight he throws onto the pickup's bed.

He breaks the ground around the rotted post stump with the sharpened end of the tamping bar. He huffs when he stabs the bar into the ground. He rocks the bar to loosen the soil and drives it into the ground again. As hard as he can. And again. He feels the jar of the work in his arms and shoulders. His head snaps forward with each thrust. He hasn't worn gloves and the steel shaft tears at his hands. He likes the way it feels. The simple violence of the task calms the confusion in him. He feels soundly alive and imagines he will continue to live.

He pries the stump out, a rotted piece at a time, and deepens the hole and sets in the new post. He shovels dirt around it and tamps the dirt tight and drops in rocks the size of his fist and tamps them down into the dirt. He works back and forth like that, first a layer of soil, and then a collar of rocks beaten into the soil. When the hole is filled level with the ground he draws what little dirt is left around the post with the instep of his boot and stomps it down. He throws his shoulder against the post and there is only the impact he feels in his shoulder. The post is solid. He brings up the rails and nails them into the new post and walks to the posts on either side of it and pounds in the spikes that've pried loose. It's late morning when he's done and he still feels gunned up, but his gut has settled, and his head seems exactly centered between his shoulders.

He puts the tools away and drops off the used post at the wood-yard. He props it in a buck and saws it to stove lengths with a Swede saw. He thinks about riding up on the Forest Service lease to have a look at his cows but knows it's already too late in the day.

He's staring at the slant of light off the Bighorns when Bennett drives into the woodlot. He sits back against the sawbuck and leans the Swede saw against the buck.

Bennett hands him a sheet of paper. He can see it's Gretchen's handwriting, but asks what it is.

"Read it," Bennett says. His face has yellowed from the beating Curtis gave him and his left eye is still mostly closed, but the rest of him just looks tired. "I already read it. It was on the kitchen table when I got up." Bennett walks to a stump and sits down and nods toward the sheet of paper. "I'd've been here earlier but I didn't get up until a little bit ago."

McEban looks down at the paper. A breeze bellies it away from him. *Dear B,* he reads.

I'm sorry and I know sorry isn't enough. I've been up all night crying and drinking too much coffee. I've packed my clothes, a few books, some cookware, and my saddle. More than I deserve.

When you read this I'll be gone. There's another man but he's only part of the reason. He's the opportunity. I meant to leave years ago but I loved the idea that I could love you, and I loved the clarity of the light against the mountains here. None of this is what any good man should have to hear.

All of it's my fault. My lack of imagination. It happened a little at a time. If I'd tried to stay I would have disappeared before your eyes. I'm sure of it. You'd be sitting at this kitchen table where I am now, more lonely than you are already. And older, and drinking more, and even less happy.

I've left you to become solid again in the world if I'm able to. If you follow me awhile, I think I can make you understand. I'm asking for a favor that I have no right to ask. Let me write another letter or two. It's the only way I can think to apologize for having married you, and it's the only way I can think to say what I need to say, and for you to have the time to listen. Please trust me. Over twenty years married and a lifetime together lets me imagine I know you, what you might do, what you'll need. Please. Just this last indulgence. There will be a letter in Bozeman at the post office.

There's really no reason not to do this,

Gretchen

P.S. Ask McEban to come with you. He will if you ask. He can drive when you're too drunk. It doesn't seem like it, but he's more stolid than you are. He was always more geared to misery than any of us.

G

The paper is yellow, lined, torn evenly from a tablet. McEban looks up at Bennett. "What do you think?"

"Don't fold it," Bennett says.

"I wasn't going to."

Bennett stands and takes the letter back and sits against the truck-seat with the door propped open for a windbreak. "I don't know when I'll be done reading it," he says. "If it's folded in half I might tear it."

"Are you going to drive to Bozeman?"

Bennett looks up from the letter. "She was right when she said I haven't got a good reason not to." He works a handkerchief out of his pocket and blows his nose. "Maybe she wants me to follow her so I can win her back. Prove I love her. It might be one of those things she doesn't even know she wants."

"How many times has that happened?"

"It could be a subconscious thing."

"Is that the way you'd bet?" asks McEban.

"I guess not."

"Do you think she's right about me being stolid?"

Bennett turns and lays the letter on the truckseat behind him. "I wasn't sure," he says. "I had to look it up but when I did I thought you were. I think it's a good thing," he says. "I mean, she didn't call you bovine."

McEban thumbs his hat back from his face and Bennett starts the truck and lets it idle a minute. "I think she thought you'd hold together better than me. I think that's all she meant."

"That's what I thought too."

"I've got some calls to make," Bennett says.

"I'll be ready when you get back."

In the morning light he stood in front of the mirror over his dresser and pulled off his T-shirt and stared for a long while at the medal where it hung against his chest, and then he dressed and went down to breakfast.

During the day he stopped his work and reached between the buttons of his shirt and pressed a fingerpad to the medal. In the afternoon he found his mother where she sat on the back porch.

"Thank you," he told her.

She only stared at him, past him. She rubbed her fingertips at her temples and asked him to bring her the bottle of aspirin and a glass of water.

That night he became afraid to sleep with the Saint Christopher around his neck. He was afraid he might snap its slight chain in his sleep. He was afraid it would be lost.

He lifted it over his head and held it dangling for a moment in the light from the hallway and then lowered it to the dressertop.

When he went to his dresser in the morning the medal was gone. There was a pinecone on the dresser and that was all. He held the cone up in the early morning light. He looked from the cone to his reflection in the mirror. He stared hard at his chest. He honestly thought he might watch his heart explode, and when it didn't he went into his closet, under the eave, and knelt by the hole where the packrats came in. His grandmother had told him to stuff a clump of steelwool into the hole to keep the rats out. She had told him more than once.

He stared down at the cone he held in his hand. It was just two inches long, egg-shaped, brown, patched with darker crescents of brown. He turned it in his hand. It was a female cone. He moved his thumb against its three-pointed bracts.

He carried the cone in his pocket, and the scales wore away from its spine and littered his pocket. In the evening he walked into the trees by the creek and turned the pocket out and buried the separate parts of the cone and that night arranged wads of tinfoil on his dressertop. He hoped the rats wouldn't know what they had and return the medal for a ball of foil. Everything's precious to a packrat, he thought. He said it aloud to make it true.

He heard his mother up in the night. He heard her in the kitchen and in the yard. He imagined her hands and face and feet growing cold as creekwater. He imagined her standing with her head back, staring into the stars, her arms extended to the heavens and held that way. On other nights he had seen her do just that. He fell asleep before he heard her come in from the yard.

In the morning the balls of foil were gone, and another pinecone was left as a trade.

He dressed and walked to the barn and knelt by its northwest corner and worked a block of limestone loose from the foundation and eased his head and shoulders through. He lay blinking into the darkness.

"You looking for a place to hole up?"

He squirmed back into the sunlight and looked up at Ansel. The man stood over him with a shovel across his shoulders.

"I'm thinking of starting a war," he said. "Against packrats."

"For sport or revenge?"

"It's personal."

Ansel nodded and let his arms fall from the shovel handle and stabbed its spade into the earth. He knelt and looked in under the barn, squinting.

"This where you plan on starting the slaughter?"

"Yes, it is."

Ansel stood and took up the shovel again.

"There's some number-one spring traps hanging in the toolshed," he said. "High on the northeast wall. You know how to work them?"

"I think I do."

"You get a finger broke, I'm not the one who told you you could use them. You understand?"

He was still sitting by the foundation stones. He nodded.

"Last time they were put to work your dad was a boy. He thought he was going to make a fortune trapping pine marten. They'd be the right size traps for packrats."

"Did he?"

"Did he what?"

"Make a fortune trapping pine marten?"

Ansel smiled and spat downwind. "If he did he's been close-mouthed about it," he said. "When you get in under there, make sure the barncats don't follow. You haven't got your root out for cats, do you?"

"No, sir."

"Just make sure."

An hour later in the toolshed McEban had the traps spread out on the dirt floor and asked, "What about my scent?"

"You'll smell worse the older you get," Ansel said.

"I mean on these traps."

"You worry about your scent for coyotes and such. You're just trapping rodents. They aren't much smarter than you."

Ansel pulled a foot-long length of sawed-off ax handle from his back pocket and handed it to the boy. There was a hole drilled through its end and a leather thong threaded through the hole and tied in a loop.

"Did you make this?" he asked.

"The thong's to fit around your wrist," Ansel said. "In case it gets exciting in that crawlspace under the barn."

McEban turned the piece of smooth wood in his hands. He fit the thong over his wrist and let the thing dangle and then gripped it and struck at the air.

"What's it for?" he asked.

"It's your ratsap."

"My what?"

"They aren't all going to be killed when you find them. The thong's so you won't lose it. You'll want it handy."

He nodded and swiped again at the air and gathered the traps and a hammer and sacked them in a gunnybag and put a dozen sixteen-penny nails in his back pocket. He got a flashlight and a jar of peanut butter from the house. He worked the block of limestone free from the foundation and wriggled under the barn and dragged the gunnybag in and wedged a scrap of plywood into the hole to keep the barncats out.

He stretched out in the darkness and waited for his eyes to adjust. He listened for rattlesnakes. Bennett had been bitten on a finger the summer before, and his hand had turned black and swelled until the skin split the length of the poisoned finger and across the back of the hand. He was in the hospital a week and when he got out seemed raw and nervous. The doctors talked for months about the hand needing to be cut off.

He played the flashlight beam against the barn joists and the near foundation stones. He splayed his elbows and crawled along the foundation on his elbows and knees, dragging the gunnybag behind him. He found the rats' nests spaced along the interior of the foundation. He stopped every ten feet to catch his breath and listen for snakes.

At each nest he held the flashlight in his mouth to free both hands, and he picked through the mess of cones and sticks and pine needles and dried horseshit and scraps of cloth. He found an old wristwatch. A girl's ring. There were wads of pink fiberglass insulation woven through the nests. But he didn't find the balls of foil he'd left on his dressertop. And he didn't find the Saint Christopher medal either.

At every nest he set a trap, at the bigger nests, two. He drove a nail into the nearest joist and hung the trapchain's O-ring over the nail and pounded the nail back over the ring. He paid out the chain, working it into the foundation joints, and smeared peanut butter on the trap's trigger plate. He squeezed the flat springs down and opened the trap jaws and set the trigger under the plate. Ansel had shown him how to do the thing. He was careful to keep his fingers under the jaws when he set the trigger against the tension. And then he settled the trap in front of the nest and eased away to the next.

McEban stands with Ansel on Ansel's front porch, and the old man turns away and walks to the end of the porch. He rolls a cigarette and leans into the rail. Woody's sprawled against the cabin wall at his feet.

"At least this isn't the first time I've pissed you off," says McEban.

"I just don't like getting old."

"Nobody likes it."

Ansel flicks his cigarette ash over the rail. "You get old you can't hit any simple son of a bitch any time you'd like. You have to stop and think about getting hit back."

"You'd like to hit me?"

Ansel looks back over his shoulder and then down at the dog. "I'd like to beat you like a redheaded stepchild."

McEban looks at Woody too. "I'd never hit you back."

Ansel tightens his face. "You're goddamn right you wouldn't. You'd be laid out flat on your back." And then he laughs low in his throat. "You have your lunch?"

"I haven't gotten hungry yet."

"How long do you think you'll be gone?"

"I don't know," McEban says.

"If you had to guess."

"You were the one who asked me whether I was going after her."

Ansel turns fully, facing McEban, leaning back against the porch-rail. "I didn't think you'd go right away."

"What did you think?"

"I thought you'd get your goddamn work done first. I didn't think you'd tell me you thought Einar Gilkyson could help bring those cows and calves down off summer pasture. That's what I didn't think."

"Einar's good help."

"The man's a friend. He's not family. You expect him to help me cull out the open cows and sell 'em with the steers? You think he's anxious to be that kind of good help?"

Ansel turns away and exhales the cigarette smoke through his nose and stares out at the county two-lane. A half mile of powdered road dust rises and hangs in the air behind a UPS truck. The dust stands red against the sweep of tan-and-aqua prairie.

McEban says, "I'll be back before we have the vet out to pregnancy test."

"You sure about that?"

"I'm pretty sure."

Ansel cocks an ankle against its opposite knee and stubs his cigarette out against the heel of his boot. He stands the foot down and grinds the butt back to loose tobacco between his thumb and forefinger.

"How old were you the other day?" he asks. "When you had your birthday."

"Forty-one."

"I guess you're thinking it hasn't been much of a year so far."

"I was thinking it could have been worse."

Ansel walks to the cabin's door and holds the screendoor open. "I'm surprised Bennett asked you to go."

"Gretchen told him I would. In her letter she told him to ask."

Ansel stares down at the porchboards. He's bareheaded and his hair is grown out and ready to be cut. "I'm going to make myself something to eat," he says.

McEban thinks he should ask the old man up to the house to cut his hair, but says, "I'll let you know before I go." He steps off the porch into the late-afternoon sun.

Ansel turns in the open doorway, still holding on to the screen. "I used to go in to the AA meetings," he says. His voice has quieted. "There was mostly townsmen and a few used-up women. They used to get together in the basement of the Presbyterian church on Thursday nights."

McEban shuffles in the sunlight at the bottom of the stairs. "I don't remember you being a drunk."

"I never was. I just went to the meetings when I was feeling sorry for myself. It cheered me up to sit in the back row and watch those poor bastards chainsmoke and whine about their lives."

"I'm not feeling sorry for myself."

"I thought you might be."

"I'm not."

Ansel nods and steps into the cabin and lets the screendoor swing shut. Woody comes awake from the porch corner and wobbles to the top of the steps, blinking, stretching his hindlegs.

"You want me to leave the dog with you?"

Ansel answers from inside the door. "I'm a cat person," he says.

McEban held the flashlight in his left hand and his ratsap in the other with the thong around his wrist. He'd worked the throat of the gunnybag through the back of his belt. It draped across his ass and the backs of his legs. He'd brought the sack to bring out the dead. Ansel had told him he didn't want the barn to smell like dead packrats.

The traps at the first two nests were sprung and empty and he smeared fresh peanut butter on their trigger plates and reset them. At the fourth nest a rat had been caught by the throat and hung in the trap's jaws, and when he released the tension the little animal tilted and fell to the ground. He pulled the gunnybag loose from his belt and held its top open and lifted the rat by the end of its tail, and the tail came away from the body, leaving just a nub. He dropped both parts in the bag, rat and tail, and reset the trap. When he crawled away he felt the small body bouncing against the backs of his knees.

He heard Ansel step into the granary above him, and the sound of the man's boots against the barnboards made him jump. He thought he might be getting as jumpy as Bennett. Even without the venom of a rattlesnake. He turned out the light and lay in the ash-dry dirt to see if he could imagine what Ansel was doing by the sound of where he walked, where he paused, how long he paused before he moved again.

He heard the man walk a horse into the far stall and pour grain into the feedbox and the horse stamp its feet and snort into the grain. He was sure that's what he heard and the surety of it settled him, and he thumbed his light back on and continued his rounds.

When he got to the next nest a rat's eyes caught in the lightbeam and shone red. It turned its head away and the trapchain rattled, and it tucked its head under its shoulder and tightened into a ball. He could see the rise and fall of the animal's body. He could hear the quick short breaths it snatched from the air. Its right rear leg was caught in the trap-jaws. The leg hung from the steel curve of the jaws, raw and hairless and limp. The rat's whole body quivered.

He kept the light on the animal and rolled onto his left side and balanced against his hip and elbow. He raised the ratsap in his right hand. It was as though he had done the thing a thousand times; it was as familiar as graining a horse. He wasn't thinking about what to do next.

He looked up the length of his raised arm to make sure his swing would clear the joists and then brought the ax handle down to the back of the rat's head. When it quivered harder, he brought the sap down again. There was a spray of blood against the foundation stones but that was all.

The rat lay sprawled and still. It did not try to cover itself.

He opened the trapjaws and dropped the little corpse into the gunnybag and worked the bag's throat back through his belt. He turned off the light and sucked at his tongue, and it tasted peppery and sweet. He ran his tongue over his teeth to make sure there was nothing in his mouth. At the very edge of his hearing he recognized the sounds of Ansel seating the lids on the grain bins and stepping out of the barn and latching its door. He curled his knees to his chest and laid his head along an arm and closed his eyes and slept.

When he woke he finished his circuit because he was a boy who had been taught to finish a job. He was a boy raised with chores. He found one more rat dead in a trap and two others caught that he killed with his sap. And then he started back the way he'd come, from nest to nest.

He pulled each trap and dragged them with him and heaped them against the foundation wall. He crawled out into the light and dragged the traps out and replaced the stone. He brushed off his jeans, front and back, and shouldered the gunnybag of dead rats. He carried the sack to the place by the creek where he'd buried the cone. He dug a hole and lifted up the bag and spilled the bodies into the hole. They tumbled out like ruined toys, their soft brown-gray bodies piled together in one furred and broken heap. He said a prayer for the rats and for himself. He prayed for strength. He prayed for the strength to someday lift a child in his arms and carry that child across fast water, from one bank to the other. And then he shoveled the loose dirt in on top of the dead packrats, the rats he and no one else had killed, and he patted the mound smooth.

＊

The sun's just set and the house comes gray and hard as galvanized tin. McEban switches on the overhead light in his bedroom and kneels in front of a footlocker centered at the foot of his bed. He opens the trunk and takes out a canvas duffel. Below the duffel are what he's kept of his father's clothes. Mostly shirts, pants, one pair of fancy-stitched boots his father wore to town, a belt, and the blue-serge suit. He's stored the clothes to save the odor of the man. It's as though his history has been archived here, in the scents of horsesweat, bag balm, motor oil, and Old Spice. He bends over the trunk and inhales deeply and imagines his father sitting up in his coffin, blinking, confused.

He reaches to the bottom of the footlocker and lifts his mother's jewelry box from under his father's clothes. He opens the box and stares at the single pinecone and the Saint Christopher medal. There is nothing else. It is what she left him. An inheritance.

He takes out the medal and slips its chain over his head and replaces the box and closes the locker and stands. He knows if he closes his eyes he will hear his mother's laughter.

He stuffs the duffel with jeans and shirts and underwear and socks. He drags it into the bathroom and assembles his toiletries into a leather kit and pushes down his clothes and drops the kit in and gathers the duffel's top and snaps it shut.

He shoulders a forty-pound bag of dog kibble from the pantry, takes down a warm coat from where it hangs in the mudroom, and folds a pair of fleece-lined gloves into its pocket. He backs through the screen onto the porch and stands the bag of dogfood beside his bedroll and brings out the duffel and locks the door and slides the key under the footmat. He sits in a porch chair and waits for the last bit of light to drain away from the day.

✳

A flight of crows flushed loud in a cottonwood at the corner of the field where the ditch turned east. Ansel stopped to watch and McEban stopped too.

"I saw you hung your traps back in the toolshed," Ansel said.

"I'm done with them."

They studied the crows resettling in the cottonwood.

"Was it everything you thought it would be?"

"I didn't know what it was going to be like."

"And now you do?"

"I guess so."

Ansel looked down at the boy. "I guess you learned why those traps've been hanging up in that shed for twenty years."

"I guess I learned that too."

Ansel rolled a cigarette and crimped it at one end and closed his mouth completely over it. When he pulled it out the paper was silvery with spit. He stuck it in a corner of his mouth.

"I saw the lights on up at the house last night." He popped a wooden match and cupped his hands around the flame.

The boy watched the man inhale and shake the match out. "You shouldn't smoke," he said.

Ansel squinted through the smoke. "Did I ask you why you went to war with the packrats?"

"No, you didn't."

"No. I didn't."

McEban looked back at the cottonwood. He couldn't see the crows he knew it held. "She's been getting up again."

"Like usual?" Ansel asked. "Did she get up and go after the kitchen?"

McEban nodded and Ansel pulled the cigarette from his lips between a thumb and forefinger and flicked the ash from its tip with the nail of his little finger.

"You think she gets up at night because she's lonely for your brother?"

McEban turned to him. He felt his face come hot. "My brother's dead."

Ansel spit and looked back at the house. "Not to her, he's not."

H e carries his soup bowl and Ansel's bowl to the old man's sink and runs them full of water.

"Thank you for the beans," he says.

"It's the hambone that makes them worth eating." Ansel scoots his chair just back from the table and pours an inch of schnapps in his empty water glass and tilts it back. "Don't worry about anything here," he says. "Those cows might come down off the mountain all by themselves."

"You feeling alright about me?"

"The schnapps helps. How're you feeling about yourself?"

McEban dries his hands on a checkered dish towel.

"My dad used to say the best place to look for sympathy was somewhere between *shit* and *syphilis* in the dictionary."

"That's what he said." Ansel lifts the bottle away from the table. "You want a sip of this?"

McEban sits at the table and Ansel pours them each a shot of schnapps.

"You miss your dad?"

"Sure I do."

"I do, too." Ansel downs his schnapps all at once and grimaces. "At least he had a chance at a family. I'm sorry you missed yours."

"If you tell me you want me here I won't go. Bennett can go by himself."

Ansel stands out of the chair and walks to a cupboard and takes down a can of Vienna sausages and snaps the lid off and thumps them loose onto a saucer. "I'm just feeling inconvenienced," he says. "The quicker you go, the quicker you'll get done with it." He sets the saucer at his feet, and Woody has the little sausages gone before the old man can straighten. When he's standing all the way up, with his shoulders squared to McEban, and his chin leveled, he says, "She was pregnant when you left for school."

McEban looks up from the oilcloth where his glass has left a ring of clear liquid. "What did you say?"

"I said Gretchen was pregnant the fall you went off to college."

"That's bullshit."

"She said I shouldn't ever tell you, but she's gone now, and Bennett never said how he felt about it at all."

"You're telling me Gretchen was pregnant by me?"

"That's what she said. I don't remember her lying a lot. Do you?"

McEban stands and puts his hat on and sits back down. "If she was pregnant, then where's the kid?"

"She miscarried. She asked me to drive her to Denver for an abortion and when I wouldn't she went ahead and married Bennett, and then she miscarried right after that."

McEban walks to a window and opens it all the way and leans against the wall. He stares into the darkness, but there is only the reflection of the room where the panes have overlapped.

"If I'd've known I would have married her right away," he says. "I'd've married her that summer."

"She thought if you knew you wouldn't go to school."

"So she married Bennett because I wasn't here?"

"I imagine she married him because he asked. And because she was eighteen and didn't want to feel like she'd forced you to ask."

Headlights play through the porch windows. They listen as Bennett downshifts into the gravel and turns in front of the cabin.

Ansel walks to the table with a dishrag and lifts the glasses away and wipes the oilcloth clean. "Bennett hasn't got a hell of a lot going for him," he says, "but at least he wasn't bashful about telling her he loved her. She never had to wonder whether he cared. There's something to that," he says. "There's people who need to hear something like that."

McEban tastes the schnapps rise up in the back of his throat and he steps to the door. Woody stands wriggling against his leg, wagging his stubbed tail, and McEban stomps his good foot and the dog sits, and then lies all the way down. He rolls onto his side and whines.

"If you want to kick that little bastard you ought to let him out where he can get away from you."

McEban turns the dog out into the night. "If I'm going to kick anything I probably ought to start with myself."

He hears the old man pull a drawer out and walk to him. When he turns, Ansel offers a new kerchief, dark blue and folded. It lays flat on the palm of his hand.

"You might need this," he says.

McEban takes a corner of it and shakes it out into a square yard of silk.

"It's a beaut." It's all he can think to say.

"I was saving it for a change in the weather. My neck gets cold, I'm cold all over."

McEban holds the kerchief up by diagonal ends and twists it and loops it around his neck twice and ties it off.

"It looks good on you."

"You won't miss it?"

"I can get another."

Bennett honks.

"Did Bennett know about her being pregnant?" McEban asks.

"I believe he did. From the get-go."

McEban nods. "You know, you don't have to do a goddamn thing I ask you to," he says. "You don't have to ride up on the mountain and bring those cows down, or get out of bed if you don't want to."

"What else would I do?" Ansel steps back to the table and pours himself another schnapps. "It'd just bore the piss out of me to sit around here and wait to die."

"I never thought about it that way," McEban says and when Ansel doesn't look up from his drink, adds, "I'm sorry I missed my chance for a family too." Ansel looks up from his glass. The fixture over the sink backlights his head and his hair catches the light in a dome of unexpected halo. He shrugs his shoulders up toward the halo and smiles. McEban steps out through the door.

He shoulders his duffel and tosses it into the back of Bennett's truck, and his bedroll and the sacked dogfood too, and whistles Woody in after them. He leans in at the open truck window.

"Why are we dragging a trailer?" he asks.

"Because I couldn't fit a horse in the cab."

"What horse?"

"Aruba."

McEban pushes back from the truckdoor. The nose of the trailer is flushed red with the brakelights.

"Why Aruba?"

"Because he's blind. I couldn't leave a blind horse home. It might storm. Have you said your goodbyes?"

The lights are on in the cabin, but the old man's not at the door or at the windows. "You're sure you want to do this?" McEban asks.

"I'm sure I can't think of what else I'd do."

McEban steps into the cab and folds his winter coat on the seat.

"I like driving at night," Bennett says. "How about you?"

McEban nods and Bennett eases them down the dirt track and onto the county two-lane. The county crews have been at work, and the highway stretches out flat and black and oily with new macadam.

The nights have cooled, and snakes, dozens of them, have come out of the borrow ditches to warm themselves on the roadways. Their flattened skins remain. Their meat, their reproduction, their cool hearts have been ground into the asphalt, but their twists of skin catch in the headlights like metallic threads of calligraphy. McEban counts twenty-six in the first five miles. An alphabet, he thinks, and then he thinks that if Ansel dies before he does there is only Bennett left to come to his funeral.

"Today your birthday?"

"What?"

"Your birthday?" Bennett asks.

"Day before yesterday."

"Happy birthday."

The mountains swell up dark before them.

"How come you and Gretchen never had kids?"

Bennett turns to him. The dashboard lights cast his face in shades of green. "Where'd that come from?"

"I was just wondering. Somebody said something about family and I was just wondering."

"We couldn't." Bennett shifts on the seat and eases the truck into the first long switchback that will raise them into the Bighorns. "It was me," he says. "The doctor said I was shooting blanks."

"But you tried?"

"Course we tried." Bennett swerves into the oncoming lane to avoid a roadkill porcupine. There is no traffic. "Maybe if we'd've had kids she wouldn't have left."

"Maybe not." McEban eases back in the seat and closes his eyes.

"Did you come with me just because she wanted you to?"

"I've come with you because I can't stand the thought you might be killed by a Nature Conservancy physicist." McEban's eyes are still closed.

"How do you know the guy's a physicist?"

"Gretchen told me."

"When?"

"When you were drunk."

"Last night, or some other time?"

"Last night. Can you pull over a minute?"

Bennett looks to his friend and into the side mirror, and the night is blank as McEban's face.

"Sure I can." He eases off the gas and coasts onto the highway's shoulder and stops.

McEban leaves the door open when he steps out. He stands gripping the windowframe.

"What are you doing?" Bennett asks.

"I get a little carsick sometimes."

"You want me to cut the engine?"

McEban steps away from the door. "Let it run. I can usually settle down if I just take a minute."

"What happens if you don't?"

"What?"

"What happens if you don't settle down?"

McEban turns to him. He looks to where Bennett's belly creases into the bottom curve of the steering wheel, how the domelight casts the man's shadow weakly against the dash. He hears Aruba stamping on the trailerboards, the grind of cricketnoise.

"If I don't feel better right away I just put up with it."

Bennett nods, and McEban stands awhile longer and steps back into the truck.

"You feeling better?"

"I'm feeling as good as I'm going to get."

He leans back and closes his eyes and feels the truck work up through first and second, and the thrust of a higher gear. His window is down and there is the tang of the nightdamp, the weight of the silent darkness.

"It's nice to be out like this, don't you think?" Bennett asks. "I've always loved driving at night."

McEban nods without opening his eyes.

In the dream he is on his back, on a bed of tossed linen. His legs are straight, slightly parted. His toes turned out. His arms lie to his sides, away from his sides, as though he has just begun to raise them. His hands are slightly cupped, palms up. He feels buoyant, as though able to lift into the air, lift against her, and she is upon him, and still.

She presses herself into him. Her thighs to his, stomach to stomach, breast to breast, palms pressing down against palms, fingers interlaced. He breathes evenly, and when he inhales his belly rises into hers. There is no weight, he thinks in a dream. Only pressure. Only this evidence he is not alone.

Chapter Five

✳

M cEban works his elbows into the ground and arches his chest and blinks into the chilled morning air. For a moment he doesn't know where he has come awake.

He remembers driving over the Bighorns in the night, and through Cody, and for miles up the Shoshone River. He remembers pulling off the highway in the middle of the night and stepping Aruba out of the trailer and pounding a stake into the soft earth and picketing the horse by a single front foot. He remembers throwing his bedroll in the meadow grass along the river and lying down to sleep. He remembers the silence.

He sits up in the dawnlight and yawns, and the bedroll falls and bunches at his waist. A mist lifts away from the river. He can hear the blind horse at the end of his picket rope, sucking at the Shoshone, shifting for balance.

Woody's dug a shallow trench beneath the truck's gearbox and lies in the trench with his muzzle on his forepaws. His eyes are open. He whines softly in his throat but doesn't move.

Two gray jays argue at the rim of a firepit. They hop the circle of blacked stones, flare their wings, and when the larger one picks out a piece of char Woody bursts from his bed and flushes them into the lower branches of a fir. He sits under the birds, baring his teeth, his hackles spiked.

Bennett turns in his sleep and pulls the throat of his bedroll over his head. There is the muffled rhythm of his snoring. Only that, and the birdnoise, and the suck and slap of the river.

McEban takes up his coat and flaps it free of frost. The sleeping bags, the truck, the pine needles, and the browning grass are blurred with it. A large blunt raven stands at the center of a decomposing stump, watching their camp, unruffled, frostfree.

McEban swivels on his butt. He'd laid his boots under his coat and he pulls them on. The boot leather's cold and nightstiff and he struggles to stand. He staggers against the ache in his hips, and stamps each foot—the good, and the bad—and the raven lifts away from the stump and banks west. McEban holds his breath. He listens to the receding slap of the big bird's wings upon the morning air.

He'd forgotten the good feeling of being out, away from convenience, away from routine. He'd forgotten the slight spread of atavism that comes from sleeping on the ground.

He limps to the truck and scoops a bowl of kibble and calls Woody away from the jays. The dog sniffs at his breakfast and stands to the side and gags up a clump of undigested grass and bile, and then begins to eat, and McEban wanders into the trees.

He snaps off an armload of dead branches and builds a fire and balances a grate over the fire and has water warming for coffee when Bennett comes awake.

"Where are we?" Bennett asks.

"We're somewhere short of Yellowstone."

Bennett stands out of his bedroll and slaps his sides and shakes his head.

McEban squats by the fire. "How can you sleep with your boots on?" he asks.

Bennett looks down at his feet. He'd gone to bed entirely dressed. "I guess I can if I forget to take them off."

McEban pours them coffee and starts a pan of bacon, and Bennett climbs into the back of the truck and paws through the toolbox. He straightens with what looks to be a crutch wrapped in a blanket and returns to his bedroll and sits. He folds back the blanket and lifts out a rifle and bolts the action open.

"What in the hell do you expect to do with that?" McEban asks.

"I expect to look at it."

The domed top of Bennett's head is the same shade of gray as the morning air, and his skull appears leveled, flattened to the fringe of hair that grows above his ears.

"If they catch you in Yellowstone with a gun they'll throw your ass in federal prison."

"What about a chainsaw?"

"I don't know about a chainsaw."

McEban forks the bacon onto a paper plate and cracks four eggs into the snapping grease, and stands away from the fire. "Slide these eggs out when they're done the way you like them," he says, and Bennett nods.

Aruba noses the panel at the back of the trailer, and McEban halters him and spills a mound of feedstore hay cubes as a breakfast treat. He thinks of Gretchen. He wonders if he'll see her again. If they'll be uneasy with one another. And then he wonders why—past a vague curiosity—he has never truly missed the possibility of children in his life.

He steps to Aruba's flank and thinks of Gretchen leading this same blind horse up the creek just three months ago. She tied him at the barn and sat against the barnwall and wept. That was the way he'd found her. It was July.

"Has something happened to Bennett?" he asked.

"It's the horse." She didn't look up. "He's blind."

"When?"

"This morning," she said. "I found him standing by the garden when I came out to weed."

"Did you call the vet?"

"The vet said he couldn't find anything wrong. Maybe a brain tumor." She stood and laid her hand flat against the star at Aruba's forelock. The horse stood drowsily, staring into its new darkness. "The vet was only guessing," she said. "He made the trip all the way out from town, and he wanted to say something before he drove back."

"Horses get better," McEban said.

She pulled out her shirttail and blew her nose on it and let the tail drop against her leg. "Nothing ever works out that way." She slipped the halter off the horse and yelled and waved and when he turned from her she snapped his heels with the leadrope.

They watched him trot away, at the weedy center of the road. He felt out with his front feet more than horses do, but that was all. He didn't balk.

"If he finds his way home I'll keep him," she said. "If he doesn't, I'll call you." Her face was drawn, empty, her eyes had lost their light. "If he doesn't find his way home I'll call you to take him to a place you won't tell me about and kill him, please."

McEban reaches out with a forefinger and traces the blotch of color on Aruba's hip that represents the imperfect outline of the island for which the horse was named. He closes his eyes and presses the bridge of his nose between a thumb and forefinger. His vision pulses red and he squeezes the red to black, and wonders if the dead dream. If they dream in color.

✳

He'd made his fort in the windbreak. Deep in the overgrowth of spruce and Russian olive and cottonwood. He'd cleared away the fallen limbs and stamped out a six-by-six-foot square in the thistles and the shade-weakened grasses. He'd scavenged rotted corral rails and broken-off posts and dragged them to the cleared place and notched their ends with a hatchet. He worked when Ansel and his father had gone to town or when they were moving cows.

He fitted the posts and rails together into a three-sided cabin because the rails were longer and the design was out of the ordinary. He did not want an ordinary hiding place.

After the flashflood he walked the creek bottom and found the mud-covered boards that had sided the toolshed. He dug the boards out of the cutbanks and carried them to his fort for its roof and spaded out squares of meadow grass and heaped them on the boards. He did not make a door.

He dug a burrow under the southeast wall, and if he lay on his back and walked his shoulders against the ground and pushed with his heels he came up inside.

He smuggled in coffee cans filled with colored stones, and a shed deer antler, and the wing feathers he'd found fallen from ravens, and a single tail feather from a red-tailed hawk. He brought in a whole horse skull. The sheath of a buffalo's horn. A foot-long length of petrified wood.

He filled empty milk jugs with creekwater and stacked them in a corner and held back candy bars he'd bought in town and filled a cracker tin with them for emergencies. He carved Gretchen Simpson's name in a rail and ran the pad of a finger in the grooves of the letters and brought the finger away and closed his eyes and touched the fingertip to his lips.

When he wasn't needed he sat in this place of his making and listened to the meadowlarks. He raised his hands through the yellowed louvers of sunlight that fell in through the walls.

Once a large bird landed on the sod roof, and strutted and scratched, and beat its wings. He could not tell if it was a hawk or an eagle, or if it was the soul of his brother. And once a rabbit hopped to the fortside, and he watched the soft brown animal nibble at the bunchgrass. He just watched, because the rabbit did not know he was there.

When he was called home for dinner he circled to the edge of the east field and crawled the bottom of the irrigation ditch and came up in a different place every time, walking home, whistling, never looking toward the windbreak.

They buy a visitor permit at the east entrance to Yellowstone and grind up Sylvan Pass and drop off toward the central caldera of the park. McEban is driving.

"You think an owl could kill Woody?" Bennett asks.

He's sorting through the sheaf of handouts the ranger gave them along with their day pass. He holds up a single sheet of pale-green paper. At its top, in bold print, is the announcement: YOUR PET AND YELLOWSTONE.

"Maybe if there were two owls," McEban says.

Bennett slides the window panel open behind the seat, and Woody springs to the top of the toolbox and sticks his head in the cab. Bennett reads from the green paper. "Says here you probably lack the ability to survive in the wild."

Woody twitches his tailstump and cocks his head.

"Says you'd no doubt fall prey to a bear, or wolves, or owls, or a bunch of other wilder stuff. Or just boil yourself in one of these hot-water pools they've got up here." He looks up from his reading to

McEban. "Do you think Woody would have time to yip if he jumped in a hotpot?"

"Is this the way the whole goddamn trip is going to go?"

"Turn up here." Bennett points to a sign advertising a scenic turnout, and McEban gears down and makes the turn onto a macadam road. The road angles up the mountainside for a mile and ends in a turnaround that looks over Yellowstone Lake. They can see the Tetons edge off the horizon sixty-five miles to the southwest. It is that clear. They can see the rock summits plainly.

Bennett steps out of the truck and pulls the rifle from the toolbox. He seats it against his shoulder and scans the highway below them. When he finds a single car he centers the thing in the crosshairs of the rifle's scope and follows its progress along the lakeshore, and when the car enters the trees and falls away from sight he makes a popping sound he means to mimic gunfire and bucks his shoulder back from the imaginary recoil. And then he centers another car in the rifle's scope.

"Stop it," says McEban.

Bennett rolls his eyes but does not move his jaw away from the cheekpiece. "It's not loaded."

"It doesn't matter. You still look like some goddamn madman."

"I just like to pretend," Bennett says.

McEban sits against the sidehill. The day is light-shot and cloudless and the sun bright above him, and his shadow humps away from his back. Below him the land spreads away from Yellowstone Lake in folds of evergreen, broken unexpectedly into faded meadows, torn here and there by sprays of aspen, golding in the short, stark days. Steam rises at Sedge Bay and, again, from a scatter of vents past Mary's Bay. The sky is snapped a single and primary blue, falling a shade darker at the horizon.

He thinks of how thin the crust lies here. Just beneath him. He's read that this lake describes the southeast border of a thirteen-hundred-square-mile caldera. The mouth of a monstrous volcano grown lush and deceptive, he thinks. He wonders if the earth's core is colored orange, or red, or white; if it is anxious for escape. He imagines he can hear that core groan and turn in its molten somnolence, waiting for weakness. He imagines he can hear the hot center of the planet— a basso hum. He imagines the earth rising into ash, pluming to the horizon. Hundreds of millions of cubic tons of ruin. He imagines a day choked to blackness. Any day.

Bennett settles beside him and stands the rifle between his knees and grips its barrel and stares at the spreading expanse of the continent's divide, snaking away to the northwest.

"When I was a kid I used to try to figure out ways to meet the president," he says.

"Which president?"

"It didn't matter. Just one with a daughter." Bennett lays the rifle to his side and leans back against the slope. "I figured I could hire some dupe to kidnap the daughter and muss her up a little. Then I'd return her. I figured the president would give me anything I asked for."

"What were you going to ask for?"

"This."

"Yellowstone?"

"All of it." Bennett smiles. "If you'd've brought beer I would have let you come up any time you wanted." He levers himself up against an elbow. "If you'd've brought Miss Rodeo America I'd have let you build a cabin."

"You have a plan for what you're going to do if you catch up to Gretchen?"

"I'm not as good at plans as when I was a kid," Bennett says.

A gray squirrel chatters in annoyance, bouncing on a bough of blue spruce. Its tail is fluffed and risen like a soft and oversized stinger. McEban hears Woody jump from the toolbox to the top of the truck's cab.

"I'm going to take a bus home when we get to Bozeman," he says. "I shouldn't have come at all."

"You think they'll let you take your dog on a bus?"

McEban raises an arm and snaps his fingers, and Woody lies down on the roof of the cab. "If they don't I'll rent a car."

Bennett stands and brushes the duff from the seat of his jeans. He cradles the rifle in his arms. "They'll probably let you take him on the bus."

Bennett rode over bareback. He was plump through the ass and gut, and his legs splayed out from the horse's broad back. The horse was an overfed pet his mother kept close to the house. She called him Tom. Bennett reined Tom in at the doorway of the root cellar and called for McEban to come out.

He leaned forward along Tom's neck and bent his knees to take the stretch out of his legs. "What are you doing in there?" he called.

McEban stepped into the afternoon sun. "I'm scrubbing." He carried a pail of water and a stiff-bristled brush.

"Why?"

"Because my grandmother told me to. There were some jam jars that didn't seal right and they leaked."

Bennett rocked upright on Tom's withers and looked to his right and left and lifted up the front of his T-shirt long enough for McEban to read *Playboy* across the top of the magazine shoved into the waist of Bennett's jeans.

McEban peered toward the house, searching for movement. "Where'd you get it?"

"My dad threw it away."

"You sure he's done with it?"

"I guess he is or it wouldn't've been in the trash. You want to have a look?"

"Did you look?"

"I did. But I'm not tired of looking."

McEban ran the pail and brush into the root cellar and closed the door. Bennett held down his hand and leaned away, and McEban took his hand and swung up behind him.

They rode to the end of the windbreak and slipped down and tied Tom off to a cottonwood. They crawled through the hedgework and stopped and listened. McEban cut a leafed-out switch of caragana and swept their tracks away behind them.

"Where are we going?" Bennett whispered.

"Here," McEban said. He squirmed into his tunnel, and when Bennett tried to follow and got stuck, he pulled him through. They sat up in the fort and Bennett swiveled his head, blinking.

"This yours?"

"I built it."

"Is it a secret?"

"Just the two of us know. Let me see it."

Bennett lifted his shirt and pulled the magazine out of his waistband. He'd sweated against the back cover, and the front and back both tore away when McEban leafed it open. They sat side by side.

"That's her pussy," Bennett pointed out. He was still catching his breath from being stuck in the entrance tunnel.

McEban bent closer to the centerfold.

Bennett reached over and turned the page. "Are you getting a stiffy?"

"No, I'm not."

"I am. I've had one all day. You want to see?"

"No, I don't. Look how smooth her skin is."

"They do that with an airbrush," Bennett said.

"What's an airbrush?"

"I don't know. It's what Jack Maris said."

"You already showed this to Jack?"

"He was with me when I found it."

McEban bent lower to the page. "I wonder if the airbrush tickles."

"Gretchen Simpson?" Bennett's voice jumped an octave and McEban snapped his head up from the magazine.

Bennett scooted to the rail where her name was carved and held his head up next to the name and rolled his eyes back in his head and stuck his tongue out toward the letters. He made his tongue quiver.

"Stop it," McEban said.

"I'll bet you got a stiffy when you were carving Gretchen Simpson's name in your fort." Bennett stuck his tongue in the air again and made it quiver harder.

"Be quiet."

"It's pathetic. I'll bet you've brought her in here. Haven't you?"

"Shut up." McEban was whispering.

He folded the magazine and sat on it and cupped a hand over Bennett's mouth. They both held their breath. There was a thumping. And silence. And then the sound of brush snapping. After a longer silence there was his father's voice.

"If you boys want to go to that barn dance at the M Bar Nine it's time to come out of there."

McEban crawled out because he didn't know what else to do, and Bennett got stuck coming after him and his father pulled the bigger boy out.

"What were you doing in there?" His father bent and cupped his hands beside his eyes and looked in through a space in the rails. McEban stepped away and Bennett stepped away farther.

"We were sitting," McEban said.

His father straightened and pushed back his hat. "It looks like a premier place for sitting."

"I didn't use anything you might need," McEban told him.

"I can see that."

"All the rails and posts were in the woodlot."

"I said I could see it." His father turned and kicked the corner of the fort with the toe of his boot. "You boys build this all by yourselves?"

"He did," Bennett said, pointing to McEban.

His father nodded. "You're kind of a guest then?"

Bennett said he was.

"I've never seen a three-sided fort before."

"If there'd've been more broken rails I would have made it into a square."

"I'm glad you didn't," his father said.

"How did you find us?" McEban asked.

His father looked at him and sucked at his cheeks. It made a sound like he'd snapped his fingers. Then he looked up to the sky. "A crow told me."

Bennett huffed and smiled at McEban.

"I wish the truth didn't sound like I was bullshitting you, but that's the whole of it. If I didn't understand crows I couldn't have found you at all. I walked right past here twice."

"I believe you," McEban said. "I think there was a crow on the roof once. A big one."

They all looked toward the wind-cracked sod piled on the roof.

"Let's get you boys some supper and cleaned up for that dance."

His father walked to the house and the boys led Tom to the creek, and Bennett turned him loose and told him to go home. They washed their hands and faces, and McEban put on a clean shirt and got one of his father's clean shirts for Bennett to wear.

When they were done with their supper they rode in the back of the pickup to the M Bar 9. They sat on the wheelwells in the pickup's bed and let the wind work at their hair. His father drove, and his mother sat next to him, and Ansel sat on her other side.

W here the water drains out of Yellowstone Lake and into the continuation of the river it breaks into a stretch of riffles, and on this day is sheared by sunlight, for a hundred yards, from bank to bank, presenting itself not as water, but as a field of shattered opals. Just precious stones turning under the weight of light.

McEban slows the truck and stops on the highway's shoulder. The cab, his face and hands, and Bennett's face and hands—where they hold them up to the light—have come alive in moth-size bursts of reflection. The very air snaps with it. It flutters in the pines, in the meadow grass. Violet, rose, salmon. Like the scales of luminescent fish falling about them. And a flash of indigo. And white. Everywhere, the slaps of white. A wildscape of light. Bennett holds his hands up higher between them. He's grinning like a boy. "It tickles," he says, and he laughs like a boy.

And then the sun's angle drops a degree and the river falls to just a slick run of slate and blue and white, the air merely clean and full of daylight. Where the riff runs smooth there's a pair of trumpeter swans. McEban hadn't noticed them. They turn and feed on the glassy surface, at the edge of the tailwaters. They upend together, their webbed feet paddling in the air, and right together, their white bodies, newly wet, sheeting water, for a moment become pearlescent. But the moment of magic has passed.

Bennett folds his hands in his lap. "Oh, God," he says, and McEban starts the truck and at Fishing Bridge turns north.

The traffic is light and the day warm and thickened with the scent of pine. He drives with the windows down. Bennett sleeps, and wakes twice when McEban pulls to the side of the road to listen for wolves. In between the stops there is only the buzz of the tires on the asphalt, the strobelike flash of sunlight and shadow cast across the road by the stands of pine.

They're short of Mammoth Hot Springs and slowing for a bison in the road when they see the girl and the ranger.

The girl sits on the trunk of a lodgepole pine. The tree's fallen diagonally across the slight barrow pit. She stares straight ahead. She doesn't blink. She holds her knees and ankles pressed together, her chin slightly raised.

Her hands and face are uncommonly smooth and dark as freshly turned earth. Her black hair is drawn into a ponytail. When she nods, the hair flashes as a burl of volcanic glass would flash.

She wears white cotton socks and Doc Martens and an ankle-length bloodred skirt and a brown-and-yellow sweatshirt with "University of Wyoming" printed across its front. A backpack the size of a five-gallon can is propped against her legs.

The Park Service truck is parked at the side of the road, and McEban pulls across from it and stops. He hears Bennett open the truckdoor and step out, but he doesn't look away from the ranger.

The ranger stands in front of the girl. He looks up at McEban and nods and steps closer to the girl. He gestures deliberately with his hands, as though they are involved in some child's game, and when the girl does not respond takes a notepad from his back pocket. He scribbles on the pad and tears the sheet of paper free and hands it to the girl, and then he does it again.

Woody crawls through the window in the back of the cab and stands on the seat beside McEban and whines. McEban fiddles with the dog's ears and thinks of the black bears who used to panhandle along the edges of the park's roads. The sows sat upright and bared their teats, and suffered their children to play at their knees. They begged for potato chips, torn bits of sandwich, sun-ruined fruit. They didn't ask for more. They traded their nakedness, their charade of domesticity, for just picnic scraps. It was before the Park Service captured them and relocated them, and killed and buried them when they returned from the backcountry. McEban thinks this young woman seems, like the bears, to ask for little. He wonders if she is hungry.

He's stepping from the truck to ask her if she'd like something to eat when Bennett bursts from the trees behind the ranger. He runs in a crouch and holds his sleeping bag at arm's length, chest-high. His hat comes loose from his head and bounces softly at the highway's center, and he doesn't stop to retrieve it, and the ranger doesn't turn. The ranger doesn't hunch or widen his stance. He writes on his notepad, his head bowed studiously. He's licking his pencil point to write again when Bennett drops the bag over his head and pulls it to his ankles and begins beating the man wildly with both fists.

The punches land where the man's head must be. And his chest and stomach and groin and kidneys, and he staggers, and McEban is running and yelling for Bennett to stop, but Bennett does not look up from the attack. He whines. Like a penned animal whines. McEban hears the dull impact of the punches. And the whining. That's all there is to hear.

The bag slumps and folds to the ground, and still Bennett does not stop. He kicks into the middle of it, and when McEban reaches him and hugs his arms to his sides, Bennett still kicks the bag. McEban pulls him away. He stands holding him, and Bennett kicks into the air, and then goes slack—and the whining stops. There's just his gasps for breath, and McEban's. They stand on the highway staring at the bag. The bag does not move. The ranger's lace-up boots, and the cuffs of his green pants, fall out of its throat and do not move.

McEban looks at the girl. She bends to her backpack and takes out an apple. She polishes the apple against her thigh.

He releases Bennett and when Bennett catches his breath he picks up his hat and seats it on his head.

"There's a culvert behind his truck," she says. She points with the hand that holds the apple.

Bennett nods and hugs up the ranger around his chest and drags the man, bag and all, into the meadow grass below his Park Service truck.

McEban watches the girl eat her apple. He hears Bennett come back onto the asphalt. He hears him turn the federal truck's hubs into four-wheel drive, and he hears the truck's undercarriage scrape rock and wood as Bennett guns it into a stand of lodgepoles. There is the snapping of branches.

When the girl is finished with the meat of the apple she holds it up by its stem and eats the core.

Bennett pulls his truck and trailer alongside where McEban stands by the girl. He leans across the seat and pushes the passenger door open. "Everybody ready?"

"I travel with my sister," the girl says.

"Where is she?" Bennett looks to his sides.

"She's dead," she says. "Could you help me with my backpack?"

Bennett pulls on the emergency brake and stands out of the truck. He comes around the front and lifts her backpack into the pickup's bed. "Can your sister ride back here?"

The girl shrugs. "The wind doesn't bother her much."

She stands and moves awkwardly to the open truckdoor, as though nursing a bruised hip, but she doesn't grimace. McEban watches her face. Her face remains heart-shaped and smooth, like the single track of an antelope. Her face looks to be just the evidence that something lovely and innocent has passed.

"You coming?" Bennett asks.

McEban looks away from the girl. "I'm not sure I am."

"He had a pulse," Bennett tells him. "And the culvert's dry."

"The nights aren't warm up here," McEban says.

"I left him in the bag. Do you think I'm capable of murder?"

"I didn't an hour ago."

They hear an approaching car, and McEban looks up and down the highway but nothing has come into view. When he turns back to the truck Bennett has gotten in behind the wheel again and the girl sits beside him.

"When we stop for supper I'll call," Bennett says. "I promise. I'll tell them where to find him. You want to be here for that?"

"I think I better," McEban says, but he feels his father's hands on him. Pushing him. Pulling. Lifting. The hands are work-roughened and hot, and when they've got him in the truck he looks down at his own hands spread against his thighs and thinks a man's hands do not lie about his life. His hands ache to be at work.

They pass through the buildings at Mammoth Hot Springs and turn out of the park toward Gardiner. He hears Bennett's laughter, but vaguely. The girl is not laughing. He turns to them. He watches their lips move, but their voices seem to have come loose from their mouths. He thinks of a badly dubbed film.

The girl reads aloud the notes the ranger has written. She reads each note solemnly and passes it to Bennett. They are a catalog of questions. Does she have a car? How did she come to be on the roadside? Does she have warmer clothes in her backpack? Does she need a ride?

"The man's a mute." There is wonder in Bennett's voice.

McEban turns and looks through the back window. Woody is curled against the tailgate. He does not see the dead sister.

"Is he okay?" the girl asks.

"I don't imagine he's a bit okay," Bennett says.

He fiddles with the radio dial, and settles on the play-by-play of a University of Montana football game.

"I mean him." She points to McEban.

"There's not a goddamn thing wrong with him," Bennett says, and the game is lost in a burst of static and he shuts the radio off.

McEban feels movement against his knee and squeezes away from the girl and looks down. At his feet, by the side of his boot, there is a hand. It is small and brown and dirty and pressed against the floorboard. He bends forward and raises the girl's skirt to the middle of her calf and uncovers a forearm. And then a shoulder. The back of a head. He thinks in a moment of panic that he's discovered some deformity—the movable parts of a Siamese child. He looks for connection. He raises her skirt to her knees.

"He feels safe under there," she says.

The boy turns to look at McEban. His face is soft as doeskin. His eyes are black. His nose is running and his upper lip slick with snot. He's doubled forward and his hands are pressed to the floormat to keep from falling.

Bennett cranes across the girl's lap. "I'll bet that's a good place to stay warm."

"It's a good place when the wind's blowing," she says.

McEban bends over his knees and grips the boy and lifts him into his lap. The boy is light, hard as cinder, and smells of sage and pinesap, and of the girl.

"He's my brother," she says.

"You got any more of your family under there?" Bennett's smiling like a clown.

She turns to him. "Not yet."

McEban works a handkerchief out of his back pocket and wipes the boy's nose and holds the handkerchief up tight and tells the boy to blow. The boy blows.

"Warm-weather colds are the worst," she says.

The boy curls against McEban's chest. McEban grips his left wrist with his right hand, around the boy, so his arms won't fall away. He leans into the window and closes his eyes. He can feel the boy squirm against him and settle.

"His name's Paul," she says.

A t the M Bar 9 Bennett and McEban loitered in the stalls with the other boys, and the girls were there too. They drank Cokes, and, one after another, tried a pinch of snoose from a tin of Copenhagen Jack Maris had lifted from his uncle Jimmy.

Above them they heard the dancers in the loft; they heard their parents' bootheels hammering against the loftboards, the adults' laughter winging in the rafters.

Jack Maris was the first to turn pale. His face ran wet, and then he puked. The rest of them ran their fingers around their gums to clear the snuff and stood apart, spitting out the loose flakes. Every one of them was lightheaded, a few staggered and sat with their heads between their knees.

Above them they could hear the singsong cadence of Chester Lennon's voice calling the dance: "A figure of eight, till you come straight. Hurry there or you'll be late. You're going like an old slow freight. Come on boys, don't hesitate."

McEban pretended to be interested in the halters that hung the length of the barn's alleyway, and he watched Gretchen from under the brim of his hat.

She stood in the barn entrance and shook a loop out of a lariat and twirled the loop and tried to jump through it. She got tangled and stood laughing. The other girls formed a half-circle around her and clapped, and some of the boys stood there too.

Gretchen was the only girl who'd dipped the snoose, and the only one of all of them who hadn't fingered it out of her mouth. She sucked at the stuff and spit a stream of brown juice to her side and built a bigger loop in the catchrope. She smiled at McEban and twirled the loop.

He tried to smile back but the smile was a failure, and it came too late. She'd already looked away to the spinning rope. The palms of his hands itched, and the backs of his eyes ached, and he thought he might have to sit down in the alleyway.

Above them, Chester called: "Circle up four like you did before. Circle left with the girl you adore."

He took a Coke out of a cooler of pop and leaned back against the barnwall and opened it. Gretchen jumped through the loop she'd made and jumped through it again. He swished a mouthful of Coke to sweeten his breath and whispered, "It's close in this old barn. Don't you think?"

All summer he'd sat in his fort and stared at her name. He pictured the girl beyond the name. He pictured them laughing together. Holding hands. In his fort he had spoken his heart. He'd practiced speaking his heart.

At night he stood alone in the dark pastures and practiced asking her to walk out for a look at the stars. He imagined his left hand as hers and stood for hours with his hands clasped at his waist, pointing skyward with his chin, saying aloud the names of the constellations he knew. Little Dipper and Big. Orion. And northeast from Orion, Gemini. And there, he'd say, is the Great Square of Pegasus. Pegasus, he'd say.

He cupped a hand in front of his mouth and sniffed the palmful of warm breath to see if it was sugary. He turned to look at the other boys. They joked and swaggered in the stalls. Gretchen was recoiling her rope.

He was swishing a second mouthful of Coke when he heard Bennett call, "Gretchen Simpson, come over here and give me a kiss."

He swallowed wrong and the Coke fizzed up in his throat and ran out his nose. He held his head away and coughed and the Coke still fizzed out of his nose. The boys laughed and Jack Maris stepped to him and thumped him on the back. His eyes watered and bubbles gathered and fell from his nostrils. When he looked up, Gretchen smiled right at him, and then she hung the lariat on a nail and walked to Bennett and tipped her hat back and kissed him on the lips.

The boys hooted, and Chester sang: "Swing your partner here and there. Swing that girl with the rats in her hair."

He could hear the boots against the boards above him, and he could hear the men and women laughing. They clapped their hands to the rising whine and fall of Chester's fiddle.

He could hear everything above him and nothing in the barn around him. It was as though he were out alone in the open, standing under a storm of heat lightning and far-off thunder. He looked up to the floor of the loft. A fine, sweet dust hung in the air, stomped loose from the cracks between the loftboards by the dancers. He walked to the ladder that led to the loft and put one foot on the first rung and looked at Bennett and Gretchen. They were still kissing.

H er sister's name is Alma," Bennett says. He fingers through the litter of potato skin and bread crust on his plate. He picks out his steakbone and gnaws at the feathering of meat along its length.

"What's the live girl's name?"

"Rita."

McEban drains the last of his beer. "When did you find all this out?"

"While you napped with the boy."

McEban leans back in his chair. "Why'd you do it?" He watches Bennett.

"Why the wilderness bureaucrat?" Bennett speaks with the bone between his front teeth.

McEban nods.

Bennett drops the bone on his plate and wags his fingers in his water glass and dries them on his napkin. "Because he had it coming."

"Him personally?"

"You haven't had to pay my taxes."

"That's just bullshit."

"You haven't been married either. Somebody had it coming."

They look across the bar at Rita. She leans into the jukebox, her hands resting on its chrome shoulders, her hips swaying slowly back and forth to a Lacy J. Dalton love song. The bar is underlighted and close with cigarette smoke.

When the song ends Rita turns to a lanky cowboy at the end of the bar and holds out her hand. The cowboy stacks a half-roll of quarters on her palm, and she turns and begins slotting them into the machine.

"Both girls are half Mexican, half Shoshone," Bennett says. He works a toothpick in and out of his mouth. "I believe Paul's all the way Shoshone."

"You call the park?"

"An hour ago. If you're just going to play in your meal why don't you slide it over?"

McEban takes a carrot stick and the sprig of parsley from his plate and sets the rest in front of Bennett. Bennett bends to the steak.

"What if he dies? Have you thought about that?"

Bennett looks up from the plate. His mouth is full of porterhouse. "His name was Linderson," he says. "It said so on his nametag."

"Where'd you see his nametag?"

"On the front of his jacket. I zipped the bag open when I put him in the culvert. I didn't want him to suffocate."

"That ought to move a jury to tears."

"You ever hear of a squarehead who couldn't take a beating?"

"I'll ask Ansel when I get home."

Bennett waves his fork. "They've probably got him laid out in a hospital bed in Mammoth. Hell, it's probably the first vacation the man's had in a year."

McEban pushes back from the table and stands. He takes up a Styrofoam box and holds it against his hip. "I'm going to run this out to the boy."

"And then what?"

"Then I guess I'll go to bed."

Bennett grins like McEban's seen him grin when they've played poker. "I thought you and Woody were off to the bus station."

McEban looks to Rita. She hasn't turned from the jukebox. He looks down at the Styrofoam container. "I changed my mind."

Bennett laughs. "And the good Lord loves you for the sweet man you are."

McEban searches Bennett's face. If they were playing stud poker he'd guess Bennett to be holding only a small pair. A pair of fives. He points with his chin to Rita. "She tell you where she needs to be?"

"She said she needs to be out on the land."

"She seems to be doing okay indoors."

Bennett leans back in his chair and watches Rita sway her hips through two choruses of a Ray Charles ballad. "She's like me," he says. "She adjusts."

When he climbed through the loft's trapdoor and stepped out onto the floor it was bright as a doctor's office. He squinted and blinked and stared into the lights. There were two wires strung through the rafters, for the length of the gambrel ceiling, with eight bare bulbs hanging from each wire.

He stood away from the top of the ladder and eased into a crowd of standing men. The men clapped their hands to the rhythm of the fiddle music and passed a pint of Ancient Age. He watched the three squares of dancers on the floor. There were four couples in each square. If he squinted, the whole big room turned into his mother's garden in the wind. That's the way the women's bright skirts swayed and thrashed about their legs. Light, bright flowers, he thought.

Chester Lennon sawed at his fiddle and sang: "Pass those girls side by side. Turn them around and make it wide."

His father danced with Anna Maris in the middle square, and his mother stood in the far corner and swayed to the cadence of the call. Her eyes were closed and her arms hugged her waist.

There were other women who weren't dancing, but they sat or stood away from his mother, lined shoulder to shoulder on bales of first-cut hay, or against the loftwall.

His nose still ran from the Coke fizzing up in it, and he wiped at it with his hand and wiped his hand on his jeans.

Chester stood at the head of the loft on a sheet of plywood laid across a raft of hay bales. "Now pass them over to that gent over there. And around that gent without any hair." Chester's face was red and sweat ran into his eyes.

When he looked back at his mother she was coming diagonally across the loftfloor, coming toward him, and she was dancing. Her eyes were still closed and she still hugged herself, but her hips swayed to the fiddle music, and she cocked up a knee and swung out the foot and half-stepped—first with her right leg, once, twice, three times, and then with the left.

The square nearest her broke up and parted to let her through. The dancers stood and dropped their arms to their sides. They smiled at first and shuffled and then hunched their shoulders. The man nearest his mother circled an arm around his wife's waist and turned her out of the way. Their faces fell blank as midday.

The women looked toward his father to see if the man would know what to do with his wife, but his father was laughing and still dancing with Anna Maris. His shirttail had come loose and flapped against his ass.

They'd parked the truck and trailer in a vacant lot behind the bar. Just a field of cheatgrass and gravel, lumber scraps, litter, gone-to-seed pigweed, a collapsed foundation, a pile of signs dumped by the Highway Department. They'd turned Aruba loose in the lot, and when he hears McEban he lifts his head and nickers.

McEban walks to the back of the horse trailer and looks in over the trailergate. There is the milky throw of light from a corner streetlamp. He finds the boy and Woody curled together on a flake of hay strewn against the manger wall. McEban swings the gate open.

"Come out of there," he says.

Paul stands and brushes off his jeans and steps out fully into the citylight.

"I thought I left you in the cab."

"I got bored." The boy kicks at the ground.

"You feeling forgotten?"

"I need a warmer jacket," he stands with a hand under each arm.

McEban strips off his canvas coat and drapes it over Paul's shoulders. The coat hangs to the tops of the boy's tennis shoes.

"You could have run the heater in the cab."

"I didn't want to make you mad," Paul says. "Where are we?"

"We're in Bozeman. You wouldn't have made me mad."

McEban finds a wooden crate and drags it to the trailer. He sits and Paul sits beside him. He sets the Styrofoam supper-box in the boy's lap.

"There's a steak and a plastic fork in there," McEban tells him. "And some fries."

"Is there a knife?"

McEban digs his pocketknife out of his jeans and opens out the long blade and hands it down.

Paul already has a mouthful of fries. "Can I have a sip of your beer?"

"How old are you?"

"I'm small for my age."

"That doesn't tell me how old you are."

"I'm nine."

"Just a swallow."

McEban pulls a YIELD sign still attached to its post out of the vacant lot and lays it in front of the crate.

"Don't backwash any of that meal into my beer," he warns.

Paul hands the beer back and wipes his mouth with his sleeve and cuts into the steak. McEban inches the boot off his left foot, strips the sock off, and rests the foot against the cool metal of the street sign. He and the boy stare down at the lumpy and moon-white foot.

"How'd you do that?" Paul asks.

"A horse fell on it."

"From out of the sky?"

"He fell over on a bad slope. It was slick. This foot was the only part of me that didn't get all the way out from under him."

"Does it hurt all the time?"

"It doesn't wake me up."

Paul nods.

"How old's your sister?" McEban asks.

"Which one?"

"The one I can see."

"Twenty-nine."

"How about the other one?"

"Alma's a year older."

Paul reaches out and McEban hands over another swallow of beer. "Are we going to stay out here all night?" he asks.

"I got us a room at the Ramada."

"Does it have a shower?"

"Of course it does."

The boy nods. His face looks smooth as jasper. McEban leans toward him and plucks a haystem from his hair. "How come you and your sisters are out on the road?"

"Rita says she wants to show me what's possible. So I won't be ignorant."

"Where did you live before now?"

"In a trailer."

"On the reservation?"

"Rita says we never leave the reservation. She says white people just don't know it yet."

He hands the beer back to McEban and pulls a deerskin pouch from under his shirt and unknots its drawstring and works its throat open with his fingers. Its sides are decorated with columns of blue quills.

"Hold out your hands," he says, and McEban holds out both hands and the boy spills the contents of the pouch onto his palms. There are pieces of bone. Teeth. A jade slick. A silver dollar. A dried strip of hide with the hair still on. A raptor's talon. A piece of moss agate patched with a chalky rind. Three Pokémon cards. A red metal El Camino.

Paul sets his meal on the ground and kneels in front of McEban's hand and plucks the agate up and holds it to the streetlight. He turns it between his thumb and forefinger. "Make a wish," he says.

"Now?"

The boy has one eye closed from squinting at the stone. "Don't tell me what you wish for," he says.

McEban looks away to the blind horse and wishes he were home.

"Are you finished?"

McEban nods and Paul replaces his treasures in the pouch and works the pouch back under his shirt. He pulls the canvas jacket tight across his chest.

"You find all that stuff?" McEban asks.

"My uncle gave me the silver dollar and the jade and the little car. I found the rest. Except for the Pokémon cards. I bought them. Can I touch your foot?"

"Help yourself."

He extends a single finger and touches the lump of knitted bone at the top of the foot and pulls his hand back and settles on the crate again. He looks up at the corner streetlamp. "I'm a regular boy," he says.

"I can see that."

"That's not what you think."

"What do I think?"

"You think you're lucky you're not me." He picks up the Styrofoam box and sets it back in his lap. "You were thinking you're lucky you aren't small and out on the road with your sisters. And half Indian. Or whole Indian." When he looks up his mouth is full of steak. "I'm right, aren't I?"

"You're close."

"You should stop it." He rocks the yield sign with the toe of his foot.

When his mother danced into the edge of his father's square she still hadn't opened her eyes. His father was twirling Anna Maris. He stood Anna on her feet and steadied her and when he turned found his wife dancing before him. In place. Alone.

He smiled and looked at the other dancers and then around the loft. His hat was pulled down and it was hard to see his eyes. Everyone was watching him. A smile tightened just under the shadow his hat-brim cast and lifted the lower half of his face into a tight crescent, and it held that way.

That was the way his father was smiling when T. C. Brokaw laughed. There was only T.C.'s laughter and the fiddle music and the shuffling of the last square dancing.

His father walked to T.C. Right up to him. T.C. was a big man and his father had to take his hat off to look up into T.C.'s face. They were so close that when they breathed their chests touched.

T.C. still tried to laugh but it got harder the longer his father stood there holding his hat against his leg and smiling that tight smile.

Chester eased off the fiddle and the last square slowed. They pretended to dance but mostly they craned over their shoulders, wanting to see what was going on.

He felt a hand on his shoulder and the hand moved him to the side, and Ansel came past him. He was stepping his knees to his waist and slapping his thighs. He danced out onto the floor.

Ansel nodded to Chester and Chester nodded back and bent into his fiddle. Ansel met McEban's mother in the middle of the floor, where his father's square had broken apart, and circled her waist and swung her off her feet. Her eyes snapped open and when she recognized Ansel she smiled wildly and put her arms on Ansel's shoulders, and they high-stepped around the edge of the loft in a reckless polka.

When they danced past him his mother's head was thrown back, and she was laughing. He looked at his father. His father still stood in front of T.C. with his hat in his hand. His mother and Ansel were the only ones laughing.

At the far side of the loft Ansel twirled his mother and handed her off to Gene Maris, and Gene started around again with her and Ansel stepped beside his father. Ansel was taller than T.C. and didn't have to take his hat off.

T.C. nodded. First to his father and then to Ansel, and then he sat down beside his wife. He turned to her and pretended he had something interesting to say.

In the morning McEban hears a woman's voice he doesn't recognize. There is also the sound of traffic, the occasional bang of room doors along the hallway, vaguely the smell of coffee and exhaust. He can feel the boy along his back, spine to spine. The boy's butt presses into the small of his back. He opens his eyes. The drapes are drawn but there's a partition of sunlight fallen into the room where the cheap rubbery curtains don't meet. Bennett's sprawled on the second bed. He's swept the pillows onto the floor and kicked the spread and blanket away.

Paul tightens in his sleep and murmurs and McEban pulls away from him and sits up, careful not to jostle the mattress. There are just the street sounds and then again there is the voice he doesn't recognize.

Rita sits cross-legged on the pallet she's made at the foot of the beds. Her eyes are closed and there's a handheld tape recorder propped against her ankles. The voice comes from the tape recorder. *"You are Rita Sanchez,"* it says. *"Your sister's name is Alma but she is dead. Your brother is Paul. He is my favorite. Your father's name was Eduardo. The devil got into him and I could not get the devil out. It was not his fault. The world tore a hole in him and he began to leak. The leak made room for the devil and the devil got in."*

McEban leans back against the upholstered headboard. Paul snuggles against the side of his leg, searching for heat, breathing evenly.

"You were born in August." The voice is calming and McEban shuts his eyes. *"I was living with your father then, when he was still filled with just himself. I was out killing grasshoppers the day you were born. They ate everything. Even the chilies. I hope the little bastards that escaped my broom died shitting fire. It was 1971. They were American grasshoppers. Better for you. They could have been Mexican grasshoppers. We lived on the border, but on the Texas*

side. Or they could have been reservation grasshoppers. There was a reservation flood the night your sister was born. It swallowed our home and that's why we moved to the desert. You were born in the heat."

McEban can hear the squeak of the housekeeping cart moving along the hallway, the whispered conversation of the maids beyond the taped voice.

"Your sister was marked by water, and finally riverwater killed her," the voice tells him. *"She was three and you were two. We had taken a picnic away from the desert. I was with her but I am no match for water. Water knows who it wants for family and cannot be reasoned with. Water also has memory. Don't worry. You are owned by the earth. You are like me. Think of your life like a sack of beans, daughter. There are only so many. The same number of beans for you and for me. If you eat too many all at once you can live for years with nothing to show for it but gas. I am your mother and I love you. Not just because I am your mother. My name is Rose. Say your rosaries and keep a pet. A goat is a good pet to keep. Goats see life as food. If you watch the life of a goat you might learn to hoard your beans, and don't worry about your brother. Paul belongs to the sky. Paul's father had no holes in him."*

"I guess that beats the farm and ranch report," Bennett says. He sits at the foot of his bed. He's patting the top of his bald head with his palm. "Do you do that every morning?"

McEban opens his eyes. The slab of sunlight falls across Rita's face and she blinks against the glare. "It helps me remember who I am," she says.

She kneels at the edge of her sleeping pallet and begins to roll it, pressing the air out with the weight of her hands. She wears just a white T-shirt and it bellies away from her breasts and stomach. "Alma wants to know how long it takes you two to get going in the morning."

Bennett swings his legs over the side of the bed. "McEban's the slow one," he says. "He's got hair to comb."

"Alma likes to get an early start."

She ties the mat across the top of her backpack and strips off the T-shirt and stands and reaches her hands toward the ceiling, lifting herself onto the balls of her feet, stretching. Her face and shoulders and breasts and belly rise into the shaft of sunlight, and the allusion of movement is so convincing both Bennett and McEban look above her outstretched arms to the ceiling. She appears to be some misplaced and fatless sea mammal rising for a breath of air. McEban looks away.

"How the hell does that happen?" asks Bennett. There's real appreciation in his voice.

Rita drops her arms to her sides and shakes her hair away from her face. "How does what happen?"

"How do you get as fit as you are?"

"I'm not afraid of very much." She smoothes an open hand over her abdomen. It is slightly swelled. As though she's been up and had a good breakfast. "Fat's just insulation from your fears."

Bennett looks down at his belly. "Apparently I'm scared shitless."

When he looks back up Rita has turned and pulled on a pair of socks. There is a tattoo covering most of her back, red and blue, from the top plates of her shoulder blades to the swell of her buttocks. It is an accurate representation of Montana, the Dakotas, Wyoming, Idaho, Colorado, New Mexico, Arizona, and the Chihuahua and Sonora states of northern Mexico. The Continental Divide snakes from top to bottom in a series of descending chevrons.

"I think you've got a whole time zone there," says Bennett. It comes out as a hoarse whisper.

Rita steps into a pair of panties and turns. She crosses her right arm under her breasts and absently scratches the hollow under her arm and then drops her arms to her sides.

"It's the only way I can keep you Anglo-fucks from building on my land," she says.

*

In the dream she holds her face next to his and winks an eyelash at his temple, along the bone of his cheek. She grips his hair, fists of it. She tilts his head back and nips the length of his throat, at his jugular, across his collarbone. And then again.

Her knees press to the sides of his waist. She grips with her thighs and her breasts swing roundly in her work. Her nipples brush his chest. She laughs, but the laughter does not slow her. It is only the sound that predators make in their sleep. The laughter of a chase. The laughter of a successful hunt. There is the snap of her clean enamel teeth. She laughs harder. And then she stops.

She lowers herself onto his chest and brings his hands to her ribs, just his fingers on her sides, and settles upon him. The whole weight of her. She grips him more tightly with her thighs, and he wonders if he will ever wake. He wonders if this is the way death harvests its night-time crop.

Chapter Six

✳

Bennett *puts down* a deposit for a post-office-box key and finds the box empty.

They walk a block over to Bozeman's main drag and window-shop and eat their lunch in an overpriced café and wait for the day's first-class mail to be sorted. When Bennett's box is still empty they pull the trailer to a city park east of the P.O., and McEban steps Aruba out of the trailer and Bennett unhooks the trailer and sits on its tongue.

The park is heavily wooded, and the trees are beginning to turn. McEban leads the horse onto a slope of overgrown bluegrass and unsnaps the halter rope.

"What do you feel like next?" he asks.

"I feel like I'd be grateful if you drove back to Yellowstone," Bennett tells him.

"You mean today?"

"I mean I just told them where to find the man. I'd like to know what they found."

Rita and Paul sit at a picnic table. The girl spreads a set of dominoes between them and Paul shuffles the blocks.

"Why don't you come with us?" McEban asks.

"I don't believe I can." Bennett leans into the tailgate. "I wouldn't mind if you left Woody, though. If I've got him and Aruba for company I'll be just fine."

"There's a creek at the bottom of this hill." McEban lifts his chin toward the slope. "You could lead the horse down. It might be a nice place to sit."

Bennett nods and drags the bag of dogfood out of the truckbed and stands with the bag against his hip. "Do you believe in evil?" he asks.

"You mean as a general thing?"

"Do you believe something could have got in me when I beat the ranger like I did?"

"No, I don't. I believe you've got in you what you've got in you. From the get-go."

Bennett looks to the picnic table. He watches Paul make a match and pluck up a new domino.

"Tell that poor son of bitch I'm sorry." He looks back at McEban. "Tell him whatever seems right to you. If you want to, tell him I'm likely to go to hell."

H is grandmother lost fifty-three pounds between Valentine's Day and the first day of spring, and her skin didn't fit anymore. It draped like uncooked pastry from the backs of her arms, at her knees, at her throat, and when she hadn't used the toilet for three mornings in a row his father decided she needed to go to Billings, Montana.

They put down the backseat of the station wagon and slid a single mattress in, and his grandmother lay on the mattress and slept most of the way. He had his learner's permit and his father let him drive from the Ranchester turnoff to Lodge Grass.

They checked her into the Deaconess Hospital, and a nurse told them they might as well get something to eat.

"We've got tests to run," she told them.

His grandmother was sitting up in the hospital bed, and the nurse was tying the hospital gown at the small of the old woman's back.

"Hand me my purse," his grandmother said.

He went to the closet and got her purse and brought it to her. She opened the purse and took out a freezer container. On a strip of masking tape stuck to the container's top was written: SUGAR PLUMS.

"You shouldn't have anything to eat," the nurse told her.

"You aren't going to ruin my whole day," his grandmother said.

He and his father slept in the same soft bed at the Holiday Inn and were sitting in the waiting room at the hospital the next morning when the surgeon came in. The man appeared simply wearied, at a loss for where he might keep his hands. His hands were incredibly white. He finally folded his arms across his chest with a hand under each arm. He told them he'd cut her open and found cancer every place he looked. He told them he'd sewed her back up.

"How long?" his father asked.

"Not long."

"Will she live till Mother's Day?"

"You should tell her she's a good mother now."

"She knows it."

"It wouldn't hurt to tell her."

"I should've told her before," his father said. "If I told her now she'd think she'd done something wrong."

He followed his father out of the waiting room and down the hall. They stood beside his grandmother's bed. Tubes ran out of the backs of her hands, and there was a tube in her nose. Her hair was combed straight back from her face and lay flat against her skull.

She came awake slowly and coughed and worked her tongue around her mouth. She tried to ask for a drink of water, but she had to try three times before they understood. His father lifted her head away from the pillow and held a cup with a straw in it to her lips.

She sucked at the straw and swallowed hard and managed a thank-you when she was done.

"I'm sorry, Cleva," his father said.

His grandmother lifted the sheet away and pinched up one corner of the surgical bandage. Her eyes were rheumy from the anesthetic.

"At least I won't have to worry about whether this scar heals up pretty," she said. "I doubt this will be the summer to try a bikini."

"We'll get you home," his father said.

"Jock," she whispered, and his father bent to her. His grandmother took her son's hand. "I didn't cry out," she said. And then she fell back asleep.

L ast night was a good time." Rita kneels at the front of the truck's seat and reaches out the window and turns the side mirror in and stares at the reflection of her face, seriously. "Good times sneak up on you," she says. "A good time's not something you can plan for." She puckers her lips and kisses into the air, and so does her reflection. Paul looks at her and smiles. He sits between them, straddling the gearshift. They are on Interstate 90 backtracking east.

"Bennett says you're a good dancer," says McEban.

"I don't think Bennett would know good dancing from swatting wasps."

"He dance with you?"

"I don't know. I dance with my eyes shut."

She thrusts her head out the window and steadies herself against the windowframe and when she sits back in the cab appears satisfied—as though she's heard something new in the wind. Something she didn't know before.

"When it was hot," she says, "my dad used to buy my mom a dollar bag of ice and she'd hold it on her lap on a long drive. I remember that and it's not on the tape."

"Is that the tape I heard this morning?"

"I just need it to get started. When I first wake up."

"I don't remember the ice," Paul says.

He's spread Rita's sweatshirt across his legs and shaken the contents of his pouch on the sweatshirt. He's sorting his treasures into two rows, one along each thigh.

"You weren't born yet," she tells him. "And the man was different." She looks up at McEban. "We have different fathers."

McEban nods and stares into the faultless autumn sky. The air tastes tart in his mouth and smells of sap and water.

There are stands of aspen bright as scraps of goldleaf, and in the hayfields leading down to the Yellowstone River the alfalfa is ripened and stacked into lumpish blocks and the horizons are littered with pairs of hunting ravens.

He shifts on the seat and Rita asks, "You think Bennett'll be alright?"

"Sooner or later he will," he says and then admits he doesn't know it for a fact.

They turn south at Livingston and drive the broad sweep of Paradise Valley toward Yellowstone Park, back and forth over the narrowing river, gaining elevation.

They work up the switchbacks onto the Yellowstone Plateau and idle into Mammoth Hot Springs. McEban parks the truck in front of the Hamilton Store, and Rita stands out and up onto the front bumper. She shields her eyes from the sun and looks toward the hot springs. The boiling water falls away from a hill's summit, gathering in pools, falling slowly, sheeting through the pastel terraces of travertine. The sun flashes against the water and sparkles in the steam that crowns the ridgeline.

"I'm going in to see Linderson now," McEban says.

"I know you are."

He leans into the bumper. "Do you want to come?"

She sits back on the hood. "Why should I give a shit if white people want to beat on each other?"

"I don't think that ranger thought about what color he was. Or you either. He was just trying to help."

"Alma's favorite colors are mauve, indigo, and lavender."

McEban kicks at the gravel with the side of his foot. "She just tell you that?"

"She says her favorite smell is sulfur."

Paul reaches up and takes McEban's hand and leans in against the man's leg.

"What will they do if they catch us wading in the mineral pools?" Rita asks.

"Probably tell you to stop," he says. "They probably won't say anything to Alma at all."

She slides off the truck's hood and hikes up the waistband of her skirt and climbs into the truck's bed. She bends over her backpack and comes up offering a book. It's a worn paperback of Barry Lopez's *Field Notes.*

"Linderson might like to look through this," she says.

"Your idea or Alma's?"

"Alma's."

She climbs down and steps out onto the blacktop toward the mineral springs. "Tell him I'll want the book back when he gets done with it."

His father and Ansel muscled the sofa into a corner of the living room and stacked the rest of the furniture behind it. Two dollars and sixty cents rattled from the sofa's springs, and he took the coins up from the floorboards and held them in the palm of his hand. His father told him he could keep what he found.

Hospice brought a hospital bed and they squared it in front of the picture window. He walked out onto the porch and looked in through the window when they laid his grandmother on the bed. He didn't think it made much of a picture.

When the nurse came he walked in with her and watched her hook up his grandmother to an I.V. and take her temperature and blood pressure, and check where the incision was oozing.

The nurse was thick through the hips and shoulders, and her breasts hung heavily against her gut and bounced as she worked, but she was gentle and precise and seemed to care. McEban turned away when she put the catheter tube in.

"I'll come out three times a week," the nurse told his father. She wiped her hands with a towelette and wrote down her home phone on a Hospice card and gave it to his father. "If you need me in the middle of the night I'll come out then too. My name's Janet."

When his father didn't say anything she patted his hand and took up her bag and left.

"Janet was a good draw," Ansel said.

His father nodded.

"If you can't keep her busy with me," his grandmother said, "God knows she looks stout enough to stack up a pasture of alfalfa."

✳

M cEban asks the receptionist at the infirmary's desk where they can find Ranger Linderson.

"Family or friends?" She means the question to matter.

McEban takes Paul up under his armpits and holds him out toward the counter. The boy kicks his feet in the air. "His son," McEban says.

"I'm sorry. I didn't know." She points to a hallway.

The door to Linderson's room is stopped open. McEban and Paul stand together in the doorway. A catheter snakes out from under the sheets and empties into a half-filled plastic bag of orangish piss. The bag is buckled to the stainless bedframe. Paul stares at the thing in horror. He folds his arms across his chest and hugs himself and squeezes into the doorjamb.

The room is freshly painted and smells strongly of thinner and antiseptic. The bottom sash of its single window is raised open. McEban can hear the chatter of magpies.

Linderson's right leg and arm are cast, and the cast leg is elevated in traction. His head is bandaged and his face and neck are bruised yellow, black, violet, and brick. He opens the only eye he can and stares at McEban. The open eye is shot through with blood.

McEban steps into the room and pulls a chair to the side of the bed and leans back in the chair and looks up at the rate of drip in the I.V. tube. He counts to seven between each drop. He watches the drops gather and fall.

"I saw the accident," he says. "You remember me?"

Linderson nods just a little and winces against the effort.

"Hell of a wreck," McEban says. He looks out the window and Linderson looks too. There's a cow elk grazing on the sweep of lawn. "I guess you're asking yourself why."

Linderson doesn't try to nod.

"Just blink if I'm right."

Linderson blinks. It forces a tear from the corner of his open eye.

"Do you have to see my lips move?" McEban asks.

Linderson blinks.

McEban leans forward in the chair. "It's because he sells real estate." He holds his voice just above a whisper.

Linderson doesn't blink. He furrows his brow—or the strip of brow that's not bandaged.

"And it's probably because he married a woman who didn't love him." McEban looks over his shoulder at Paul. The boy still stands in the doorway staring at the bag of piss. McEban leans over his knees, closer to Linderson. "His wife took off with another man. She left just yesterday and a few days before she left I slept with her." He straightens. He keeps his voice low but tries to speak each word clearly. "I'm his best friend."

Linderson blinks twice.

"I'm sorry for what happened, and he says he's sorry, too."

Linderson blinks again and McEban can't think of anything else to say, so he waits for a count of seven and stands and walks to the foot of the bed. He takes up Linderson's chart and flips through the pages and hooks it back on the metal footboard.

"You'll likely limp awhile," he says. "Probably until after the holidays. And that right arm isn't going to work the way you'll want it to." He steps away from the foot of the bed and extends his arms. "I've been busted up lots worse," he says, "and look at me. I don't look too bad."

Linderson smiles around the open gap where his front teeth should be. And then he sucks at the air.

"Ribs too?"

Linderson blinks.

McEban walks behind the chair and leans into its back. "Maybe I'm not the best example of a full recovery."

Linderson blinks.

"Give him the book." Paul is whispering.

McEban nods and pulls the book from his back pocket and steps forward and lays it beside Linderson's unplastered arm. The ranger looks down at the book and then back at McEban.

"That's from the girl," McEban says. "She didn't have anything to do with what happened. You understand?"

Linderson blinks.

"She was just like you. She was just there." McEban looks up at the screen of a television mounted high in a corner of the room. Its tube is gray as polished slate. "I don't imagine reception's worth a shit up here."

Linderson blinks and McEban puffs his cheeks and blows and widens his eyes for the exasperation of poor reception. He steps toward the boy and turns. "I am truly sorry," he says, "but it could've been worse. I don't know whether that's something you've thought about."

Linderson blinks.

He stood alone with his grandmother. She asked him to open a window and he did, and she breathed in deeply.

"I always hoped to die in the spring," she said. She closed her eyes and sniffed at the cool air. "A spring death gives a family all summer long to work it out of their system," she explained.

He asked her if he could get her anything to eat.

"You anxious to be on your way?" She opened her eyes.

"I just thought you might be hungry."

"I'm hungry for love," she told him, and he got up beside her on the bed and rested his head against her withered breasts and looked out the window with her.

When she fell asleep he stayed, pressed to her. There was the faint echo of her heartbeats in his ear, and his head rose and fell with her breathing. She smelled like soured leather.

He stared out the window—at his grandfather's tombstone, and his brother's too. The stones caught the sun at the ridgeline across the drive.

R ita is already back in the truck when McEban and Paul get in. Her socks are off and her feet are wet.

"How was he?" she asks.

"He was damaged."

"Did he appreciate the book?"

"He was speechless."

She brings up a foot and rubs it dry. "I know that's supposed to be funny but it wasn't my fault."

"I told him it wasn't your fault."

"Alma wants to go hotpotting."

McEban is thinking of how Linderson's one good eye followed him from the room. "What's hotpotting?" he asks. He starts the truck but doesn't pull out into traffic.

"It's where we find a hot spring that won't scald us to death or where geyser water runs into a river so it's body-warm." She tucks her legs under her to sit higher on the seat. "We could get in and soak."

McEban looks down at Paul. The boy has spilled his treasures onto his lap again. "You want to go hotpotting?" he asks.

"I don't like to get wet," Paul says without looking up.

McEban smiles at Rita. "Tell Alma she can take a bath when we get back to Bozeman." He backs the truck out onto the highway.

"Hotpotting's for fun." She's risen up on her knees. The sun flashes in her dark hair. "Haven't you ever done something just for fun?"

"I'm having fun now. Besides, Bennett's waiting for us."

"Bennett's waiting for the mail," she says.

McEban looks to the west and thinks unexpectedly of laughter. He thinks of the sound of clear water over water-polished stones. The Gallatin Range stands treeless and stark against the horizon, and he knows that the Gardner River, Panther Creek, Indian Creek, Winter and Straight Creeks all fall away to the east. The sounds of water and laughter, he thinks. He shrugs and tries out a short measure of his own laughter and turns south, toward Old Faithful.

Along the Gibbon River there are swaths of burned timber on both sides of the highway. It's been twelve years since the Yellowstone fires, and the trunks and branches of the needleless pines stand gray and charred and naked above the new-growth timber and plush of wild grasses.

He slows the truck in the meadows along the Gibbon. A dozen buffalo churn the riverbank to mud. The spring's calves are nubby-eared and raucous.

Rita spreads a park map open on Paul's lap, and the boy helps hold it open. She points to a canyon south of Madison Junction.

"It's the Firehole River," she says. "I don't think they'd call it the Firehole if it isn't."

Ansel slept on the couch and McEban slept on the floor in front of the couch.

His father had volunteered to stay through the nights, but his grandmother told him cancer shouldn't kill more than one of them at a time.

"I'll not have you in here to watch me rot," was exactly what she said. "I'm not prepared for that too."

"What would you have me do?"

He'd been out irrigating and had slipped his boots off on the front porch. He stood beside her bed in his stocking feet, looking down, his thumbs hooked in the back pockets of his jeans. He smelled like the pastures he worked.

"I'd have you stay out in weather." She looked up at her son, and then turned to the window. "Ansel's old enough to want to be here, and the boy's too young to think it can happen to him."

"I'll come in when the work's done."

"You let this place slip and you'll have me for a ghost."

"I won't."

"I know you won't," she told him.

His father got down on one knee and took the old woman's hand in both of his and shut his eyes and pressed his forehead to her hand, and she let him keep it there. She didn't pull away.

Ansel got up every two hours through the night and turned on the bedside lamp and drew an unneedled syringe full of the morphine solution and squirted it under her tongue. When she gagged he cupped his hands in front of her face, and walked to the bathroom with his hands still cupped, and washed them, and came back, and did it over again.

When she needed to use the bedpan Ansel helped her then too.

They spoke in whispers, and sometimes laughed, and McEban lay awake to hear what they said.

"I want to be buried on the hill out front," she whispered. "Between Angus and Bailey."

Ansel drew a chair to her bedside. "What did you think we were going to do with you?"

"Just so you know." She rested a hand against his knee. "What day is it now?"

"It's Good Friday."

"Don't worry," she said. "I won't die on a holiday. I won't leave you with that."

"I wasn't worried," Ansel said.

She lived through Easter and by the end of April was light enough for Ansel to pick up and hold in his arms while McEban ducked under them and changed the sheets. Her chin and cheeks and shoulders all came up sharply against her gray skin. When she slept she moaned in her sleep, and cursed, and ground her teeth.

On a still, moonless night she gripped Ansel's shirtfront and pulled him close. He sat on the chair by her bed. Her voice came harsh, high up in her chest. "You could put an end to this," she said.

"No, I couldn't, Cleva."

"You're a low coward." She still held Ansel close. Pulled down to her face. Her teeth were clenched against the pain. "I'd do it for you," she told him.

"No, you wouldn't."

"Then I'll ask the boy."

"You wouldn't do that to the boy."

She dropped back in her bed and let her hand fall away and Ansel straightened. He dipped a washrag in a bowl he kept by the bed and wiped the sweat and tears from her face.

"That wasn't like me," she said.

"Can I kiss you?"

She blinked hard to clear her mind. Her eyes held a flash of fright. "Have you always wanted to?"

"I want to now."

She nodded and Ansel kissed her on the forehead, and she blinked into the gauzy light thrown up from the nightlamp, but the fear had fallen out of her eyes.

"I remember who I am now." She tried to smile. "Now, I'll be just fine."

"You've never been anything but fine," Ansel said.

It was before dawn when his mother came in. She came in every other day. She wore just a nightgown. No robe. No slippers. Her hair fallen about her face. She always came in after Ansel lay down for a little sleep on the couch.

She crept in on the balls of her feet and carried a bucket of sudsy water and a brush and fistful of rags. She got down on her hands and knees and scrubbed the pineboard floor, and the walls as high as she could reach, and wiped the chrome bedparts, and the tending tables, and took out the trash.

She worked fast, and sometimes she hummed while she worked, and he and Ansel watched her through the slits of their eyes and pretended to sleep.

When she was done, and the room smelled of detergent and Lysol, she knelt at the foot of his grandmother's bed and pressed her palms together in front of her face and prayed. He watched his mother's lips move while she prayed but couldn't hear the words she whispered.

When she was gone, Ansel would rise and squeeze the morphine under his grandmother's tongue, and, if she was bloated with fluid, inject a drug into one of her tubes that made her kidneys bleed the fluid off.

Once his grandmother nodded to the hallway, the way his mother had gone. "That poor woman would've been good at any work other than this ranch."

Ansel said, "I guess you and I got lucky we weren't stuck in the wrong kind of life."

The canyon is steep and shaded and the sound of the Firehole River swells up from its bottom. Rita sits at the edge, where the level ground drops away. They can smell the water.

"I'm not going down there," Paul says.

"Alma says it's a good spot."

The boy steps forward and looks down the slope. "I don't care what Alma says."

"It's too bad we didn't have the same father," Rita tells him and pushes off and slides out of sight on her heels and butt.

McEban and the boy stare over the side. They can hear her giggles, the snapping of branches, a single scream, more giggles.

From the bottom she calls, "I'm fine."

"You going?" McEban asks.

The boy still looks over the side. "I said I wasn't."

"Remember that movie where Butch Cassidy says to the Sundance Kid, 'Hell, the fall will probably kill you'?"

"I haven't gone to a movie yet."

"Well, that's what he said."

"I'm fine up here," the boy says.

"You're sure?"

"I'm sure not going down there."

McEban sits on the spot where Rita had pushed away and digs his bootheels into the sidehill below him. "I bought a bag of groceries before we left Bozeman. It's in the toolbox," he tells the boy. "There's bread and cheese and milk if it's not spoiled. You want me to make you a sandwich?"

Paul gets in behind the steering wheel. He sits sideways on the truck's seat. The door stands open. "I don't eat a lot," he says.

McEban nods and looks down the chute Rita's made through the duff and scree and rosehips. He takes a deep breath and holds it as long as he can, and when he can't hold it any longer he closes his eyes and pushes off.

He hits the canyon's floor and rolls once before he needs another big breath. He stands and brushes off his backside and takes a step to make sure he can. He wishes he'd kept his eyes open. The heel of his right hand is skinned. Rita calls to him, ahead in the trees.

He cups his hands to either side of his mouth. "I'm all the way down," he calls. He turns around to face the upslope. "I'm down," he calls again.

He weaves through a dark stand of pine and finds Rita squatting by a pool at the river's edge. The main current is beyond the backwash and broken into rapids. The rush of water is loud in the air and the air is damp and cool. She sweeps a hand across the surface of the pool and stands.

"It's perfect," she says.

She crosses her arms to the bottom of her T-shirt and pulls it over her head. She steps out of her skirt and panties and wades into the still water. McEban watches the map of the Rocky Mountains flood, and she turns at the far end of the pool. "Aren't you coming?"

There's a stretch of mud and mud-covered river rocks between them. "I don't want to get my boots wet," he says.

"Then take your boots off."

He sits on a fallen lodgepole and works off the boots and peels his socks off and drops them in the boots and stands the boots together beneath the log.

When he reaches the river he's limping badly. Without support his clubbed foot has suffered on the uneven stones. He stands on an apron of sand with his weight shifted to his right leg. He holds his left foot away from the sand.

"Those feet shouldn't earn the same wage," she says.

"A horse fell on this bad one."

"Maybe you should get it cut off."

"I'm thinking about that now."

He looks into the pool. The bottom is sandy and broken into hundreds of effervescent fumaroles.

"Alma says that foot has bad karma."

"Is she in there?"

The surface of the pool is pricked alive with the rising gas.

"She's in the hottest part." Rita sweeps her hands through the water. "She says in a past life you tripped Christ with that foot."

McEban hasn't thought about living more than one life at a time. "Why'd it take him two thousand years to even the score?"

Rita smiles. "He thought he'd let you sweat it awhile. You coming in or not?"

McEban looks down at his mud-splattered jeans. A pocket is torn and hangs from the front of his shirt. "I don't look as good naked as you do."

"Did a horse fall on the rest of you?"

"Different horses fell on different parts."

"Bet I've seen worse."

He thinks he'd like a rest before he walks back over the mud-slick stones, and is tired of standing, so he strips his clothes off and wades in quickly and sits and wriggles his ass in the sand. It takes a minute for the pleasure to register. The steam venting through the water tickles his legs and ribs and back. He imagines the sensation to be the same as falling through pine boughs. Just the tips of their soft needles pricking his skin. Or that's the way he'll explain it to Bennett, whether Bennett asks or not. He relaxes his hands from where he's cupped them over his genitals and his arms float to the surface.

"Maybe you should have kept your clothes on," Rita says. She's staring down at her breasts. They're just barely submerged and fuzzed with bubbles.

He looks into the timber. "I thought you said you'd seen worse."

"I thought I had. Alma says you look like guys did coming home from the Crusades." She still stares at her breasts. "Don't you think they look bigger?"

"About a third bigger," he says.

"You didn't even look."

"I didn't have to." The Saint Christopher medal lifts and settles against his chest and catches gold as an aspen leaf. "Everything looks bigger under water."

"Rodney always loved these guys." She rolls her shoulders and her breasts bounce and the bubbles shake free and rise.

"Who's Rodney?"

"My boyfriend." She looks up smiling. "Alma thinks he'll kill me. That's why I'm on the road." She presses her palms against the bottom to lift her butt away, and brings her knees up against her breasts. "You'd probably like to fuck me, wouldn't you?" she asks.

He looks back at her. "I don't believe I would."

She straightens her legs and lets her arms float to her sides. "Practically everyone I've ever met wants to."

"I don't."

"What's wrong with you?"

McEban bows his head to study the uneven reflection of his face. "I don't know," he says.

"I wouldn't let you, anyway. I just wanted to make sure there wasn't any ugly energy out here. You have any brothers or sisters?"

He looks up at her, blinking. "I wasn't listening."

"Do you have any brothers or sisters?"

"I had a brother."

"Where is he?"

"He's dead."

"I'll tell Alma. She gets lonely for other dead people. What's his name?"

"His name was Bailey."

"What's your first name?"

"Barnum."

"That figures."

"My dad went on vacation once to Denver," he tells her. "The circus was in town."

He closes his eyes and lets the water work into him, work his sins away. Or that is what he'll tell Bennett.

Just before dark they stand steaming out of the pool and get into their clothes and scrabble up the slope to the pickup. They grip themselves up hand over hand, pulling themselves from one needled bough to the next. They sit in the bed of the truck in the gathering dusk and smell their hands and rub the pitch from their palms and eat cheese sandwiches and drink from the carton of milk. Paul has found two Mounds bars in the glovebox. The candy's so stale McEban has to saw it into pieces with the blade of his pocketknife, and they hold the pieces in their mouths until they're soft enough to chew.

They spread out McEban's sleeping bag on the truckbed and lie down and cover themselves with a tarp. They stare into the press of stars.

"How was the water?" Paul asks.

"Like sitting on those stars," Rita says.

H e stood beside his grandmother's bed and dug in his pocket and brought out a rose-colored stone. It was only as big as his thumbnail. He turned it and they watched it catch the evening light.

He sat on the side of the bed, and when he offered it to his grandmother she took it between her thumb and forefinger.

"Is it candy?" she asked.

"It's just a stone."

"A stone?"

"I found it," he said. "And other ones too. I leave 'em in the rock tumbler Ansel helped me build. I put in some rockgrit and after a few weeks of tumbling, the edges and rinds wear off and they're polished."

His grandmother touched the rose-colored stone to her tongue. "It could be candy."

"It's the prettiest one I have."

She took his hand and laid the stone in his palm and closed his fingers around it.

"Don't you like it?" he asked.

"Of course I like it."

"I made it for you."

"I can't take it with me," she said.

"You could keep it until then." He opened his hand and looked down at the stone. "Until you can't take it with you."

"And then what?"

"Then I'll keep it," his father said. He had come in off the porch. He picked the stone out of his son's hand. "I'll keep it in my pocket." He looked down at the old woman. "You won't catch me without it."

The Hospice nurse came out of the bathroom and closed up her bag and folded her wind jacket over her arm. She nodded to his father and he followed her into the kitchen, and McEban went to the end of the hallway where he could watch them and still keep out of the way.

The nurse ran a glass of water and drank it and set the glass on the counter. "It won't be long," she told his father.

"You said that a week ago."

"She's a tough old woman."

"You should have been here when she was on her feet."

"Do you have a picture of her?" the nurse asked. "Besides that wedding photo on the mantel?"

"I don't have a camera."

"You don't have a picture of your mother?"

"I don't need one."

She rolled her sleeves down over her forearms and buttoned her shirtcuffs. "I'd like a picture of her," she said. "I'd like to keep her fresh in my mind."

"You come around whenever you like," his father said. "I can tell you every inch of her."

The nurse crossed her arms over her breasts and looked into the hallway at McEban and lowered her voice. "I think you need some counseling," she whispered.

"For what?" his father asked. His voice was too loud.

"For the grief." She looked back at his father. Her arms were still crossed. "The counseling's free."

"What I need is help branding my calves in a couple of weeks."

She stared down at her soft white shoes. "Maybe someone to talk to the boy then. Or your wife."

"I talk to them. If I'm not around they can talk to each other."

She looked up squarely into his father's face. "Cleva says she doesn't want a memorial service."

"That's not something we do."

"A service helps."

"Who does it help?"

"It brings a sense of closure."

"I don't know what that means," his father said.

In the morning they make a second round of cheese sandwiches and finish the milk and start back to Bozeman.

Rita sits quietly, cross-legged on the truckseat, with her eyes closed. She plays her taped biography, and then she plays it again.

It begins to drizzle in Gardiner and they stop briefly to buy groceries, and cups of coffee for McEban and Rita, and a soda for the boy.

By Livingston the day has turned to a steady rain. The wipers struggle and squeal. Water stands on the interstate and hisses against the truck's undercarriage. The sky presses down dark and bruised and storm-glutted to the horizons.

They park at the back of the horse trailer and get out and hold their jackets over their heads, and McEban swings the trailergate open. They stand in the downpour and stare in at Bennett. He sits against the manger with Woody curled in his lap. Aruba is haltered and tied in the lefthand stall. There's a pile of fresh horseshit at the horse's heels and it steams. Aruba turns to the sound of the gate opening and then back to the manger.

Bennett offers up a scrap of stationery, waving it above his head, and McEban steps into the trailer and takes it from him. The noise of the rain on the trailer's roof is deafening. He can see Bennett speak but cannot hear what he says. McEban leans closer. "Trailer me to Jackson Hole," Bennett screams and hugs Woody up against his chest and bows his head and draws up his knees.

McEban shuts up the trailer and gets into the truck and Rita straddles the trailer's tongue and guides him back under it and drops the tongue over the ballhitch and snaps the safety chain in place and runs to the cab. They're wet enough in the cab, McEban and Rita and Paul, that the windows fog. McEban hands Rita the letter and clears the inside of the windshield with his sleeve and turns on the heater and pulls into traffic.

"What's she say?" Rita asks. She holds the letter in one hand and combs the other back through her wet hair.

"I don't know yet," he says. "Read it out loud."

Rita wipes her face with the belly of her T-shirt and smoothes the letter against her wet skirt and holds it up close to her face.

" 'Dear Bennett,' " she reads.

I never thought I'd die in a motel room but last night I woke and there was an angel at the foot of my bed. She stood to the ceiling, with the standard white wings, but had a face that was fierce and sad. I asked her to open the window a little and she said I was just dreaming. And then she told me that God deplores staleness, and that any person's specific meltdown—mine, or yours—is seen as tragic only in the short view. She said it doesn't mean they don't care for us. It's just they expect some evolution for their care. She said souls who refuse to change are lumped into the same category as crocodiles and sharks, and are generally believed to need another billion years, or so, to evolve into animals worth cuddling. She said animals who don't change are the ones who take your hand off when you try to pet them. She said I was that kind of animal and then she left. She was right, and I'm sorry, and none of this is true. There was no angel. There is only my guilt, and the stories I make up to try to live with that guilt. I cannot remember my dreams.

Rita looks up from the letter. "I don't feel good about Bennett being back there by himself," she says.

"You want him up here?" McEban asks.

They're stopped for a light on Bozeman's main street. She stares out the window—at the people squeezed against the Baxter Hotel, out of the weather—and bends over the letter again.

Certainly, it must feel familiar for you to be after me. I've made you search for me most of our lives together without letting you find me. It's not something you could have planned against. When we were young I came to you. I begged you to take me in. I begged you with my body and my laughter. I thought if I could convince you to adore me that it would be enough. That's how young we were. I am so sorry.

I'm crying again. Harder than the morning when I left and it doesn't feel good this time. This time I'm crying for my

crimes. I hated you for your gratitude. I punished you because
you were easy to punish. I let you ruin yourself under the
weight of my punishment. In time I saw our life together for
what it was and did nothing. I was a crocodile. I was afraid to
change and fear is the root of all evil. I don't need dreams or
angels to tell me about fear. That's what my life has shown me.
I ask for your forgiveness. I pray you know what a decent man
you are. I pray you may forgive me for never learning to love
you and trying to convince you it was your fault. The angel
inside me knows the loneliness she's caused. She knows it's not
a long fall from wonder to despair.

Paul curls down on the seat between them with his head in
McEban's lap. Rita stops reading long enough to pull off his wet shoes
and socks and tuck his feet under her leg. For a long time she stares out
at the storm-soaked valley they are passing through. And then she reads
the last of the letter.

I hear you making excuses for me. I hear you saying that
we're all only human. I think we only trot out our humanness
to make sense of our cruelties. It's what we fall back on to forget we are angels and believe we are crocodiles. It's what I've
said to relinquish my responsibility for having fallen. I pray my
absence will allow you to heal. I'll write again in Jackson.
Gretchen

Rita folds the letter and places it in the glovebox and laces her fingers together and stretches her arms before her, palms out. Her knuckles
crack. She looks through the back window to the small curved window
in the trailer's nose.

She leans forward and shakes her arms over her knees. "There's a lot of electricity in that thing," she says. "I feel like if you plugged me in I could light up Billings."

"They were together a long time." McEban cracks his window and still can't get the air to the bottom of his chest. "We all were."

"This is the kind of thing that gets somebody killed."

He breathes in deeply and holds his breath. "It's just a sad letter."

She takes the letter out of the glovebox and reads it again, silently to herself, and folds it back into the glovebox and shakes her arms loosely from her shoulders. "Pull over when you find a good place." She shudders and shakes just her hands. "Pull over now."

"I will when I find a wide spot."

"It's wide enough here." Her voice is shrill and her eyes are wild in her face.

Paul sits up in the seat and McEban coasts onto the highway's shoulder and stops the truck. They've just turned south toward Gallatin Gateway.

Rita springs out into the borrow ditch and runs as hard as she can for several hundred yards away from them and turns and runs back just as hard.

"She needs to do that sometimes," Paul says.

"I can see she does."

"You look sad," the boy says.

McEban's eyes brim and he sucks at a noseful of snot. "It was just a sad letter," he says.

Rita glares in through the side window and stomps past the cab and walks to the back of the trailer. They can hear the trailergate open, and after a minute, close.

"Maybe you need to take a run too," the boy says.

The sky is clearing to the west and the rain has stopped. McEban pulls a dry denim jacket from behind the seat and covers Paul's legs and works a cotton handkerchief out of his back pocket and blows his nose.

"I'm no good at running." He watches Rita return along the side of the truck. "If I don't feel better in a while," he tells the boy, "I might get out and hop around a little."

Paul smiles and pats McEban's leg and Rita gets in and rolls down her window. "It smells good out," she says.

"What did Bennett say?"

"He said he needs a drink."

"He say anything else?"

"He said he'd feel better if Alma rode with him."

McEban waits for a semi to pass and pulls into the big truck's wake.

"We'll get him a whiskey in West Yellowstone."

"Don't let me read that letter for a while," she tells him.

The semi throws up a rooster tail of spray and McEban turns the wipers on high. "Do you think she'll be happy?" he asks. His eyes have damped again and he turns his face slightly away. "Do you think she's happy now?"

Rita draws her knees up against her chest and circles them with her arms. "I think she believes in her new man," she says. "I think she has to." She rests her chin on the caps of her knees. "If she couldn't believe in something I think dying in a motel room would seem just right."

B y the middle of May his grandmother couldn't eat, and he went into the root cellar and brought out a jar of plums, and one of peaches, and one of pears. He lined them in a row according to their color—darkest to the right.

He dipped tablespoons of the syrupy juice out of the jars and held the spoon to her lips, and when she could part her lips he dribbled the juice into her mouth and wiped away what came out the corners of her mouth.

"I love you, boyo," she told him.

He nodded. Her cannula whistled and she blinked slowly and stared at the ceiling with her clouded eyes.

She lifted her hand and tickled the back of his forearm. He looked down at her hand, at the yellowed nails. It was easy to imagine the hand as just bone. Goosebumps rose on his arm.

His father and Ansel stood behind him, against the big window.

"Make sure you just visit," his grandmother said, and when he looked puzzled she rolled her head toward the window.

"She means up the hill," his father said.

He looked past his father, out the window to the stone markers at his brother's and grandfather's graves. They stood silhouetted against the skyline on the rise.

His grandmother let her hand come to rest against his arm and tucked her chin to have a look at him. "It's not where you belong." She smiled. "You are our fruit." She was still smiling. "The fruit of stone."

In West Yellowstone they stop for a light and hear Bennett pounding against the side of the trailer. McEban honks once and the pounding stops and when the light changes he pulls through.

At the corner of the next block there's a liquor store, and McEban idles past the drive-up window and evens the trailer with the window.

"There was a man I knew in Cut Bank who's like Bennett," Rita says. She kneels backwards on the seat, watching the trailer.

McEban watches the trailer in the rearview mirror. The trailer rocks on its springs, and they can hear the stamp of Aruba's hooves against the floorboards.

"What was his name?"

"Louie," she says. "He had tantrums. Nobody could tell when he was ready to pop. He just popped."

McEban watches a red-haired man in the side mirror. He leans out the store window and mouths a conversation into the side of the trailer.

"One afternoon in the spring Louie threw a tantrum and couldn't stop. The force of it punched a hole in the Hi-Line and a tornado twisted in to fill up the hole. I saw it from start to finish. I was about ten. We were staying with my uncle."

McEban nods. He watches Bennett's arm poke out between the metal slats in the trailer's side with a twenty-dollar bill slotted between his index finger and the next. The red-haired man takes the twenty and pulls his head and arm back into the store.

"The tornado snatched up a Hereford calf and tossed it into a backyard in Browning. That's a thirty-mile toss," she says. "It wasn't a normal tantrum."

The barman reaches a bagged bottle out the window, and they watch Bennett grasp the bottle and pull it into the trailer.

"Keep the change," McEban says.

"What?" Rita asks.

McEban starts the truck. "That's what Bennett just said. He said, 'Keep the change.' What happened to the calf?"

"There wasn't enough of him left to make an eighty-cent hamburger," she says. She turns on the seat and fishes the seatbelt out and buckles herself in.

In the dream her hair falls to either side of her face and over her face. Her eyes are dark and flat and struck indistinct. There is the odor of her breath. Her breathing smells as his hands smell after he's worked in a garden, of a rich and sugary soil. She is that close.

She wets the lids of his eyes with the tip of her tongue, just that, and rests the length of her wet body against his. Her breasts roll against his chest, cushioning. Her nipples come hard as stones. There is the damp, electric brush of her cunt-hair striking against the smooth skin below his navel. The slip and skid of skin upon skin.

And then she pushes away from his chest and tilts her hips and arches her back and takes him into her. All at once.

Chapter Seven

✳

They top the Continental Divide out of West Yellowstone and gather speed on a high plateau of mostly Forest Service scenery: stands of mature pine, reseeded clearcuts, browning meadow grass, a cloud-broken sky. The air smells of elevation and the wind is up and out of the northwest. Paul pushes upright in the middle of the seat and rubs his eyes. He brings his knees to his nose and sniffs his jeans.

"I'm not all the way dry," he says.

"I have to pee," says Rita.

"We'll be in Ashton in half an hour," McEban tells her.

The boy taps him lightly on his thigh. "I think she means now."

McEban turns the truck into a campground and parks by the cinder-block toilets. The timber presses in around the campsites, and the wind lifts and drops the pine boughs and they sweep the air into the sound of falling water. There are no other campers.

Rita slides her panties to her knees and steps her right leg out of the elastic bands. She throws the door open and hikes up her skirt and swings her ass out over the threshold. She grips the armrest with her right hand and the metal doorjamb with the other and digs into the floormat with her toes. She rolls her eyes to illustrate the pleasure of her toilet.

There is the sound of the engine ticking as it cools, the wind, and the softer sound of her urine on pine needles. McEban stares into the trees.

"This embarrass you?" she asks.

"When you've got to go, you've got to go," he says, but doesn't turn his head.

"You look like you want to poke your eyes out."

"My eyes are just fine where they are."

She shakes her fanny in a series of small shudders and steps back and down and pulls up her panties. She lets her skirt fall and lifts it away from her thighs and lets it fall again.

Paul slides across the seat and out and Rita climbs into the truck's bed.

"Some people might've used the outhouse just over there," shouts McEban.

She opens the window panel behind the seat and sticks her head into the cab. "Outhouses smell like shit."

McEban stands out of the truck. He watches her work a pair of sneakers from her backpack. When she has them laced she rises on the balls of her feet and bounces once, and then again, and steps over the tailgate and onto the ground.

"I'm going for a run," she says.

Paul leans against the far side of the pickup. He's only tall enough for his head to show over the panel. They hear her swing the trailergate open and step Aruba out.

"She isn't usually this comfortable around live people," Paul says.

They turn to watch her against the wall of wind-fluxed evergreen.

She leads the horse and he trots behind her. He throws his forelegs out as though he's trained to pace. Woody's lined out at his heels. Her skirt blouses away from her knees and her hair snaps at her shoulders.

They watch her duck through a gap in the pines and disappear and the animals disappear after her. The scene is reduced to green and tan and blue, and, above, the ivory press of a rounded shelf of cumulus.

Paul steps onto the top of the tire and over the sidewall. He kicks out of his shoes and pulls his T-shirt over his head. When he's found dry clothes in Rita's backpack he skins out of his damp jeans and underpants. "Besides me and about six dead people she doesn't really like anybody very much," he says. He zips and buttons the dry jeans. "She likes dead people because she says you can trust them. She says dead people don't pretend to like you unless they really do."

He buttons the front of the flannel shirt he's put on and fishes a sweater out of the backpack.

McEban lifts the bag of groceries from the toolbox. "You hungry?"

"You ask that a lot." The sweater's brown and his eyes appear darker above its dark collar. He sits against the toolbox and opens his hands in exasperation. "There's people she didn't like at all when they were alive," he says, "but she gets along fine with them after they die."

A week after they buried his grandmother and stood her granite marker up in the sun and wind he was at work with Ansel and his father. They were out on the east slope of the Bighorns, and they were horseback.

They flushed the mother cows and their calves from the willow bottoms and the brush-choked breaks where they'd lain up for the night. They moved them down into the sage and nativegrass and wildflower foothills, and fell in behind them, and kept them moving down.

When the calves tried to break away from the gathered body of cows, the horses threw their lathered shoulders back and forth over their front feet and worked the flanks of the herd like sparring partners, keeping them bunched—the cows and calves—hating them for their lives of passive leisure, proud to be horses with a trade.

Ansel's colt laid his ears along his skull and chattered his teeth and rushed the cow's heels and steamed in the morning air. Ansel laughed and rocked back in the saddle and turned out his toes.

"Look at this working roan son of a bitch," he shouted and slapped his lariat against his thigh and reined the horse, just with his fingertips, just when the colt needed the experience of the man.

There was the smell of broken sage, and fresh cowshit, and turned soil, and leather, and the air was struck thick with pollen.

His father chanted, "There cow, now cow, hey, hey, hey," and whistled through his front teeth and kept his horse just below them on the sidehill, kept them bunched away from the rimrocks, moving steadily against the fall line.

They walked stones loose and the stones rolled where they could, and where there was just shale, the shale shattered and slid.

The flies swarmed in the warming air and fed at the cows' faces, their asses, at their chafed and swinging teats.

The new calves bucked and bolted and squeezed against their mothers' sides. And there was the general complaint they made—the mothers, and their soft children—in their lumbering descent. The sun broke out of a low cloudbank and put an edge to the shadows and glinted in the pint of sour mash Jock pulled from his saddlebags, again, and then again.

The boy looked at Ansel but Ansel looked only to the work, so he spurred his horse wide of the herd, ahead of the men, and opened the wiregate to the lane. He swung back onto his horse and squared the horse in the lane beyond the gate.

Ansel crowded the cattle through and McEban's horse paced and bobbed its head and nickered, and Ansel's colt answered. And then his father tipped back the last of the pint and tossed the bottle under the brace at the gate and said what a comfort it was to have a kid who thought he was handy as a man.

They rode behind the settling cows in the dirt lane, and swung in hard behind them in the corrals. They went to work sorting the calves from their mothers, turning the mothers out, two and three at a time, where they stood hunched in the pasture and bawled.

His father overcrowded a rangy heifer and she got a leg and shoulder through the rails and thrashed and snapped a rail and came up just bruised and joined the others. He snatched his hat off his head and swung it in the air, and yahooed, and dropped the hat, and his horse stepped on the crown. McEban felt the heat of the morning on him, pressing down with weight.

McEban scuffs the horseshit out of the trailer, and they sit on the edge of the trailerboards and balance slices of white bread on their knees and take them up one at a time and smear them with peanut butter. Bennett is curled against the manger. The whiskey bottle is capped and tucked under his arm. He snores and murmurs in his sleep.

Paul digs a Leatherman out of his pocket and fans open the choice of tools. He closes the handles behind the crescent of metal meant to be a can opener and centers a can of tuna between his feet and stabs the opener into it.

"It's got a knife and pliers and a saw blade too," he says.

"I can see that it does. Where'd you get it?"

"Rita usually keeps it with her. Aren't you still wet?"

"I'm fine," McEban says. "I'll be dry before it gets dark."

He watches the boy pick chunks of tuna out of the can and thumb the chunks into the peanut butter. When he's covered one side of his sandwich with fish he presses the two pieces of bread together and bites into it.

"I've never seen that combination before," says McEban.

"It's good." Paul looks up, chewing.

"I'll bet it's not."

"Try it."

Paul holds his sandwich up and McEban manages a timid bite. "It's not bad," he says.

"I told you." He skids the can over with the side of his foot and McEban picks at the fish, but keeps it separate from his sandwich.

"Where did you used to live before now?" McEban asks.

"In Lander. We lived in a trailer in Lander. With our mom." Paul looks into the grocery bag. "Did you buy any smoked oysters?"

"I will next time I shop."

The boy nods. "She died," he says.

"Your mother?"

He nods again.

"How did she die?"

"She had diabetes. They had to cut off one of her feet. Afterward, she said I was her foot and Rita was her head." He works the peanut butter away from the roof of his mouth. "After that she got a lot worse. We were with her when she died."

"Was it a long time ago?" McEban asks.

"It was just January second." He opens his sandwich and rearranges the tuna and closes it again. "I saved up and bought her a scarf for Christmas. I wish I'd've bought something she could've used."

Bennett turns in his sleep and they look to see if he's come awake. He hugs the whiskey bottle more tightly to his chest and settles, and McEban wipes his hands on his jeans and pulls a carton of grapefruit juice from the grocery bag and takes a long drink. "Is your dad alive?" he asks.

"I guess, but I don't know where."

Paul leans over and picks the tuna can up out of the dirt.

"Mom said she only saw him once and then he disappeared." He plucks out the last chunks of tuna and eats them slowly. "She said he didn't drive away, or get a job in Colorado. He just disappeared. While he was soaking in a tub of hot water. She said she was sitting on the toilet seat talking to him about the price of propane gas and he just disappeared." He looks at McEban and shrugs. "She told me she thinks he was an angel. She said that when she was still alive."

McEban hands the grapefruit juice to the boy. "This'll cut that peanut butter," he says. "Do you believe the thing about your dad?"

"Sometimes I do." He takes a long drink of grapefruit juice. "Sometimes at night. Is your mom dead?"

"She lives in Albuquerque with a chiropractor. I've never met him," McEban says. "She sends a Christmas letter every year. She always writes that she's a woman in need of adjustment."

"My mom went to a chiropractor once, in Lander."

Paul hands the juice back to McEban. They can hear the sound of Rita and the animals in the timber.

"Do you know Rita's boyfriend?" McEban asks.

"Rodney? Sure I do."

"What do you know about him?"

Paul sucks the tuna juice from his fingers, one finger at a time.

"He worked at the One Stop in Lander with Rita. He was going to college in Laramie but then he came home. Rita said they were in love for exactly one year. From one Fourth of July to the next one. And then Rita said she got drunk and fell in love with herself. That's what she said, and that's what she told Rodney." He looks up at McEban with a forefinger in his mouth. He works the finger around his gums. "Alma thinks Rodney wants to kill Rita."

"What do you think?"

"I don't know," the boy says. "I've never been in love."

"Do you think he's following us?"

Paul takes the juice carton back and drinks and folds the top shut. "Alma sings to him. Rita says Rodney can hear Alma's song."

"Why does she sing to him?"

"Rita says Alma doesn't like loose ends."

The boy tilts the grocery bag down, searching for a treat. "When we get somewhere with a stove, can we boil some eggs?"

"Sure we can." McEban sets the carton of grapefruit juice back into the bag and stands. He steps away from the boy. "Is Rodney crazy?"

Paul lifts his shoulders toward his ears and lets them drop. "I've never been crazy either," he says.

Gene and Anna Maris parked their truck by the barn, and the Hansons, and the Reillys, and the Simpsons too. The boys and girls alike took up stockwhips and lariat ropes and waded into the cows and calves and helped with the sorting.

When a calf turned back over Bennett and knocked him down and got free into the pasture, Ansel spurred his roan colt into the distance behind the calf, and built a loop and rode him down, and swung once, and dallied, and dragged him back.

The calf's tongue hung from its mouth and it wailed and blubbered and tossed its head and slavered and fought the rope.

The men fired the propane torch and lined the branding irons in the metal trough under the flame. They laid out the vaccination guns, and the dehorning tools, and the vials of vaccine, and the powder that would stanch the flow of blood.

They tilted down two four-by-eight sheets of plywood from where they leaned against the barnwall and laid them over sawhorses on the shaded side of the barn. The women filled the rough tables with bowls of tinfoil-covered food, gallon-size Thermoses, picnic plates, and plasticware.

The women who didn't have infants in their arms, or at their breasts, rolled up their shirtsleeves and bent through the corral rails and stood ready for the work.

He looked back to the house to see if he could find the outline of his mother. He didn't see her on the porch, or at a window, and when Nancy Reilly saw him looking she smiled, and he looked away and stepped down from his horse.

He handed Brian Reilly his bridle reins because the man's foot was broken and wrapped, and he needed work that got him off the foot and on top of a horse.

"Help me set these stirrups out to the length of my legs," Brian told him, and he ducked under his horse's head and unbuckled the stirrup strap on the offside.

"How many holes down?" McEban asked.

"Four should do it," Brian said. "I'm sorry about your grandmother. And so is the wife. Bennett cried all night the day she died."

"Thank you," McEban said.

He looked at his father. He had his horse parked away from the work and sat the animal, weaving, gripping the saddle's horn, smiling into the sunglare.

"I've never seen your dad drunk before," Brian said.

And McEban nodded because it was the truth, and he was glad a grown man had said it out loud.

Bennett wakes at dusk and crawls to the trailergate and swings his legs out and sits.

"Are you ready for supper?" Rita asks.

She squats on her haunches, turning hotdogs with a sharpened stick. She's built a fire under one of the campground grates and let the fire burn down to coals. She's stirred macaroni and cheese and creek-water into an aluminum pot and broken open a package of hotdogs on the grate around the pot. McEban and Paul sit across from her on a length of fallen pine they've rolled to the fireside.

Bennett reaches back for his bottle and stands out of the trailer. He holds onto the gate. "Do we have catsup?"

"Just mustard," she says.

"I can't eat a hotdog without catsup. Where's my letter?"

"In the glovebox," she says.

He starts along the trailerside and falls once and gets back up. They can hear him open the truckdoor and the leafsprings shift and the door close. He staggers to the fire and sits in the dirt next to Rita and opens the letter on his lap. "Did you read it?" he asks.

"Twice." She sits back on a smooth stone behind her and takes up a paper plate of blackened hotdogs and balances the plate on her knees.

Bennett sucks his upper lip between his teeth and lets it go. He holds the letter to the fire. McEban can see the careful loop of Gretchen's handwriting through the milky paper.

"I read it the second time to make sure I'd remembered it right from the first time." She takes a hotdog off her plate and folds a slice of bread around it and hands it to her brother.

Bennett tilts back a sip of whiskey. "When you see Alma how does she look to you?"

Rita studies him as he stares into the fire. "Like pond ice," she says. "Alma looks like the ice at the edge of a pond when it's splintered and the sun's out."

"Is that the way you think we all look?" he asks. "After we're dead?"

"I think it's the way Alma looks."

Bennett squints against the firelight. "Do you see anybody else that's dead?"

"Not regularly," she says. "But sometimes."

Bennett takes up a stick and pokes at the coals. The coals pulse orange and red and silver, as though gasping for breath.

"I think your wife loved you as much as she could," Rita says. She holds a hotdog by its end. She nibbles at it and wags it toward Bennett. "I think she stayed with you because she felt superior to you, and when she couldn't anymore, she left. I don't think she feels superior to anything anymore."

The night presses in against them, against the wavering bulb of firelight in which they sit. Bennett drops his head back and stares up into the darkness.

"I still love her," he says.

"I still love Rodney," she says. "Rodney made the same mistake. Every morning he woke up next to me he thought his life couldn't do anything but improve."

Bennett levels his head. "Who's Rodney?"

"Her boyfriend," McEban says. "Alma thinks he's going to kill her."

Bennett stares blankly at Rita and then to the sheet of paper in his hands. He nods and rips the letter in half and then again, and leans forward and lays it on the coals. The paper curls and blackens and bursts into flame.

"Goddamn it." Rita pokes at the flaming paper with the sharpened stick. "I just got those coals spread out right."

"Do I look like I could start over?" Bennett asks.

She looks up at him. The nightside of her face is flattened against the darkness. "What do you want to start over?"

Bennett shrugs. "Just about everything, I guess. I looked in the truck mirror to see if I looked like I had any energy left, but I couldn't tell under the domelight. I feel used up."

"You've been drunk for a day," she says. "Nobody looks good when they're drunk."

"Take that into consideration," he tells her. "And remember I was beat up just a couple of days ago."

Rita sets the pot of macaroni off the grate and kneels at Bennett's side. She shuts her eyes so that when she opens them and looks it will be like the first time. She lifts his chin toward the firelight and studies his face. The swelling has gone down, but there's still a hammock of purple under his left eye, and the lid droops, and the left side of his jaw is bruised from its hinge to the point of his chin.

"You look tired," she says. "And you need a bath." She sits back against her heels. "I don't think any of us can start all the way over."

Ansel and Brian Reilly roped the calves by their heels when they could, and around their necks when they missed the heels, and dragged them to the boys.

The boys waited in pairs at the center of the corral. McEban worked with Jack Maris, and the Hanson brothers worked as a team, and Gretchen Simpson worked with Bennett because McEban hadn't gotten to her first. He watched his father more than he watched anything else and tried to act as though he didn't.

His father missed three calves, and caught his horse's front feet once, and finally reined his horse away, and took out a second pint of whiskey from his saddlebags.

Ansel dragged a calf to McEban headfirst, and said about the boy's father, "That's none of your business," and McEban bent over the calf and gripped its front leg, and the flap of hide at its flank, and lifted against his thighs, and let the calf drop on its side. He knelt against its neck and bent its foreleg back at the knee and took the catchrope off its neck. He looked to where his father sat his horse and drank.

"It feels like my business," he said.

Ansel nodded down at the calf. "Right there's your business. What you've got in your hands."

Jack Maris sat in the corral dirt behind the calf and pulled its top hindleg back to his lap. He pushed with his boot sole against the lower hindleg, and scissored the animal in place.

The day was dry and the corral worked to dust, and the dust hung close to the ground. He could taste it in his mouth, could see it mixed with the sweat on his hands, ground into his clothes, and the feel and smell of it got all the way into him. He looked only to the next calf that came his way.

Gene Maris and Dan Hanson ran the irons. They wore leather gloves and walked to the calves with the brands glowing red, and the iron cooled as they walked, but not enough.

They stepped a boot up onto each calf's hip and pressed the iron into the wiry red hair, and the hair burned, and the hide did too, and the smoke made the boys' eyes water. Sometimes it made them cough.

The calves bucked against the ground and bawled. They bulged their eyes until the whites showed plainly all the way around. Their tongues hung from their mouths, and the red dirt stuck to their tongues.

The man with the iron stepped back and almost always bent down and rubbed the palm of his glove against the brand to make sure it was right. These were men with their own stock; men who would bring their cows into their home corrals tomorrow, or the day after, or on the weekend, and all this would be done again.

Anna Maris ran the vaccination gun, and whichever of the men had his hands free first stabbed the razored circle of the dehorning tool over the horn nubs and twisted it into the calf's skull, and popped the little buds of horn onto the ground. If the blood didn't stop the man shook in the styptic powder and stood away, and waited, and when the boys turned them loose the calves jumped right up, and when they didn't the boys helped them to their feet, and ran them through a gate into the pasture where they trotted to their mothers, and tried to nurse.

If it was a bull calf there was more to do.

Anna Maris shook her hair away from her face, and reloaded her syringe, and laughed, and said, "This is the only time it doesn't go against the girls," and Dale Simpson knelt down and slit the sack, and fished out the nuts, and cut and feathered the cords. His wife stood behind him with a coffee can and he dropped the nuts in the can for the nutfry they'd have that night.

Rowene Simpson shook the can at McEban, right under his nose, and said, "Mess with my daughter and this is where you'll come to find your little oysters." Then she said as much to Jack Maris too.

McEban snuck a look at Gretchen and she smiled at him, and he looked back down at the can of wet and bloody nuts.

And then his father fell off his horse and lay faceup in the sun and they all stood away from their work. For just one moment. And then Anna Maris and Dan Hanson walked over to him and hooked him under the armpits and dragged him into the shade of the barn. They propped him against the barnwall and never said a thing, and in another hour the work was done and it was only one in the afternoon.

They washed up at the hose bib by the barn, and Rowene Simpson brought his father's hat out of the corral. She reshaped its crown and knelt by him and tipped the hat down over his eyes. She wiped around his mouth with the corner of a bandanna she'd damped at the bib and stood and joined the others.

They sat on benches at the homemade tables to have their dinner. They gripped one another's rough and work-thickened hands and bowed their heads, and Ansel said, "God bless every one of us according to our need," and then he thanked the Lord that no one needed stitches, for more twin calves than stillborns, for good grass, enough winter snow to keep the creeks up, for good-natured horses. "And for

Cleva," he said. "She was the best of us." He cleared his throat, and added, "I wish to someday be the man she saw in me."

Every one of them said, "Amen."

There was potato salad and corn on the cob and white bread and chicken and baked beans reheated in a Dutch oven that Nancy Reilly had set in the branding trough.

They ate with their hands and with spoons, and they laughed while they ate. They wiped their butter-slick fingers on their jeans.

"I got this recipe from your grandmother," Rowene Simpson said about her potato salad. "I'd've never thought to put the olives in."

Dale Simpson looked up and said, "It's only God who gets the pleasure of her now," but his mouth was full and his wife asked him to repeat it and he did.

Nancy Reilly asked McEban if his mother was feeling weak again this year, and he said she was.

"I'll save out a plate for her. It's no fun feeling weak," Nancy said, and she looked up toward the house.

They're asleep under the tarp in the pickup bed when the barking starts. The moon is set and the night has fallen soundly dark. McEban takes up the flashlight he's laid by his hat and sweeps the night with its beam.

He finds Woody backed against the truck tire. The dog's hackles are spiked and he growls and drools and won't look away when McEban calls his name.

Bennett has the toolbox open and McEban hears him bolt a cartridge into the rifle's chamber. "Try to get a light on what's out there," he says.

"Is it Rodney?" Rita asks.

McEban turns the light toward the sound of her voice and back into the night. She's taken Paul up under an arm and moved to the tailgate.

They hear snuffling and a series of rasping coughs. Bennett shuts the toolbox and steps up onto its lid. "If it's Rodney," he says, "the man's dying of tuberculosis."

They hear Aruba neigh and whistle and stamp in the meadow grass, and Woody crouches lower and whimpers and snarls.

"I think we might lose that horse," Bennett says.

"Shit," says Rita, and when McEban puts the light on her again the boy is gone.

"Where is he?" he asks.

"He's gone for the horse," she says.

McEban stands and snatches the rifle from Bennett and slides over the sidewall. "Get the girl in the cab," he says and thumbs the safety off. "And the dog too."

He seats the rifle against his shoulder and holds the flashlight up under the forestock and sights along the side of the scope. He keeps both eyes wide and moves into the night a step at a time.

He hears the snapping of brush and the horse hit the end of its picket line and fall and get back up and run in a circle.

He sweeps the flashlight and rifle back and forth. The beam throws an empty cone of yellowed light. It catches in the pines and meadow grass. There is only that. And the sounds of the horse and the huffing of the wild thing come in out of the night.

He wishes he had checked his watch. He'd like to know if it's an hour until dawn or more. If he's mauled, he thinks, he'd like to know how long he will have to lie in the darkness. His flesh feels hot and his blood throbs at his temples and in his neck. He sniffs the air for the odor of blood. His ears ring.

He hears the truckdoor slam behind him and Bennett's voice. "It's probably just a bear," Bennett shouts.

McEban thinks of the eyes that surely must be on him. Dark eyes, dark nose, dark fur, black lips, white teeth. He thinks of the brain behind the eyes. He knows it is a mind bent singularly on its own satisfaction, its own hungers. Primitive, without remorse.

Skin covers meat, he thinks. Protein. Broken skin presents a meal. A snapped bone reveals the bonus of marrow. Only that. And a belly full of blood brings a sound and satisfied sleep. He wonders where he will find the boy. He prays the boy isn't torn open and dragged away into the deep timber.

He hears steps to his right and swings the light and rifle and blinks to clear his sight. He hears the approach of footfalls, hears them quicken, the drumming upon the earth. He feels the vibrations move into his calves and thighs, and he widens his stance and bends at the knees and holds his breath and grits his teeth. He can hear his teeth squeal. Enamel sliding against enamel.

Sweat runs from his armpits and down his back. His scalp pricks and itches and he narrows his eyes. He centers himself over his lowered ass. He is crouched that way, sweating, his arms gone leaden when the boy trots the blind horse out of the brush and into the light.

McEban relaxes his finger from the trigger and turns the barrel away and puts the safety on. He exhales and sucks full of the night air and it makes him choke. He turns away and coughs and tries to spit. He licks his lips and tries again.

Paul has stopped the horse before him and leans along its neck and whispers sweetly and clucks his tongue.

"Aren't your feet cold?" he asks.

McEban looks down to where he stands. A small stream parts neatly around his calves. He steps up onto the bank. "I forgot to pull my boots on."

The boy slides from the horse's back and steps to its head. He's fashioned the end of the picket rope into a crude hackamore, and still twenty feet of the rope trail away. He pulls the rope to them, and the horse swings its hindquarters and rolls its blind eyes. Paul whispers to the horse and loops the rope against his open hand.

"There now," McEban chants, "that's the man." He steps closer so the horse can scent him. He holds the light on the boy's hand and they watch the rope coil against his palm. The hobble comes up out of the grass unbuckled and wet with dew.

"Were you scared?" McEban asks.

"Yes, I was." Paul ties off the coil of rope. "And then I got sort of calm. Were you scared?"

"I never got calm."

The boy looks over his shoulder into the dark. "Did you see what was out here?"

"No, I didn't."

"I never did either."

McEban holds the flashlight to his side and they look down together and bend to have a better look at the single track. The footpad is broadly triangular and the toepads arched to the middle toe and the foreclaws straight and deeply gouged.

"It looks bigger because the ground's wet." McEban steps to the side and finds a second track with the light.

"Is it a grizzly?" the boy asks.

"Yes, it is," McEban says. He still stares at the track.

"I wouldn't have come out here if I'd've known."

McEban brings the light up to Paul's face. "I probably wouldn't have come after you." He smiles and the boy smiles too.

They hear Bennett start the truck and the throaty flush of the engine and see the headlights stretch into the timber and not quite reach them.

McEban steps back across the creek. "Lead that horse up close behind me."

"I will for sure," the boy tells him.

*

In the afternoon they played horseshoes and napped on blankets in the shade. The men drank beer, and so did Rowene Simpson, and the rest of the women and the kids drank soda pop.

In the late afternoon the women cleaned the calf nuts at Ansel's sink. They rolled them in batter and deep-fried them in two inches of lard and let them cool on a spread of paper towels.

His father came awake and Rowene asked if he was hungry, and he said he was just thirsty so she handed him a beer.

They sat on Ansel's porch and ate the nuts with their fingers and enjoyed the end of the day, and at dusk Brian Reilly was left, and so were the Simpsons. Everyone else had gone.

Brian asked his father if he was going to take up smoking too, and his father said he thought learning to drink was hard enough.

Brian said he'd help him get the hang of it and got up and fished a Miller High Life out of the cooler and sat back on the porch.

The evening came down warm and windless and McEban thought he'd never seen his father so relaxed.

When they were out of beer Ansel said he was tired of company, and his father said he wasn't, and Brian Reilly backed his truck around.

"We'll run into Ishawooa for another six-pack or two," his father said and looked at his son, "and maybe a bonfire by the river for the kids."

"Suit yourself," Ansel said.

Brian asked who would ride up front with him and Rowene said she would. Everyone else rode in the back and held their hats in their laps and watched the spread of stars grow brighter as they drove away from the porchlight and into the night.

His father leaned against the tailgate, and McEban and Gretchen and Bennett and Dale Simpson sat against the cabwall. Gretchen sat between him and Bennett and they pressed into her, and everyone watched his father.

His father had his catchrope coiled on his knees. He spun out a loop and stared into the grassy trough of the barrow pit.

Dale Simpson said, "It never hurts to practice."

His father said practice was what he needed. His hair blew over his forehead and he smiled at his son, and McEban tried to remember the last time he'd seen his father have such a good time, and couldn't, so he smiled right back, and tried to have a good time too.

Bennett drives with his window up and the heater on and the whiskey bottle stuck between his thighs. "Did you see anything?" he asks.

"There were some tracks," McEban says. "The boy says he saw something move."

"My bowel," says Bennett. "That's what would've moved if I'd've gone out there." He elbows Paul. "How're your pants?" he asks, grinning.

"They're fine," the boy says, and Bennett laughs and lifts up the bottle again.

They drop off the timbered plateau into the fertile, deeded farmland at Ashton, Idaho. A roadside sign catches in the headlights. It advertises the town as the Seed Potato Capital of the World. The streets are empty of traffic and they guess all the potato farmers to be in bed, and they idle through town and turn back east toward Wyoming.

It is not yet dawn and the cultivated fields to the sides of the road fall darkly away. No one sleeps. Rita and Paul are squeezed side by side in the middle of the seat. They blink and rub their eyes and stare through the windshield eastward for the first hint of day. McEban leans into the passenger doorpanel.

Bennett stops the truck in front of a roadside bar in Driggs, Idaho, and stands out with the headlights on bright and the motor running. He pounds on the bardoor until an old man turns on the porchlight and cracks the door open. Bennett talks to the man and follows him in and comes back out with a gallon jar of pickled hard-boiled eggs and a fist of beef jerky.

He stuffs the jerky in his shirt pocket and hands the jar to Paul, and the boy centers it on the seat and keeps it in place with a knee on either side.

"Help yourself to breakfast," Bennett says and, when no one does, grips the lid and turns it. The whole jar turns. "Clamp down," he orders, and Paul scissors the jar between his legs and Bennett twists the top off. He scoops out an egg and holds it up in the dashboard lights. The smell of sulfur and vinegar fills the cab. "To your health," he says.

He eats three, one after the other, and Paul eats one. Rita leans into McEban and closes her eyes, and after a while begins to sing. McEban has to tilt his head to hear the words. She sings just above a whisper. "Have mercy on us Lord, have mercy on us. Let your mercy, O Lord, be upon us, for we have placed our hope in you."

He means to ask her where she's learned the words to "Missa Solemnis" but doesn't want to interrupt. And he's tired of the sound of his own voice.

They top Teton Pass as the sun breaks the southeastern horizon seemingly all at once. The day is cloudless and the sky blanched pale, and Bennett swerves against the glare and paws down the visor and double-clutches and they drop a gear. Rita holds her hands before her and squints into the sun. She can see the fan of bones, from her wrists to her fingertips, the flesh become just a rosy blur.

The gearbox whines and Bennett pumps the brakes into the canted switchbacks, and still they drop faster than the sun can rise, back into the shadowed valley, the peaks surrounding the valley sun-slapped and glowing amber.

Halfway to the valley floor the sun gains the sky again and the Snake River glows as an uneven rend in the green country below them, and then they're in the little town of Wilson at the bottom of the pass and the smell of their burning brakepads fills the cab and it is fully dawn.

Bennett drives the ten miles to Jackson slowly, veering across the center line, correcting into the gravel at the road's side. He's taken up the bottle in his right hand, and points to the behemoth log homes that break up the hillsides and crowd the river bottom.

"They tell me the billionaires are buying out the millionaires down here," he says. "Can you imagine selling real estate in this little burg?"

"I can't," McEban tells him.

At the edge of Jackson they pass a drunk asleep in his car and half a dozen joggers out loping at the roadside. The breakwater tourist shops stand closed.

A gang of old men loiter in front of a downtown café, waiting for the coffee to brew.

Bennett stops the truck at the traffic light at the southwest corner of the main square, and because he's pointed east and the sun feels good on his chest, he continues east on Broadway past the Church of Latter-Day Saints, past St. John's Hospital, and out toward the elk refuge. When he's miles from the nearest building he parks on the shoulder of the two-lane.

McEban unloads Aruba and the horse bends to the thick grass at the roadside. Woody finds a patch of broken ground and stretches out on it, and McEban brings him a bowl of kibble.

"What time do you think the post office opens?" Bennett asks.

"Nine probably," McEban says.

"How long do you plan on doing this?" Rita asks.

Paul stands beside her and she pulls a comb from a pocket in her skirt and kneels in front of him. She combs his hair until it snaps with static and rises away from his head, and she licks her fingers and smoothes the hair down flat.

"How long do I plan on doing what?" Bennett sets the jar of eggs on the truck hood. He's rolled up his sleeve. He grips them out two at a time, and when he thinks of it underhands one to Woody. The dog gets up and sniffs the egg and cocks a leg and pisses on it.

"Driving from post office to post office," she says.

"As long as it takes. Except on Sundays. I guess we'll rest on Sundays."

"Why?"

Bennett studies the egg he holds. "Because she asked me to." Brine drips from his elbow and he wipes the elbow against the bulge of his gut. "Anyway," he says, "new misery's more interesting than old." He pops the whole egg in his mouth and caps the jar. "You want these?" he asks, and when no one answers, he sets the jar on the truckseat and gets in beside it.

"I might go back into Jackson and see which bar opens first."

McEban has started up a balded hillside. He stops, huffing, looking down at the truck. "We'll come in to town in a couple of hours," he calls.

Bennett waves and turns the truck in an arc that dips him through both barrow pits. Paul stretches out in the dirt next to Woody and Rita starts up after McEban.

"Alma says there's a good place to sit at the top," she calls, and he turns and waits for her to catch him. They sit in the sage at the crown of the hill and watch the land north toward Yellowstone. The glaciers on the Tetons flash in the morning light.

"Where's the elk?" she asks.

"They come down in these meadows when the snow drives them out of Yellowstone."

"Does somebody feed them?"

"Off the backs of wagons," he says. "There's some handsome teams of draft horses that pull the wagons. I've come over to watch." He plucks a grass stem up and sucks on the shaft. "When it greens up in the spring the elk wander back."

"Where do you think they'd go if no one fed them?" she asks.

"I guess they'd die."

"Do you ever wonder what it would be like if you weren't here?"

"Just me, or everybody?"

"Everybody."

"It'd be quieter." He leans back against his elbows. "And there'd probably be a lot more dead elk."

"I think it was the men who put up the fences who crowded them into the park." She sits with her knees drawn up. With her slim brown hands clasped over her knees.

"Maybe it'd just be quieter," he allows.

They watch Paul find a can along the roadway and set it on a fence-post and back off and gather a pile of rocks. He picks out each rock, one at a time, and collects himself like a big-league pitcher, and winds up, and tries to knock the can off the post.

The sun warms the hillside and McEban sits up and strips off his canvas jacket and spreads it behind him and leans back onto it.

"Alma says it's the sound of our disbelief that makes more racket than anything else," Rita says.

"Has she said what we don't believe?"

"She says we don't believe we're going to die."

"I believe I will," he says. "I just don't want to suffer before I do."

"She says you won't."

He looks to Rita. "Is she sure about that?"

"Alma's always sure. She's just not always right."

McEban slumps back fully and closes his eyes. He listens to the sound of the wind, a horsefly, the swish of the boy throwing rocks, and when he looks up Gretchen stands over him. He can see her clearly. Her red hair catches in the sun like hot copper. She stands with a foot at either side of his chest and smiles down at him. She holds a small round stone in her left hand, and when he smiles back at her, she lets it drop.

He watches the stone fall. He watches it enter him just below his sternum and he feels it pass, without a sound, through his body, and continue falling. He lies listening, waiting for the stone to strike a surface, and when it doesn't he opens his eyes and blinks into the violet-blue sky.

"Was I asleep?" he asks.

"For an hour," Rita tells him. She still sits with her knees drawn up.

He nods and stands and takes up his jacket, and she follows him down through the sagebrush to the road.

"You ready to go to town?" he asks Paul.

"I want to hit the can first."

"Why don't you bring it with you?"

McEban catches Aruba's halter rope out of the grass and swings up on him and turns him in the borrow ditch. He reaches down for Rita's hand and pulls her up behind him.

"Walking or riding?" he calls to Paul.

The boy is coming back toward them with the can.

"I don't feel like riding," he says.

"Will you bring Woody's bowl with you?"

"Sure I will," the boy says and takes up the bowl and breaks into a skipping run in the waist-deep grass, and his smile flashes bright as glacier ice.

His father'd missed a SOFT SHOULDER and a DEER CROSSING sign by twenty feet each, and got to his knees against the wheelwell so he could better see the signs come up out of the night.

Brian Reilly hung his head out the cab window and shouted, "What're you going to do if you catch one?"

"What's he want?" his father asked.

"He wants to know what you're going to do if you catch a sign," Dale said.

"Dally off hard and fast," his father said.

"To what?" Dale was laughing, and the wind caught his laughter and swirled it against his face.

"To my dick," his father said, and when Brian wanted to know what was said, Dale shouted, "His dick," and didn't even look down at his daughter and the boys didn't look at Gretchen either, but she felt bright-hot against their sides. The men laughed, and the boys sat wide-eyed, working hard at their smiles. They sipped at their cans of pop. Gretchen smiled too but tucked her chin.

At the bend in the two-lane, where it curved through a gap in the red rocks, his father looked directly at him and winked.

"Pay attention," his father said. "This'll make a good story someday."

The man rose against his cocked right knee and threw a high backhanded loop into the night and spun on his bootheels and leaned back against the stiffened rope and the rope paid out through his hands at fifty miles an hour, and the knot in the end snapped up against what was left of the meat of his hands. He bore down and was jerked against the tailgate, and over, and the darkness swallowed him whole.

Dale threw down his beer can and stood and beat on the cabroof, and Brian locked up the brakes. There was the smell of rubber and transmission fluid and rope-seared flesh.

They backed along the shoulder, and the boys and Gretchen knelt at the tailgate and when they saw his father come red in the brakelights shouted, "Whoa."

When they got to him Dale asked, "Jesus Christ, Jock, do you think you can move?"

"I probably can," his father said.

"Why don't you try?" asked Rowene. She was kneeling by his shoulder.

"Maybe I will when I feel more confident about it."

Jock lay on his back in the new grass and stared straight up into the night. They all stood around him except Rowene, who was kneeling. They cast shadows in the brakelights and Brian Reilly finally sat down in the hem of road cinders and laughed and couldn't stop.

"He's missing a boot," Gretchen said.

"Just the one?" his father asked.

"Yes, sir."

"Is the foot still there?"

"Yes, it is," she said.

Rowene said, "Why don't you see if you can find the boot?" and Gretchen started down the borrow ditch sweeping through the grass. Dale Simpson knelt at Jock's head and lifted him up against his thighs.

McEban knelt on the ground by his father's side, beside Rowene.

"What did I catch?" his father asked.

Dale said, "A curve sign."

"Isn't that a hell of a thing?"

They all nodded. McEban could see the shadow of his head move up and down, and he tilted his head to tilt the shadow.

Rowene got his father's fingers peeled away from the catchrope, and Bennett got the rope off the sign. Gretchen found the missing boot.

His father held his hands before his face. The fingers were curved down toward the heels, and the right thumbnail was gone, and most of the skin from the palms. "They're in better shape than I thought they'd be," he said, and they all agreed they expected more blood.

"Can you straighten the fingers out?" Rowene asked.

"They'll probably do that for me at the hospital."

"I'm going to get you up now," Dale said.

His father nodded.

McEban and Bennett cocked the man's knees and bent his feet back under his butt, and Dale lifted straight away from the ground. When his father was up and weaving in the brakelights McEban gripped his left arm, and Bennett gripped the right. Brian Reilly lowered the tailgate and said, "Walk him over this way if you can."

His father looked down at his son and said, "I just got up this morning missing your grandmother. That's all there was to it. This won't happen again."

"At least you didn't get your dally made," Rowene said and they all laughed, and his father sat down again in the borrow ditch with his bloody hands in his lap.

Bennett's truck and trailer are parked on the lawn in Jackson's main square. They're cordoned off with yellow police tape and a Teton County sheriff's car is nosed in at the curb. The cop car's door stands open and its bank of rooflights flash blue and red and yellow.

McEban reins Aruba under an archway of elk antlers and through a milling crowd of onlookers and up to the yellow tape and lets him stand.

The sheriff sits on the tailgate with his Stetson thumbed back from his face. The toolbox is open and the chainsaw and tarp and clothes and groceries and bedroll and rifle are strewn on the truckbed. The man puffs his cheeks and blows and plucks a can of snoose from his shirt pocket. He settles a pinch of it in his lower lip and puffs his cheeks again.

"You tired, Jerry?" McEban asks.

The sheriff looks up at McEban and Rita and turns his head and spits a stream of slick brown juice over his shoulder. He's a long, thin man and when he spits his narrow shoulders hunch up near his ears. "That horse looks like he's blind," he says.

"He turned up that way this summer. You like living over here?"

"Not as much as I thought. Housing's expensive. Ansel still alive?"

"He was when I left," McEban tells him.

Woody jumps into the truckbed and wags his tailstump and rolls onto his side and offers the sheriff his belly. The man scratches at the sides of the dog's pecker and looks back to where Paul stands beside the blind horse.

"You join a commune, or did you get married?" the sheriff asks.

"I'm on vacation," McEban tells him.

He swings his off leg over Aruba's neck and slides to his feet and ducks under the police tape and stands against the truck, looking in.

"You find what you were searching for?" he asks.

"I was looking for drugs."

"If I'd've known we were going to see you I'd've tried to get you some."

"That's not funny," the sheriff says.

"What'd you do with Bennett?"

"I sapped him down with my pistol barrel and cuffed him and had a deputy run him over to the jail."

McEban steps back from the truck. "I guess that was after he ran this outfit up on your public lawn."

The sheriff stands and points north. "It was after he stood on a bench over there and waved a whiskey bottle around and read aloud from some letter he got."

"Did he take a swing at you?"

"Hell yes, he took a swing at me. You ever hear of me striking a man if I didn't have to?"

Paul steps up next to McEban and hooks a finger in a beltloop of McEban's jeans, but McEban doesn't look away from the thin sheriff. "I don't remember your dad to ever hit a man whether he had it coming or not," he says. "Maybe you should have been a plumber like your dad was."

The sheriff turns and spits again. "I liked plumbing fine. I told my dad I did. It's getting under people's houses I didn't like." He stands and bends and picks the rifle out of the mess. "I get claustrophobic," he says. He bolts the rifle open and finds it empty and closes the action. "This yours?"

"It's Bennett's. What do I have to do to get him away from you?"

The sheriff leans the rifle against the toolbox. He slips his hands in his back pockets and stares into the crowd at the edge of the yellow tape. "I never liked him," he says.

"Nobody likes him except me and Gretchen," McEban says.

"That's not why I whacked him, though."

"You already told me you whacked him because you don't like to get under people's houses."

The sheriff stares down at McEban. "You'd have to make his bail to have him," he says. "And guarantee me you'll drive him out of town and bring him back when a court date's set."

"I can do that."

"You going back over to Ishawooa?"

"Not today," McEban says.

"Where are you going today?"

"I don't know for sure."

"Jesus Christ, McEban. You're in the middle of a goddamn mess here. If I was somebody else it could've been worse than it was."

"Do you have his letter?" McEban asks.

"His what?"

"The thing he was reading from."

"I have it in the car."

The sheriff steps onto the trailerhitch and to the ground, and

McEban follows him to his car. The man leans into the front seat and comes out with the letter and envelope in a plastic Baggie. He hands it to McEban and McEban squints through the plastic at the envelope's postmark.

"Casper," he reads. "We're going to drive over to Casper next."

"Bennett needs help. I hope I'm not the first person you've heard that from."

McEban smiles. "I help him every chance I get."

"I believe you." The sheriff folds in behind his steering wheel and closes the door and leans back through the window and spits on the pavement and wipes his lip. "After I let you have him will you call in over here to let me know where you are?"

"If I think of it."

The sheriff spits again and turns off his rooflights. "I'm sorry I rooted through your toolbox like some goddamn ape."

"Thanks for saying so."

"When you get your horse loaded, pull over to the jail. After Bennett sees the judge I'll sign him out to you." He watches Rita in the truckbed folding her clothes into her backpack. "She a friend of yours?" he asks.

"She and the boy were hitchhiking."

"No shit." The sheriff's face falls blank in surprise. "I didn't think anyone got around that way anymore." He starts his car. "I helped myself to an egg."

"A what?"

"You've got a jar of them on the front seat. I guess I like them better'n ice cream." He looks into his rearview mirror and then back at McEban. He juts his chin out toward the Baggie. "There's a letter in there for you too."

McEban holds up the plastic envelope. "What'd it say?"

"I didn't read it. It's sealed up." The sheriff eases the car away from the curb. "If you see Gretchen say howdy from me."

"I'll do it," McEban says.

In the dream she closes her eyes and rocks her hips easily, and her face falls soft and unworried as a child's, soft as her breasts, soft as her thighs. She thrusts her breasts out to him and he takes them in his hands and circles her nipples with his thumbs, and her mouth parts and she rocks harder against him, as a rider would in the middle part of a race, paced, and in control.

He moves his hands, both hands, to the swell of her hips and rises against her, and her mouth falls wider and her face is glazed in sweat and her black hair mats at her forehead and upon her cheeks. The cords stand taut in her neck and her shoulders show the strain and her breasts sway. She shudders and stops and shudders again. She slumps against him and he bucks his hips into her, and a keening comes up low in her throat.

He can feel her heart in his own chest. He can feel the pulse at her throat. The room smells of damp oats and marshgrass and clover and the salt-sweet lather of honest beasts. He wraps his arms around her and holds her, and will not let her fall away.

Chapter Eight

✳

McEban comes out of the Jackson jailhouse and opens the truckdoor and steps in behind the wheel. He leaves the door standing open.

"You weren't in there very long," Rita says. She and Paul have waited in the truck. The boy's lined the contents of his pouch along the dashboard. A Pokémon card is propped upright in the ashtray.

"I guess Bennett's not the first drunk ever locked up in Wyoming," McEban says. "They've got the paperwork down pat and the judge wants to go elk hunting."

"Rodney tries to drink too much but he hasn't got the stamina for it," she says.

"I don't want to hear about Rodney."

"What do you want to hear about?"

"Where did you learn 'Missa Solemnis'?"

"My mother was Catholic."

"So was mine, but she wouldn't know Beethoven from Bo Diddley."

"How come you do?" she asks.

"The old man that lives on my place has a record player." He turns to her. "His name's Ansel. When I was a kid I used to sit up with him sometimes at night."

"My mother had a record player too."

McEban picks the Pokémon card out of the ashtray and holds it to the sunlight. It flashes like a little swatch of rainbow.

"That's Charizard," Paul says.

"Is he a good one to have?" asks McEban.

"If he was a baseball card he'd be a Mark McGwire."

"Can I see the letters?" Rita asks.

McEban nods and replaces Charizard and Rita pulls the Baggie from the glovebox and unfolds the letter to Bennett.

She holds it up against the dashboard. "It'd be nice if this whole thing had a good ending," she says, "but I don't think it's going to."

"Is that your opinion or Alma's?"

"Alma doesn't have to tell me everything." She bends over the letter.

Dear B.

The bad news is I'm unable to see you. This evening, for a test, I tried to picture you clear in my mind. I didn't bring a photograph for reference, but I shouldn't need one. I tried very hard and there was nothing. Just movement at the very back of my mind. It was like staring into the creek when it's choked with runoff. Before this hurts you please shut your eyes and try to see me. It's just where we've gotten. If you can see me at all I'll bet it's when I was younger, and happy. We've been invisible to each other for years. All of this is only a loss of sightedness— for me and for you.

The good news is the way I hold you in my heart. You are vivid in my heart, and large—like the mountains are when they're covered with snow and the sun is bright. In mid-winter. That is the way I see you in my heart. And bold. And brave. And gentle. And miles ahead of the rest of us.

Know that I pray for another chance but not in this lifetime. I pray the Buddhists are right about more than a single life and I may be given a chance to love you better than I have. I've lived too badly to hope for redemption in this life. And I am not strong enough. I'm only capable of moments of honesty, and even then I cannot hold on to them like I want. And because I'm too weak to reconstruct us from the ruin I have made there is now this other man. I love him partly because it's easier to start over without all the lies, without the secrets we made early on. I left to be free from the weight of my inconsistencies, my failures and lies. I've given myself this brief time to feel young again. I'll no doubt fuck this up too, but it will take some time, and I'll be older and perhaps more resolved to the lack of hope.

I pray you might find a woman you can see and smell and hold. I want that for you. I want it for you because I love you, and I want it for you to ease the guilt of having found it myself. I'm not crying now. That's who I am—a woman who is done weeping for her life. Close your eyes and try to picture me the way I am. That's the picture you should hold in your head. I am too much the chickenshit to want to know how you hold me in your heart.

That's all there is. I mean these letters as a gift, and if they aren't I've screwed that too. We own nothing in our lives but perspective. Stay away from home until you can see yourself there alone. Stay away until you are clear in your own imagination.

G

Rita looks up from the letter. "I once saw a woman in a carnival juggle half a dozen torches," she says. "I watched her husband. Everybody else watched the woman. I don't think her husband wanted to be there but he hadn't gotten tired of watching her yet. He was still proud of her."

"Maybe that's what Bennett sees when he thinks of Gretchen," McEban says.

"Did they argue a lot?"

"I guess about as much as anyone who's married."

"I think she should have made a tape recording," Rita says. "A recording of an argument would be a good thing for her to have. Maybe not now, but if she gets old it's something I'll bet she'd like to listen to. She could have made one for Bennett too."

"I don't think she should have used the F-word," Paul says.

"Nobody used the F-word," Rita says.

"The woman who wrote the letter did."

"I say it all the time," his sister tells him.

"I don't like it when you say it either."

Rita holds up the letter to McEban. "Can I read the one she wrote to you?"

He shrugs and she tears the envelope open and smoothes the letter over Bennett's.

Dear Barnum,

It's taken me a long time to stop hating you, but you can't be blamed for what you haven't known, and really, you're mostly guilty of crimes of inattention. You are as cowardly as I am and have suffered most of the same consequences. You've allowed your life to just happen to you. Without a struggle.

You need a place of your own, Barnum. Somewhere your grandparents, and father, and brother don't still live—and now I've passed away from you as well. I don't mean I think you should move. I mean you have to move away from just living in their memories. And mine. You have to make a place that's all new for you. You cannot live in the minds of the dead. Anyway, not altogether.

Ansel won't last forever, and when he's gone you'll be alone. I don't think you can live without someone to love. I don't think you can live without some sort of family of your making.

If you're reading this, thank you for coming with Bennett. He is as trustworthy about correspondence as he is about everything else. He wouldn't open your mail if you asked him to. If you haven't come he will return with this letter unopened. I don't think he knows I've hated you. I don't think he would want to find out.

I will miss our talks but I no longer fantasize about our life together. We've lived it.

With love,

Gretchen

Rita folds the letters together and slips them back into the Baggie and then into the glovebox. She stares at the cinder-block jailhouse.

"I like it that she calls you 'Barnum,'" she says.

"I like it too." He stares into his lap where his hands are clenched into fists, the knuckles drained white. "I've always liked it."

"Why did it take her a long time to stop hating you?"

He raises his hands slowly and grips the wheel. "I guess because we've known each other our whole lives."

"That would do it." She smiles. "But I don't believe you."

"You can believe what you want."

They watch the sheriff lead Bennett out of the jail, past the flowerpots and across the sidewalk. He bends to unlock the cuffs and Bennett stands rubbing his wrists, looking into the trees across Willow Street.

"You have a nice jail, Jerry," Bennett says.

"They built this about fifteen years ago. The old one used to be in the courthouse."

"It's a treat to have the newer plumbing."

"This is liberal country down here. For Wyoming anyway. Will you shake my hand?"

The sheriff extends his hand and Bennett shakes it and turns to the truck. Paul and Rita scoot together on the seat to make room for him. McEban helps the boy scoop his pieces of bone and teeth and rocks and the toy car into the quilled pouch and reaches into his shirt pocket and brings out a can of smoked oysters.

Paul turns the can in his small hands. "When did you get these?"

"When you weren't looking."

McEban takes a toothpick from the same pocket and Paul works the key loose from the bottom of the can and peels back the lid. He takes the toothpick from McEban.

The sheriff leans against the truckdoor.

"It was nice to see you boys." He tips his hat to Rita. "You too, ma'am."

"Don't let your meat loaf, Jerry," McEban says and the sheriff steps back and spits.

They can hear the tobacco juice splatter against the curb. "'Hi' my old man for me, if you see him," he says.

"I'll do it," says McEban.

He starts the truck and Paul spears out a single oil-slicked oyster and offers it to his sister, and she shudders and turns her head away. He shrugs and opens his mouth wide and sticks out his tongue and shakes the oyster off onto his tongue. He closes his mouth and blinks slowly, pressing his tongue to the roof of his mouth.

McEban turns onto Pearl and then Cache Street and is out on the sage flats north of town, past the airport, when he looks at Bennett.

Bennett sits with his hands folded across his belly and his eyes shut.

"Are you sleeping or meditating?" McEban asks.

"I'm counting my blessings."

"That shouldn't be taking so long."

Bennett opens his eyes. "Did they make you pay my bond in cash?"

"All five hundred dollars of it. The ATM wouldn't let me have it all at once. I had to go back twice."

"I'll pay you when we get home."

"I'm not worried about it," McEban tells him.

Bennett turns on the seat. "Jerry looks just the same as he always has. I recognized him right away."

"How's your head?"

"I got a pretty good goose egg. You want to feel it?"

"Maybe the boy wants to," McEban says.

Bennett bows his head and Paul fingers the knot and pulls his hand away and goes back to work on his oysters. "It feels like it hurts," he says.

The sun is behind them and the valley bottom shines aqua and silver. The Tetons rise up to their left and throw peaked blocks of shadow over the Snake River and the sage flats along the Snake.

"Gretchen have anything interesting to tell you?" Bennett asks.

"She said you wouldn't look at my mail."

"That's why I'm asking."

"She said she's all done hating him," Rita says.

"McEban?" Bennett asks.

"That's what she said," Rita tells him.

Bennett opens the glovebox and takes out the letters and holds them for a few miles pressed against his chest and puts them away again.

"She said she thinks I'm gentle," he says. "And brave." His eyes, the blackened eye and the good, run with tears. "I wish that didn't surprise me."

"She said she thought Barnum was a coward," Rita says.

"She called him 'Barnum'?"

"Yes, she did."

Bennett nods. "Up by Moose there's a good place to buy wine. It's a place called Fahy's."

McEban turns off toward the river and parks at Fahy's, and Bennett goes in to have a look at the wine selection. There is just the building and the parking lot, an outdoor barbecue, and miles of sage in every direction. Smoke lifts and hangs away from the open cooking grates, and the smell of hot food falls against them like a holiday. Paul's stomach grumbles and he looks up smiling.

McEban hands the boy a twenty-dollar bill and tells him to treat his sister to dinner.

"We have our own money," she says.

"Then the next time we get a chance you can buy me a meal."

"I will," she tells him.

They watch two men in aprons and cowboy hats work the outdoor food, turning steaks, stirring the big castiron cauldrons of beans and stew. Rita stands out of the truck.

"Do you want anything?" she asks.

"I'll be over in a minute," he says, and when she and Paul have left he finds a pay phone at the edge of the parking lot and dials home.

Ansel picks up on the third ring.

"Rocking M," the old man says.

"This is McEban."

"Then you know where you called. Are you broke down?"

"I'm in Jackson Hole. I thought you might've missed me."

"I miss Woody more. Put him on and I'll howl at him."

"I expected you to be outdoors."

"I hurt my hand," Ansel says. "I came in to tend it."

"How'd that happen?"

"It happened when I was doctoring your new horse."

"The little mustang?"

"He's the only new horse I know about. Are you drunk?"

"You could've waited until I was home."

"He didn't want to wait. He came up to the house and laid over on his back and asked me if I'd cut him open and poke his gut back in and sew him up inside and out."

"How do the cows look?"

"Fat as Bennett. When are you coming home?"

"That isn't why I'm calling."

"Then why are you? Is Gretchen with you?"

"She's still ahead of us."

"She always has been," Ansel says. "From day one."

Bennett comes out of Fahy's with a case of wine and drops the tailgate and slides it in.

"I guess I called to make sure you're still alive," McEban says.

"Well, I sure-as-by-God am."

The line goes dead and McEban stands holding the receiver, watching the sunlight grind against the shadows along the river.

He'd caught a ride home with another boy also come up for a long weekend to help with his family's cows. The other boy's name was Todd Jamison and Todd dropped him at the culvert where Horse Creek ran under the highway, and he waited until the car was all the way gone and stood in the dark and listened to the night sounds.

The lights were off at Ansel's when he passed and at his parents' house farther up the creek. He heard coyotes yipping and stopped to listen and thought how ragged their lives must be, and then wondered if they felt the same way for him. A voice said, "Good evening," and he jumped sideways and almost fell and saw Ansel standing by the side of the dirt track.

Ansel stepped to him and shook his hand and asked how he liked being a college boy, and he said better than he thought he might.

"What are you doing out here?" he asked.

"Listening."

"Do you every night?"

"Every night I want to. You home to help the cows off the mountain?"

"I go back next Tuesday," McEban said.

The coyotes swelled up in chorus and they listened until the little dogs backed off into a smattering of yips.

"Sometimes I wish I had good friends like that," Ansel said.

"Like those coyotes?"

"Like them."

They goodnighted each other and McEban let himself into the dark house and crept to his bedroom and undressed in the dark.

In the morning the smell of coffee came up sharp and earthy, and he wondered if his father was at the kitchen table or if he was already dressed and out of the house.

He flexed in his bed and pressed his feet against the footboard. He pictured the drive home from Laramie and thought of his new life in a dormitory with hundreds of boys and realized he missed the noise of them and swung out of the bed.

He heard a tractor and looked out his window and watched Ansel scraping the corrals and knew Ansel meant to spread the manure on the poorest corner of the south pasture.

When he turned he saw his mother's jewelry box on his dresser and walked to it and looked down at it—for a long time—and then tilted back its hinged top.

A pinecone and his Saint Christopher medal lay side by side on the worn dark velvet of its top tray. He took them out and held one in each hand to make sure they were real. When he was satisfied they were he replaced them.

He dressed and walked to the tackshed and stood in the doorway with the jewelry box against his hip. The saddles were lined on their racks and shone dully in the morning light. Their cinches and latigos were laid back over their seats, the hairpads and blankets stacked to the side. The room smelled of neat's-foot oil and of horses.

His father sat on the floor with a pack saddle between his legs. He leaned back against the log wall. The saddle's rigging lay across his lap.

"You must've got up early," McEban said.

His father nodded toward the jewelry box. "She left that for you."

"My Saint Christopher's was inside. I thought it was lost."

"Was there a note?"

McEban shook his head.

"Me neither," his father said. "At least she left you a piece of jewelry to remember her by."

"There was a pinecone too."

"Your mother always had her own sense of humor."

The sun fell in through the windows and lay amber on the floorboards. His father's feet lay in the sun.

"Where is she?" McEban asked.

His father worked the oily rag over the leather's rigging, and turned the dry side up, and poured more oil on the rag. "It's amazing how the weather works against this tack." He looked up at his son. "South, I guess."

"Did she say she was going south?"

"She didn't say anything. The morning after you left for school I got up and she was gone. That's all there was to it. Her clothes were gone too."

"That was a month ago." He shifted the box against his hip.

"Yes, it was."

"Then how do you know she went south?"

"Because I'd go north," his father said. "I would've called to tell you but it wasn't like there was anything you could do about it."

Oat dust and horse dander stood through the sunlight. It gave his father a grainy look. Like the photograph of his grandparents on their wedding day, he thought.

"Are you going after her?" he asked.

His father wiped his forehead with the back of a hand, and his skin shone oily in the morning light.

"I'm staying," he said. "There's too much work to do for me to go."

They camp in the Teton Forest and Bennett drinks a bottle of the good Merlot he'd bought, and opens a second one. The night is warm and the mosquitoes come down hard on them and Paul and Rita go to sleep under the tarp in the back of the truck. Halfway through the second bottle of wine Bennett says, "I always thought she loved you more than me."

McEban lays a length of deadwood on the fire, and the embers settle and a raft of sparks lifts into the night. "If you thought she loved me so much then why did you marry her?"

"Because I could. Because I got the chance to and I did." Bennett digs his heels into the pine duff where they sit and pushes up straighter against the duffel he's using as a backrest. "I don't suppose anyone ever told you about the kid you almost made?"

"Ansel said something. Is that wine just yours?"

"Help yourself."

McEban takes an enameled cup from the box of cookware set out by the fire and half-fills it with the Merlot.

"When did Ansel say something?" Bennett asks.

"Just before this trip."

Bennett looks up through the firelight. His face is alive in a gyrose of shadows and flame. "I would have loved it," he says. "Gretchen never told me whether it was a boy or a girl, but if it would've lived I would have loved it too."

"Is that why she didn't come to my dad's funeral?"

"She didn't want you to see her pregnant," Bennett says.

"And then I went back to school."

Bennett struggles onto a knee and uncorks a third bottle and fills both their cups. "A week after we got married she started to cry, and when I asked her what she needed she said she just needed to be left alone. She took the truck and drove up to the Bighorns."

"Where in the Bighorns?"

"Somewhere high, I guess. Probably somewhere near the skyline. She said she found a place out of the wind and sat down and missed you until the baby fell out of her. She said it was like a fish swimming out and that she'd never look at a river the same. She said there was a lot of blood."

"And when I came back?"

"You came back and she didn't want to tell you. She made me promise I wouldn't either."

"I'm sorry."

Bennett looks at McEban and shakes his head to clear it. "If it hadn't been for you I'd've never stood a chance with her," he says. "If she hadn't loved you like she did she'd've never settled for me."

"I am truly sorry," McEban says, but Bennett's head has fallen to his chest and McEban gets to his feet and shrugs out of his coat and covers Bennett where he sleeps.

✳

McEban stood with his father at the corrals. They leaned into the rails and watched Ansel on the tractor. He tipped the bucket on the frontloader and dragged it back, and when he'd scraped a layer of dried shit into a sizable mound he scooped it, and dumped the scoop into the back of the pickup.

He idled the tractor along the rails, and eased off the hydraulics and let the bucket drop, and cut the engine. He pulled his cigarette makings out of his shirt pocket, and creased a paper, and leveled the tobacco in.

"You about done scraping shit?" his father asked.

Ansel drew his tongue across the paper and rolled the cigarette tight and stabbed it into a corner of his mouth.

"I should unload what I've got."

"It'll be here when we get back. The truck's not down on its springs."

Ansel snapped the head of a wooden match with the edge of his thumbnail and cupped the fire and lit his smoke. He shrugged his shoulders and rolled them forward and blew smoke toward McEban. "Your dad tell you why the station wagon's gone?"

"I just did," his father said.

"Seems we're down to grocery shopping for ourselves." Ansel stepped off the tractor and drew hard on the last of his cigarette and ground the butt out with the toe of his boot. "I'm glad I was too ugly to ever get married."

"No one explains marriage to us when we're young," his father said.

Ansel scuffed at the dirt with the side of his boot. "If we're off for the mountain I better get a change of clothes." He looked up with his face opened in a new thought. "Hell, Jock," he said. "You could start all over again. This whole country's overstocked with widows and grass widows, and I imagine there's those who want to be."

"I didn't learn enough this time around," his father said.

Ansel smiled like that was the bitter truth. "It'll be nice up on the mountain."

They watched him walk away and when he was out of earshot McEban asked his father if he felt like taking a drink. The question made his stomach knot, but he couldn't get away from asking it.

His father narrowed his eyes and then let them come right in his face. "I told you I was done with that," he said.

McEban is up before dawn and has them packed and Aruba loaded, and they top out over Togwotee Pass at first light, through pine and spruce—the acidic-sweet odor of evergreen—descending toward Dubois, the Wind River roiling white and green and black below them, falling out of the Rockies and onto the plains.

"How high were we at the top?" Paul asks.

"Just shy of ten thousand feet."

"I think my ears need to pop."

"I wish there was another way to Casper," Rita says.

"This is it," McEban tells her.

"I know it is," she says.

Bennett is asleep against the doorpanel and hiccups in his sleep. The day is clean and blue and warm, and appears a full season away from winter, but McEban feels chilled and cannot shake the chill. He feels the uneasy weight of past winters, the slide into darkness. His body tightens with the memories of the lean, odorless nights, of days so leaden with cold they press the earth frail. He feels soft and toothless and watched by predators. He looks at Bennett and wonders what the coming winter will bring. He thinks if they are both alive he'll tell Bennett he loves him. He'll tell him that he's as good a friend as a man could ever want.

Past Dubois the land spreads away from them unfenced, striped in ocherous bands of yellow and rust-colored soils, broken into ridges of struggling prairie grass. Paul reads aloud the roadside sign announcing their entrance onto the Wind River Reservation.

Rita bows her head to her knees, and when she doesn't bring it up, McEban asks the boy if she's okay.

"She's praying," her brother says.

"Do you think she'll pray for me?"

"I think she'll pray enough for all of us."

McEban drives another fifty miles and the land hasn't gotten much better. He's outside Riverton and Rita still holds her head between her knees. He can hear the soft babble of her conversation with God.

Paul hangs his hand over her back and drags his thin fingers up and down her spine. He looks at McEban. "Rita says Alma leaves when we're on the reservation."

"Where does she go?"

He stares down at his sister's bent back. "Rita thinks she goes visiting and loses track of time." The boy looks away at the northern horizon. "I miss my mother a whole lot."

"I'll bet you do."

The boy looks up at McEban. "I think Rita misses her more."

They turn southeast at Shoshone and Rita sits up and slumps back against the seat. She looks simply lost and young, and separated from the familiar. Her eyes are large in her face.

"Where are we?" she asks.

"We're still on the way to Casper," McEban tells her. "Is Alma here?"

She shakes her head no and he slows, and they watch five antelope cross the highway and crawl under a fence and fan away from their passing.

Past the bar at Moneta Rita says, "I can't stay in this truck any longer."

"It's just seventy miles," he says.

"I can't go that far. Not today."

McEban turns onto a dirt track and drives them out to where the road is collapsed into a dry wash and circles the truck and trailer through the pale dirt and sage and withered grasses. Bennett comes awake and sits blinking into the glare and when they stop stands out of the truck all at once.

"If that Jackson letter wasn't her last I'll have mail waiting in Casper," he says. "This isn't Casper."

Rita slides out after him and holds on to the door. "It's my fault," she tells him. "I'm homesick and another town's just going to make it worse."

Bennett stares up at the sky.

"You be alright out here if I go in by myself?"

Rita nods and McEban steps Aruba out of the trailer and stands cranking the trailer's tongue off the ballhitch.

"Leave us the gear and groceries." He looks at Rita. "And a bottle of wine."

Paul opens the toolbox and hands down the sleeping bag and tarp and Rita's backpack and McEban's duffel and the groceries. Bennett stands two bottles of wine by the bumper. He turns again, studying the empty horizons.

"I might not get back till morning."

"Try to stay away from the law," McEban tells him. "We don't know the sheriff in Natrona County."

Rita moves to the back of the pickup and tilts her head to her shoulder and stares sideways at the sky. The clouds are broken and torn as feathers are torn, and broadcast west to east. They catch the sun and gleam white at the edges.

"What will you do if there's no letter in Casper?" she asks.

"I'd just like the chance to say goodbye." Bennett thumbs his right nostril flat and turns and blows the left nostril free and wipes his nose on his shirtsleeve. "I'd like to see her just one last time. That's all." He looks down at the dry ground. "She was right about the pictures we keep in our heads."

"I wish the child would have lived," McEban says.

"So do I," Bennett says. "I've always wished it had."

They left the Forest Service gate open and rode up through the lease. When they found cows they started them down the mountain and kept climbing and topped out above timberline and stood the horses and let them blow. They continued in bright sunlight along the limit of the timber.

He rode behind his father and led the packhorse, and Ansel rode up tight behind the packhorse.

"If I had to do it all over again," his father said, "I think I'd just live up here. I think I'd sell the ranch and come up high for as long as I could stand it."

An eagle chittered and shrieked and his father lay back against the cantle and squinted into the thin air. His horse crowhopped and he snapped upright and pulled the horse's head up and laughed.

They rode through a finger of wind-gnarled pine and tied the horses to the corral rails next to the trapper's cabin they used as a high-country cowcamp.

His father took up a shovel and went to work deepening a basin in the muck below a seep, and McEban followed Ansel into the cabin.

It was dirt-floored and windowless and sod-roofed, and Ansel couldn't stand up straight under the purlins or even under the ridge, and neither could he. He thought for a second of the high-ceilinged classrooms at college, and imagined himself there.

Ansel bent at the woodstove and scooped the ratshit out of its oven with a stick. "I wonder just how tall the stumpy little fucker was that built this place," he said, and then, "Why don't you get our bedrolls in here if you need something to do."

McEban laid out their bedrolls on the pole bunks and carried in the panniers and stacked them by the stove.

"What horse do you want kept in?" He knew the answer but wasn't yet so old he was beyond checking.

Ansel was pulling the castiron skillets, and enamelware, from a plank box by the stove.

"You can turn everything loose but that bay your father's on. We'll picket him tonight or he'll quit us as quick as your mother has." Ansel stopped his work and stared down into the box. He held a fistful of knives in his right hand. "I'm sorry," he said.

McEban didn't know how to reply and was relieved when his father stepped in with a bucket of water and set it on the back of the stove.

Ansel fixed them a supper of fried potatoes, egg-battered steaks, and a can of creamed corn, and they ate sitting in the evening sun under the cabin's front overhang. The stovepipe ticked and groaned and there was the general grind of a steady wind.

"Are our horses still caught?" his father asked.

"I'll get to them in a minute," McEban said.

"What if we rode over to the Wheel?" his father asked. "These dishes would be here when we got back."

Ansel got up on a knee and stacked their plates, one atop the next, from where they lay in the dirt. "I feel like I might stay," he said. "You and the boy go. I'll dung up these dishes while you're gone."

His father stood and when Ansel just went to work at the basin on the stovetop he walked out to where the horses were tied. McEban followed him.

"Something wrong with Ansel?" his father asked.

"I think he's just tired," McEban said, and his father said he knew how that felt and they stood up on their horses and rode side by side on the western slope of the balded skyline. Their shadows, and the horses' shadows, fell away from them to the east, in dark and elongated suggestions of men and the horses they rode.

Where the land was creased the soil had eroded into frayed gutters, like the ends of unraveled lariats, and the sage was thick and low-growing in the snaking depressions, and the horses picked their way through, and lunged when they had to.

Where the soil was gone altogether they rode on chalk-colored limestone, and stopped their horses at the edges of escarpments, and looked down for hundreds of feet, and out into the blanched basin below.

There were spiraled fossils in the bedrock, and lengths of curved hash marks, and when he asked his father what the animals had been that left their bodies' prints, his father said he didn't know.

They rode beside wind-pitted knobs of rock, broken free of the nativegrass, barnacled with yellow, black, and blood-colored lichens, and rough to the touch.

There were chipmunks, and ground squirrels, and ravens in the air, and in the trees below them, and on the ground. And when they rode out of the wind they could see fifty miles to the Absarokas.

His father stopped his horse north of the Wheel and took his binoculars out of a saddlebag and glassed the ridge where the Wheel was laid out, and just below it, and said he'd hate to interrupt a man at prayer or ceremony.

"What man?" McEban asked.

"The Crow come up here," his father said, "and the Cheyenne and the Arapaho too."

"When?"

"I guess whenever they want to. Mostly it's just tourists. Like we are now."

"Is there anyone there?"

His father put the binoculars away. "Just us," he said, and they rode down past the Wheel and tied their horses in a stand of stunted pine, and walked back to the outer ring of rocks.

"Haven't I brought you out here before?" his father asked.

"This is the first time."

"That'd be my fault." He clasped McEban's shoulder, and he looked at his father's hand and knew it to be clumsy with the fastening and unfastening of buttons, the counting out of coins, with keys, clumsy in the turning of the pages of a book, in any display of emotion.

They walked the circumference of the Wheel and McEban counted twenty-eight spokes of near-white rock coming out of the central cairn, and six smaller cairns spaced along the rim.

"How far across?" he asked.

"About eighty feet." His father bent at the waist and plucked at the waist-high chainlink fence. "This never used to be here."

"Why is it now?"

"Because the world's gotten hip-deep in assholes."

The wind picked up and lifted the offerings tied and woven into the fence. There were kerchiefs, and red and blue and yellow strips of cloth, pouches, amulets, bundles of sage and sweetgrass, lengths of bone, painted feathers. They snapped and dropped and whispered in the wind.

McEban pointed to the central cairn. "Is that a lance?"

"It looks like it," his father said and lifted his chin to the southwest. "A guy told me there was a seventy-foot arrow laid out with rocks down by Meeteetse that points right on the compass to this Wheel. And another rock arrow close by here pointing directly back."

"What for?"

"I don't know what for. I told you I was just a tourist."

"How far is it to Meeteetse?"

"About seventy miles."

They sat side by side on a boulder outside the Wheel and watched the sun fail behind the Absarokas, and the sky swell orange, and mulberry, and rose.

A raven landed in the Wheel, and chucked and cawed, and walked to a length of rolled cloth in the central cairn and plucked at the fabric.

The feathers and bundles of sage and strips of cloth on the fence rose and fell, and rose again.

"Do you believe this place is special?" McEban asked. "Like magic?"

His father turned to him, the sunward side of his face brought soft and smooth in the last slants of light. "I believe there's a whole lot I don't know," he said and turned back to watching the raven. "I don't blame your mother, and you shouldn't either." He widened his knees and spat between his boots and kept his head bowed. "This life wasn't right for her," he said. "I'm surprised she stuck it out as long as she did."

"Did you ever bring her up here?"

"Once I did. When we were young and all this was new to her."

"What was she like when she was young?"

His father looked at him because he hadn't expected the question. "She was in love," he said.

They rode their horses back to the cowcamp in the gathering dark, and picketed his father's horse, and turned the others out to graze. They stood their saddles on their forks against the cabin and his father brought a flashlight out of one of his saddlebags, and they went in through the open door and found their bunks.

"How was it?" Ansel asked.

"It's different every time," his father said. "You want that door open?"

"Or the roof off," Ansel said. "Did you pray for her?"

There was just the sound of his father pulling his boots off and getting out of his jeans. McEban thought maybe Ansel was talking to him and tried to think of an answer, and then his father said, "I wished her well."

"There's just the three of us up here, Jock," Ansel said. "Nothing you say's going to get in the paper."

His father turned in his sleeping bag. He thumbed the flashlight on and shone the beam on Ansel, and turned it off again. The burst of light made the dark come more dense.

"I pictured her in better times," his father said.

"Then it was like a prayer," Ansel said.

When Bennett is gone Rita uncorks a bottle of Merlot and takes a long drink and sets the bottle in the shade the trailer throws and strips off her T-shirt.

She's looking at McEban. "I don't care anymore whether my habits bother you."

"I'm not as bothered as I used to be." He doesn't look away.

She smiles. It's the first time she's smiled all day. "That's disappointing." She bends at the knees and lifts a stone up against her belly. She walks out onto the prairie and turns with the stone still against her and backs away farther and drops it between her feet. A breeze lofts her skirt and bends the blanched grasses against her legs.

"What are you doing?" he asks.

"I'm making a medicine wheel."

"Like the one at the top of the Bighorns?"

"A smaller one." She steps off four paces to the east. "Just out to here."

McEban stands out of the shade. "Have you built one before?"

"Never," she says. "But I don't think we have to believe in God to have our prayers answered either." She rakes a hand back through her hair. "Alma asked me to do it. A long time ago, and now I don't have anything better to do."

Paul steps up beside McEban and McEban smiles down at the boy and shrugs, and then snaps his shirt open and shucks out of it.

"Show us where to line out the stones," he says.

She drags a heel through the chalky soil to describe four spokes and the wheel's circular perimeter, and McEban muscles four large stones to the points where the lines intersect and stands sweating in the sun.

The boy kneels and rolls the closer stones into place, and Rita squats and lifts with her legs. She keeps her spine straight and her head up, and her shoulders and arms and backmap and ribs run slick with sweat. Her breasts sway and plump with the lifting. She blows and smiles and bites at the air and wipes her hands on her skirt.

McEban searches a hundred yards out for the heavier stones and grips them up, one at a time, and staggers toward the wheel. When his hands and arms go numb he drops the stone and shakes the blood back into his arms and takes the stone up again when he can. He feels himself warming, filled with the mild season, and when they're done the sun is at the horizon and a bank of cumulus swells orange and rose and crimson and effulgent and their skins glow in the soft throw of light.

Salt has dried across their shoulders and their ribs are striped with it. They lick their upper lips and smack their mouths and pull on their shirts. A breeze has come up and the evening is cooling.

They sit against the trailer and Paul makes them sandwiches of Wonder bread and Velveeta cheese and a hard salami. They pass the wine and drink from the bottle. The boy chokes and coughs and bends forward on his hands and the wine runs from his nose. McEban pats his back and pulls a cotton handkerchief from his pocket and wipes the boy's face. And then the boy tries the wine again and is fine with it.

Before it's fully dark McEban breaks a half bale of hay open for Aruba and feeds Woody the salami rind and a slab of cheese.

Rita and Paul gather a mat of dried grass and spread the tarp over it and take off their shoes and lie down. McEban lies next to Rita and pulls his bedroll over them all and they stare up into the stars stamped against the night sky. The moon is not yet risen and the night is fallen in against them. In the weak starlight they smell sweet and briny and mineral-rich, like some lithic spar just shattered open to the air.

Rita tells them of a river not far from where they rest. "The Popo Agie." She tells them that the river disappears. "The whole river," she says. "Fish and foam and all. Underground." She tells them no one knows where the river goes and that it simply reappears from the earth and spreads out in its bed, filled with its artesian secrets.

They lie watching the sky turn slowly around the Pole Star, and McEban thinks he hasn't known that water keeps secrets. But he knows he misses the sound of Horse Creek, the sound of rain on a barn's roof.

"How will we know if it works?" Paul asks.

Rita turns to him. "If what works?"

"The wheel."

Her eyes catch in the starlight and flash. "Alma says it works if we dream of water. Or wind. Or both."

"Is Alma back?" McEban asks.

"It's something she said before she left."

"What if I don't dream?" the boy asks.

"Everybody dreams," his sister says.

In the morning the eastern sky lies gray and white and hard as some great fish, and the air is cool and windless. They crawl from under the bedroll and pull on their jackets and walk stiff-legged into the wheel of rough stones and stand yawning and slapping their arms against their sides. Paul shifts from one foot to the other.

"Did you dream last night?" Rita asks.

"I can't remember," the boy says. "Did you?"

"Just in fits," she says, and then, "Alma's back."

Paul nods and walks away from her and behind a sandstone knob to take a piss.

"You didn't listen to your tape this morning," says McEban.

"My player's gone dead."

"We can get fresh batteries in Casper."

"I might take a break from it." She squats and squares a stone more perfectly in a line of stones. She looks up to McEban, still squatting. "I don't really hear the words anymore," she admits. "Not all the time. I just like to listen to the sound of my mother's voice."

They hear the truck before they see it, the whine of its engine, and look to the coil of road dust lifted from the prairie, rising into the steel-colored sky.

"What are you most afraid of?" Rita asks.

McEban watches the boy walking back toward them. He shifts his weight. "I was afraid the night the bear came through camp."

"Did you think he might kill you?"

"I'm afraid of anything that sleeps half its life away," he says, and adds, "I'm afraid that's what I've done."

Bennett backs under the trailerhitch and cuts the engine and steps out of the truck carrying a wholesale-size jar of jalapeños. He walks toward them snagging the peppers out one at a time and snapping them away from their stems with his front teeth.

"What happened to your eggs?" asks McEban.

"Nothing happened to them. I just thought I should have a serving of vegetables," he says.

"Was there another letter?"

"Just an envelope. She sent it from Valentine, Nebraska."

"There wasn't anything in it?"

Bennett sets the jar of peppers in the dirt and holds up his left hand and wags its smallest finger. "There was this," he says. Gretchen's wedding ring catches dully in the light. "She must've forgot to put it in with the last letter." He steps into the wheel. "Was this already here?"

He walks to the center stone and straddles it and lines himself up with the northern spoke. His face is bloated and the pouches under his eyes are puffed, and reddened, but he's mostly sober.

"We made it," Rita tells him.

"For what?"

"For something to do."

Bennett nods and belches. "Did anything magical happen?"

"You came back for us," she says.

In the morning Ansel fried eggs and ham and they caught up the horses, and his father led his horse to the crown of the ridge and called for McEban to come up too.

"Do you have a dollar?" his father asked.

"Sure I do."

"Give it up."

McEban fished a wadded bill out of his jeans, and his father smoothed the bill and snapped it and folded it into his shirt pocket. He pulled a blue envelope out of his jacket and handed it to his son.

"What is it?" McEban asked.

"It's a present. It's your birthday, isn't it?"

He unfolded the stiff paper and read the names and the dates. "It's the title to your truck," he said. He honestly did not understand.

"Sign it," his father told him, and turned, and McEban signed the document against his father's back.

The man swung up on his horse. He gripped the horn and jerked the saddle to his right, and settled. "It's the only thing I've got that's paid for," he said. "I'm in partners with the bank for all the rest."

"I don't need it," McEban said.

His father's horse pawed at the stony ground and lifted its chin to work some slack in the reins.

"You're my son," he said. "It'd feel good if I knew you went back to college on your own wheels."

"I'm just nineteen."

"That's what I'm telling you," his father said and spurred away and then stopped his horse and turned. "It doesn't hurt to take a banker to lunch now and then. That's something you'll need to know. You've got my debt coming your way too."

They went through the Forest Service gate and closed it for the winter, and his father and Ansel rode the cattle out of the draws, and he led the packhorse and made sure nothing turned back up the trail. He took the truck title out a couple times and read over it and put it away.

They stopped by a spring and ate sandwiches of the battered steak left over from the night before, and by evening had the cows and calves spread through the grown-up pastures along the north side of Horse Creek.

They sat their horses and watched the colors bleed from the sky.

"This is the best time of the year," his father said.

"I like it all," Ansel said.

"That's because you don't mind what kind of work you do."

"What kind of work do you like to do?" Ansel asked.

His father laughed and thumbed his hat back from his face. The underside of the silvered brim drew and held the last of the weak evening light. His father's face appeared, for just that moment, as un-weathered as a boy's.

"I'd like to work the ocean," he said. "I always thought I'd make a whale of a fisherman."

Rita and McEban sit side by side in the bed of the truck and lean back against the toolbox. The airstream is buffeting and Rita gathers her hair and pulls it into a ponytail and ties it fast with a leather thong.

The horizons fall to the edge of the sky and the land stretches away in sweeps of brown and lighter shades of brown, knobs of gritty rock weathering endlessly to sand, anthills, low-growing gully brush, wind- and elevation-stunted sage, and scarps of hardier stone. Raptors circle in the midsky, below a gridwork of contrails. They pass through swells of rot and crane over the sidewalls to see the smears of roadkill— bowel, blood, shattered bone, the tire-pounded scraps of tissue.

There are one and then two roadside bars with their own zip codes, and hundreds of pea-green Burlington Northern cars lined out behind three black engines straining northwest. Power lines cross the highway and thread away to the horizons. And there are miles of twelve-foot-high snow fence running parallel to the road, advertising the prevailing winds.

"She's doing the only thing she can do," Rita says, and McEban bends closer to her, not sure he heard her right. "Gretchen," she says.

"I know it. I know she is."

Rita hunches her shoulders up and keeps them that way, her arms crossed over her belly. "I just thought you needed to hear it said out loud."

McEban looks north toward Ishawooa and wonders when he'll return. He wonders if Gretchen might come back for something she misses. A book. An article of clothing. A linen tablecloth. And then he thinks that Bennett will never return home. Not by the end of this week. Not ever. He looks at Rita and nods.

Bennett ramps them onto I-25 at the northern edge of Casper, and they loop around the city, skirting the oil tanks and the tin-sided service buildings.

East of Casper the land rolls into waves of better grassland. Billboards appear peripherally and meager as scraps of cardboard, blown upright and frail.

The North Platte River runs north of the highway and its banks are crowded with cottonwood, gray-trunked, most of them flushed a dull yellow, or yellowing.

McEban nods and snaps his head up and nods again and sleeps. He comes fully awake as Bennett is gearing them down into Douglas. He struggles into a crouch and holds on to the edge of the toolbox. He watches through the windshield as Bennett pulls in and parks beside an aging convenience store.

Bennett steps out of the truck and looks up at McEban. "I've got to puke," he says, and disappears behind the store and is back again wiping his mouth.

He opens the toolbox and pulls out the tarp and wraps it around his shoulders. He looks up at McEban again and smiles. "I just need a little nap."

Paul runs a tight circle in the gravel parking lot, Woody chasing at his heels.

"What do you want to do?" McEban calls, and the boy stops and the dog runs into the backs of his knees and knocks him off his feet. He rolls in the gravel and laughs and gets up brushing the dust from his jeans.

"I'd like to go down by the river," he says.

"Are you hungry?"

"Not yet."

"How about a fishing rod?"

"I don't have one," the boy says.

McEban pulls two sections of a spinning rod out of the toolbox and stands the corked grip between his feet and rubs the metal end of the tip section against his scalp to grease it and seats the end in the female ferrule and snaps it tight. He pays the line out through the guides and ties on a leader. He hands the rod down to the boy with a Tupperware cup of lures.

"Is this yours?" Paul asks.

"Yes, it is."

"I'll be careful with it," he says, and turns and whips the rod in the air.

McEban hears Bennett open the trailergate and close it and feels the trailer rock as Bennett settles down for his nap.

"What about you?" he asks Rita. She sits yawning on a wheelwell.

"I'm tired too," she says and slides over the sidewall. She steps into the truck cab and lies out on the seat.

McEban finds a laundered pair of shorts, socks, a shirt, and his toilet kit at the bottom of his duffel. He bundles it all in his jacket and walks the hundred yards to a bar that sits nearer the highway.

The inside of the bar is dark and smells of spilled beer, cigarette smoke, sweat, and roasted peanuts. He leans against a wall until his eyes adjust.

The walls are papered with posters advertising rodeos, country-western concerts, and fund-raisers for God. On a CD player behind the bar Garth Brooks sings of the friends he's got in low places.

"You dying of thirst?" the bartender asks.

"I'd drink a beer," he says and sits on a stool and digs a wad of crumpled bills out of his jeans.

"You want a shot of anything to go with that?"

"Not to begin with."

The bartender sets a glass of beer in front of him and a bowl of warmed peanuts still in their shells. "We're known for our nuts," she says, and grins.

McEban nods. Besides the bartender he's the only one there.

"Where are you from?"

"From over outside of Ishawooa."

"That's Shoshone Indian," she says. "Do you know what it means?"

McEban looks up from his beer. The bartender leans against the backbar, staring at him. She is a particularly unattractive white woman.

"I've heard a bunch of different things," he says. "Mostly, I've heard it means coyotes yipping at the moon."

"It means to lie down," she says. "Against something hard. It means lying down on a hard place."

She takes a long drag from her cigarette and exhales through her nose. She wears lavender lipstick and eyeliner, and a sleeveless lavender pullover, stained nearly black where her collapsed abdomen has pressed into the bar sinks. There's a tattoo of a saguaro cactus on her left shoulder.

"Place-names are a hobby of mine," she says. "I don't know how you can be from a place and think it means something it doesn't." She leans forward and flicks her ash into the sink.

"I'll call the Chamber when I get home," he says.

"Good thing I told you." She scratches at the cactus tattoo with her lavender nails.

"You have a bathroom?"

She points behind him and sucks at her cigarette.

He squares a cardboard coaster on the top of his glass and walks to the bathroom and strips off his shirt and soaps it into a rag. He scours the hair and spittle and oilstain from the sink the best he can. He turns his head back and forth under the faucet and wets and shampoos his hair and combs it straight back from his forehead and brushes his teeth and shaves.

He's standing naked in front of the hot-air hand dryer when the young man comes in. He's standing on the tops of his overturned boots to keep his feet dry. He's soaped and rinsed his armpits and crotch, and the rinse water runs down his sides and the insides of his legs.

He nods at the man and the man nods back and walks to a urinal. McEban pushes the button on the dryer and adjusts the nozzle and stands up on his toes with his hands clipped on his hips. He stares down at his pecker wagging in the hot air and has backed his ass to the dryer when the man turns from the urinal. He nods again, and the man nods back and bends at the sink to wash his hands.

"Guess you wish I'd gotten a motel room."

"I'm glad you saved your money," the man says and turns off the faucet. "It's the cleanest anyone's ever gotten this sink."

The man's hands hang to his sides. He looks at the dryer and then pulls his shirttail loose to dry his hands. He wears his hair in braids and they fall to the sides of his face. His jeans are faded at the thighs and his boots are clean but unpolished. He tucks in the tails of his red shirt and when he looks up and smiles he flashes a single gold crown in the front of his mouth.

"Don't worry," he says. "If I'd've thought you were trying to fuck that thing I'd've walked out back to piss." He pivots out through the door and is sitting on a stool sipping at a bottle of beer when McEban comes out and takes up his draft. The bartender looks up and nods. She leans at the end of the bar leafing through a *Cosmopolitan*.

"They're known here for their nuts," the man says, and sticks out his hand.

"My name's McEban," McEban says.

"Rodney One Spear." He takes McEban's hand. "How's Rita?"

"She's asleep in the truck."

Rodney still holds McEban's hand. "I probably look bigger when I'm not around."

"You planning on killing anyone?"

Rodney lets McEban's hand drop and holds his beer up in the blue-green glow of a Hamm's sign and watches the bubbles rise into the bottle's neck.

"I plan on finishing my beer and driving back to Laramie."

"You going to school?"

"Economics. I'm finishing up a master's."

"This is a long drive from Laramie for a beer."

"Rita owes me eight hundred dollars. I wouldn't ask, but I just lost the part-time job I had."

McEban turns to the bar and sips from his beer and watches their reflections in the backbar mirror.

"How hard were we to find?" he asks.

"There aren't a lot of white men trailering a blind horse around the state."

McEban nods. "You take a check?"

"If you've got one handy."

McEban slips his checkbook from a back pocket and bends to the check. "Rita remembers you as a good deal more bloodthirsty."

"I guess a big old scarecrow with braids keeps the men off her. She's not bad-looking."

McEban tears the check loose and hands it to Rodney and Rodney squints at it. "What's the B stand for?" he asks.

"It stands for my first name."

"I imagine this'll cash without me knowing."

"I imagine it will."

Rodney finishes his beer and steps down off the stool. "Rita's got a good heart."

"Is she pregnant?"

"About three months."

"You the father?"

"I didn't get my last name because I got shitty aim," Rodney says. "If she asks you tell her I'll have a good job by the time the baby's on the ground. Tell her I'll help with the costs."

"Is there anything else you want me to tell her?"

Rodney runs a hand around the inside of his belt where his shirt isn't tucked in right. "Tell her this weather isn't going to hold forever. She ought to find someplace warm before the temperature drops."

McEban holds up his empty glass and the bartender moves down the bar.

"And a shot of Wild Turkey," he tells her.

Rodney stands at the door.

"Thanks for the check," he says. "I loaned Rita the money when her mom was sick."

"What about Alma?"

"She's the real deal." Rodney looks down and scuffs at a pile of peanut shells and looks up again. "It wouldn't hurt to keep a place set for her at your table."

When he woke the next morning the house just smelled of the men and women who had always lived there.

He dressed and put the title to the pickup truck in his mother's jewelry box, and when he didn't find his father in the kitchen he made a peanut-butter-and-honey sandwich and stepped out onto the porch.

He still had almost half of the sandwich left when he walked into the barn. The early fall light came in low through the cottonwoods and tinted the air an apple green. The flies were up in the weak heat and the barncats mewed and rolled at his feet.

He saw his father sitting back out of the sunlight against the third stanchion in the row of stalls, and he walked back to the man and dropped the sandwich half and forgot to swallow and choked. He blinked hard to clear his eyes.

His father sat on the barnboards with his left hand in his lap and his right hand fallen away and still gripping the pistol he owned. His head was fallen to the right shoulder of his blue suit and there was blood on his throat, and in his shattered mouth, and on his chest. There was a splatter of blood on the stanchion behind the man's head, and what he guessed were bits of his father's brains and skull.

He stepped around the man and the flies lifted into the air and settled, and he squatted down and his father's face looked worse on the shadowed side.

He backed out of the barn and sat down heavily in the light because his legs wouldn't hold him. And then he crawled to the corrals and pulled himself up by the rails. He tried to shout and Ansel saw him trying and shut down the Ford tractor. He tried to shout again but there still was no sound, so he pointed and stood at the rails while Ansel went into the barn and came back out.

He watched Ansel walk to his cabin and return with the blanket from his bed, and he followed him into the barn. They rolled Jock into the blanket and Ansel squatted and hefted the whole limp thing up in his arms. McEban ran ahead and held the truckdoor open and Ansel muscled the corpse onto the seat and got in beside it.

"You drive," Ansel said. He looked back into the pickup's bed. "I wish I'd've got that manure shoveled out."

Ansel held Jock in close against his side, with his arm around the dead man's slumped shoulders. The blanket fell away on the dirt road and his father's ruined head lolled and bobbed against Ansel's chest, and Ansel cupped his hand against Jock's cheek with his fingers in the blood-matted hair, and held the head tight, and stared through the windshield and ground his teeth. It made a sound like the emergency brake was still on and McEban checked.

"Don't you start whimpering," Ansel said. He said it like he was mad, but McEban knew he wasn't.

They parked at the undertaker's and Ansel stepped out of the truck with his arms around Jock's chest, and McEban took up his father's legs and they carried him inside.

A fat woman in a pink polyester suit stood up from behind a desk and screamed and fainted dead away, and they stood with his father until the mortician came out.

The mortician looked at his secretary and said, "She's new to the job," and took Jock's legs away from McEban, and helped Ansel carry the body into the back.

Ansel came out as the secretary was pulling herself up at the corner of her desk, and he helped her to her feet. He said to McEban, "Your dad always wanted to be cremated. Am I right?"

And McEban said, "That's what he always said."

Ansel held out his hand with the egg-smooth rose-colored stone on his palm. "That's all we found in his pockets," he said.

It's nearly dark when McEban walks to the pickup and bends in through the passenger window. Rita's curled on the seat, a denim jacket thrown over her shoulder.

He sips crème de menthe from a styrofoam go-cup and sucks the cooled evening air in across his teeth. He feels clearheaded, charged with sugar and the right amount of alcohol.

"Stop staring at me," she says.

"I thought you were asleep."

"I don't like to be stared at whether I'm awake or not."

"I met Rodney."

She sits up, rubbing her eyes. "One Spear?"

"I don't know any other Rodneys."

"He ask you for the money I owe him?"

"I wrote him a check."

"Thank you for doing that." She folds the jacket on her lap and rests her hands on it.

"Didn't seem like he wanted to kill you, or me either. He seemed like a nice guy."

She shrugs. "I tend toward the dramatic sometimes. So does Alma." And then she shifts on the seat to better look past his shoulder, and McEban turns to look too.

Bennett stands at the convenience store checkout counter with a package of Oreo Double Stuffs and a bag of Fritos in one hand and his 30.06 in the other. The rifle is leveled at the teenage clerk behind the counter. Both of them stand red-faced and straight. Bennett is talking. The clerk holds his hands in the air, to either side of his head. There is no one else in the store. There is just that, a mute scene taking place in the lighted cube of the store, the night gone black at its edges.

McEban doesn't hear the cup of liquor drop from his hand, or smell the splash of green stain. He doesn't feel his feet as they strike the gravel parking lot, and yet Bennett and the clerk and the rifle grow larger in their frame. And he cannot hear what Paul is saying to him. He tries. He tilts his head as he runs. The boy stands just before him, come into the middle distance, smiling, holding up a stringer of trout. McEban looks down at his legs. He can see them moving, his knees pumping toward his waist.

When he snaps his head up Paul has turned away from him, looking at the store, and beyond the boy there is Bennett. He backs through the doorway, his face turned to them, smiling over his shoulder.

McEban watches the red-faced teenager drop behind the counter, and he looks down. For just one instant. He looks down to find that it is Paul he has taken up in his hands. He has gripped the boy, and lifted him into the air. He feels himself pivot. He feels the weight of the boy slip from his hands and he watches the boy spill to the pavement. He watches the spinning rod snap under the boy's side. He watches the fish rise into the air, splayed along the stringer, their caudal fins fanned in stiff chevrons.

For just one instant there was the feel of the boy in and out of his hands. Rita will tell him later he was still running toward Bennett. She will tell him that when the clerk came up from under the counter he was still red in the face and the fluorescent lights were dull on his cheeks and forehead. She will say that she clearly saw the pistol buck in the young man's hands, and the plate-glass window scatter and the storelight splinter before them.

Ansel drove them to the sheriff's office and they stood across the desk from the man with blood on their shirtfronts, and on their sleeves, and Ansel told him what they'd found. He told him what they'd done, and if he didn't believe them he should come have a look for himself.

"Do you want a cup of coffee?" the sheriff asked.

They both said they didn't and walked next door to the attorney Jock used. Ansel told their story again.

The attorney pulled a file from a glass-faced cabinet and pushed his glasses to the top of his nose and wet a finger and leafed through the pages. "This is your father's will," he said to McEban. "The Rocking M is yours. Every single blade of grass."

McEban told the attorney to halve the deed with Ansel and that he'd come in at the end of the week and sign what needed to be signed.

"Maybe you should think about that," the attorney said, and McEban said he didn't have to. He said if the ranch was his he could do what he liked.

They walked to the truck and stood by the truck and looked in at the blood on the seat. The sun was stark and bright off the concrete, and there was a parking ticket flapping under a wiper blade.

Ansel leaned in through the side window and pulled a crowbar from behind the seat and walked to the front of the truck and beat on the hood until he was winded. And then he beat on it until he was done.

McEban wired the hood down to its latch and got in the truck and pulled away from the curb.

"I wish your daddy would have got to be a fisherman," Ansel said.

The night sky is black and blistered with stars and the starlight stings his eyes, and at the edge of the night there is Bennett's face, and Rita's, and the boy's. Soft, and shifting, like moonstruck clouds. There is the smell of asphalt, and cordite, and trout. And there is the sweet metallic odor of blood.

"What happened?" he asks.

Bennett has his pocket knife in his hands and is cutting McEban's shirt away from his shoulder.

"You're shot," Bennett says.

"When?"

"Right now."

McEban looks at the store. It is dropped to the very edge of his vision. He imagines he is looking through the wrong end of binoculars, but he can see the clerk standing in the frame of the front window, and the pistol in the young man's hands.

"Do you think he means to do it again?" he asks.

"Not tonight he won't," Rita says.

He watches her face rise away from him and he watches her walk directly to the clerk and stand in front of him. He watches her reach up with her right hand and grip the barrel of the pistol and hold it there, against her chest. She holds it until the young man averts his eyes, and loosens his grip, and sits down hard in the broken glass. He can hear the glass scrape against the tiled floor. He can hear the young man weeping. He can hear it plainly.

"There's something I have to tell you," he says to Bennett.

"There's a lot of blood," Bennett says. He strips his shirt off and wads it and presses it into McEban's shoulder.

"A lot of blood isn't always bad," McEban says.

"Yes, it is. It's always bad."

"I need to tell you about Gretchen and me."

"There's not one damn thing you need to tell me," Bennett says. "Not now, not ever."

In the dream she has fallen asleep and sprawled herself on the bed, and he stands by the side of the bed. He thinks to cover her, but knows his heart would break if he couldn't watch her sleep as she lies.

The moon has set and the night presses in. He lights a candle on the table by the bed, and the flame gutters and the darkness staggers against the walls and holds there, and her damp body glows.

He breathes himself full of the night, of her odors.

He sits on the edge of the bed and takes her hand in his. He presses the scallops at the base of her fingernails to his lips, one at a time, her hand curled over his own.

He turns her hand open and smoothes the palm. He stares dumbly at the map of lines. Life line. Health line. Heart line. He searches for evidence of their lives, his life, and her own. He whispers against her skin. He prays for a map of their souls.

Chapter Nine

❋

The old man holds a book up close to his face and silently mouths the words. He sits by McEban's shoulder, straight-backed and flat-lapped, in an overstuffed chair.

He's a sledge-headed old man, square-jawed, with gunmetal-blue eyes and slate-gray hair. His hair and eyebrows sprout wildly away from his skull. He wears a white shirt buttoned at his throat.

"Are you a priest?" McEban asks.

The old man lowers the book. He takes the right sidepiece of his eyeglasses and drags the glasses away from his face. He squints at McEban.

"I'm Gunnar," he says. "Have I changed so much I look religious?"

"You still outside Chadron, Nebraska?"

"So are you. Bennett drove you in here a night and a day ago."

"What are you reading?"

"Poetry. I've lost the patience for novels."

McEban looks up to the blood-filled IV bottle that hangs from a

sixteen-penny nail driven into the wallboard above his head. The tub-
ing snakes from the bottle's mouth into a needle taped to the inside of
his forearm.

"Are you still a vet?" he asks.

"I'm retired. Lucky for you I'm not long retired. Luckier still I ran
my practice out of my house."

"Is this horse blood, or cow?"

"It's mine," says Gunnar. "Seems we're sized out with the same
brand."

The old man gets up at the sound of a teapot whistling and walks
to the stove. He pours hot water into a cup-size French press and stirs
the coffee up into the water and lets it stand. He turns the heat on
under a stainless saucepot. "I made you some broth," he says. "It'll be
another day before you can handle whole food."

"Why am I in your kitchen?"

"Because it was easier to muscle that bed down the stairs, than you
up. I'm sorry about your dad."

McEban pushes into the mattress with his heels and his left elbow
and sits against the pillows. "That was twenty-two years ago."

"Well, I never said so before."

McEban blinks at the bandage that wraps his right shoulder. He
moves his arm slightly away from his side, testing the shoulder. It seems
just stiff. "This doesn't hurt like I thought it might."

Gunnar plunges the coffee to the bottom of the press and pours a
cup and leans back against the stove.

"I've kept a good dose of painkillers in you," he says. "And enough
antibiotic to cure a racehorse of the clap."

When the soup boils he tucks a dish towel under McEban's chin
and spoons the broth into McEban's mouth, one steady spoonful at
a time.

"How bad am I shot?" McEban asks.

"Your shoulder bone was fine," Gunnar says. "I trimmed out the ragged flesh and sewed you closed. Turns out the bullet went through and into the side panel of Bennett's truck."

There's a scratching at the kitchen door and Gunnar gets up and lets Woody in.

He says, "Lie down," and the dog does, and Gunnar sits again on the edge of the chair by the bed and tilts up the bowl and spoons out the last inch of broth.

"Where's Rita and the boy?" McEban asks.

"She's upstairs asleep. The boy is too."

"Where's Bennett?"

"He drove out of here the night we carried you in." Gunnar sits back in the chair. "He parked his rig in under the trees by the river. He said he thought the cops might be looking for it. I gave him the loan of my car. You want more broth?"

"I'm done."

Gunnar walks the bowl to the sink and runs it full of water. He turns back to McEban.

"Bennett said to tell you he thought he'd located his wife. He called this morning. I forget her name."

"Her name's Gretchen."

"You ever get married?"

"No, I haven't."

"Who's Rita belong to?"

"Herself," McEban says.

Gunnar nods. "How's my brother?"

"He's the same way he's always been."

"It must be that Ishawooa country," he says. "It strikes me that the lot of you do pretty much as you please."

"You miss him?"

"Who?"

"Ansel."

"I didn't know I was supposed to," Gunnar says.

He lit Ansel's oven and pulled a kitchen chair in front of the oven. He dropped the door and rested his stocking feet on it and drank his coffee. It was Thanksgiving and his father had been in the ground for six weeks. Ansel had called and said there was more work than he could manage, and McEban had driven home in his own truck.

He was nineteen and felt like a man. He felt limber and strong and limited by the responsibilities he knew were his. He felt the boundaries of his life strung around him as tautly as new wire. He felt the barbs on the wire.

Bennett came in without knocking and stood by the door and stomped his feet. When McEban didn't turn he stomped them again.

"Did Ansel take the stocktank heater into town?" McEban asked.

"He said he'd be back with it fixed by this evening. Or with a new one if it can't be fixed." Bennett pulled off his gloves and blew on his fingers. "I can't remember it getting this cold in November," he said. "Not all at once."

McEban flexed his toes. His feet were thawing and itched and he bent to scratch them. He'd been at work since dawn. "It's always some guy in town you hear bitching about the weather."

"I could live in town," Bennett said. "On a morning like this one town'd be just fine." His face had grown fat enough to furrow between his brows and crease at the corners of his eyes. "Are you going to stay in school?"

"Probably through the semester," McEban said. "I don't know whether I'll stay when we start to calve."

Bennett pulled a second chair to the oven and held his hands out to the heat. "Are you going to stay pissy all day?"

"I'm just making conversation."

Bennett looked at the coffeepot and the carafe was empty, and McEban saw him look and offered his cup.

"I'm fine," Bennett said.

They sat for another few minutes and Bennett said, "We didn't invite you to the wedding because we didn't think you'd come."

"I wouldn't have."

"That's what we thought."

McEban set his cup on the oven door and stood away from the stove. "I'm going to ride the north side of the creek and bring what pregnant cows I find down to the buildings."

"Won't they come down when you feed?"

"I want to make sure they're down. My dad wouldn't wait for them to come in on their own."

He bounced on the balls of his feet and it drove the warmth up as far as his knees.

"I'll ride up there with you," Bennett said.

"I guess you can do what you want."

They pulled on two stocking caps each, one over the other, and tied bandannas over their mouths so they wouldn't suck in the frozen air, and stamped their riding boots into fleece-lined overboots and buckled the overboots, and buckled on their chaps, and walked to the barn.

They caught up two horses and saddled them and stood up into the saddles. The horses groaned, and reined out stiffly, and swung their heads, and chomped at the steel bits that warmed in their mouths.

"I'm sorry," Bennett said.

McEban looked at him. His eyes watered in the cold and the tears froze on his cheeks. "I didn't think things would turn out the way they have."

"She didn't either," Bennett said.

They picked their way through the bared and brittle timber in the creek bottom, and the horses' hooves threw back clots of ice and snow, and the clots stood out in the dusting of snow like rinded gemstones. The tops of their thighs stung in the cold and their faces above the bandannas went raw. They shifted their reins from one hand to the other, as their hands numbed, and raised up in their stirrups, and thrust their empty hands in under their nuts, and sat back down on them to keep them warm.

They whipped the heifers they found out of their daybeds and started them down the creek. The cow's lashes and muzzles were frosted white, and their bellies hung low and taut, and their shit was frozen in their tails.

"I heard on the radio it's supposed to warm enough to snow," Bennett said.

"How much snow?"

"Enough to make the news, I guess."

And then the wind came up out of the west and the temperature rose, and they pulled off the bandannas and the air didn't rake at their lungs. The snow came in on the wind. It was wet and heavy and the flakes spun through the air as big as quarters. It melted against their cheeks, and stuck to their chests and arms and legs, and to the horses too.

Where the north fork of Horse Creek emptied out of its canyon McEban put his brown horse up the slope. He meant to gain the bench above the alluvial gutters. He gripped the horse's mane in his right hand and pulled himself forward off the horse's kidneys to help with the climb.

The brown horse slipped and fell to his knees, and scrabbled in the loose and frozen rock, and dug in with just the toes of his hooves, and slipped again. The wind came in gusts and the snow drove sideways down the drainage, and the horse stood for just a moment quivering against the sidehill, blowing in the snow-lashed air.

"You might want to come down off there," Bennett called from below.

McEban turned over his shoulder to say something like, no shit, and the horse tried the slope again, and lost his hindquarters, and came over backwards slow enough it seemed like a dream. McEban let loose of the mane and kicked free of the stirrups.

He thought that he wouldn't get dragged to death. That he wouldn't die in little bits. That's what he was thinking when he landed facedown, and the horse came down on top of him, and rolled away into the wind.

McEban comes awake in the night and lies still and listens to the gas heater tick and ping, and Gunnar's steady, bass snore. Woody stretches in his sleep, and there is the scrape of his nails as he sweeps the linoleum in a sudden burst of dream-chase. That is all there is. The house is pressed quiet and McEban wonders about the accumulation of snow. He has always been able to feel the weight of snow, the added silence that it spreads.

His shoulder throbs but the pain is not so stark it will keep him awake. More than the pain there is a sense of emptiness. He feels a curve of warmth against his good side and cracks an eye and lifts the sheet away and finds Paul asleep against his ribs. The boy's arm lies across McEban's chest. He's gripped up the Saint Christopher medal in his sleep and holds it in his small fist.

McEban drifts back to sleep and when he wakes a second time the room is gray with dawnlight and Gunnar is bent at his arm. The old man pulls the IV needle free and thumbs a ball of cotton against the vein.

"You figure I'm filled?" McEban asks.

Gunnar bends McEban's arm back against the cotton ball and stands away. "Your color's come up good." He yawns and stands a leg to his side and farts.

Paul sits up in the bed smiling at McEban. "Are you hungry?" he asks.

"A peanut-butter-and-honey sandwich is what I'm used to."

"I could make you one of those." He gets to his knees on the bed.

"When did you squirm in there?" Gunnar asks.

"When it started to snow," the boy says.

Gunnar walks to an uncurtained window and stares out into the soft light.

"This'll be the end of my garden. Except for the rootcrop," he says.

"How much did we get?" McEban asks.

"Three or four inches. It'll no doubt melt off by noon."

Paul scoots off the end of the bed and stands bare-legged at the kitchen counter. He wears just a pair of Jockey shorts and a T-shirt. He lines up the peanut butter and white bread and a plastic squeeze-bottle of honey. The honey bottle's shaped like a bear.

McEban swings his legs over the side of the bed and stands, and the room spins and lifts away and he sits back on the bed.

"You have to piss?" Gunnar asks.

"Like Jack the Green Bear."

"That's something my brother would say."

"That must be where I got it."

Gunnar hooks an arm around McEban's waist and steadies him to the bathroom off the hallway. He centers him in front of the toilet and stands beside him, his arm still around McEban's waist.

"I'm going to need you to look away," McEban says, and the old man stares into the corner past the medicine cabinet until McEban gets his stream started.

"Sounds like your prostate's in good shape."

"It's about the only thing left on me that hasn't been in an accident."

"How hard's Bennett trying to get himself killed?" Gunnar asks.

McEban looks up from the bowl.

"I don't think he's thought it out."

"What about you?"

"I just came along for the ride."

They both stare down at McEban's pecker.

"Do you think he means to hurt his wife when he finds her?" Gunnar asks.

"Alma doesn't think so."

"Who's Alma?"

"She's already dead," McEban says.

Gunnar nods. "You going to stand here forever shaking that thing?" he asks, and before McEban can answer the phone rings and Gunnar leans him against the bathroom wall, between a towel rack and the door, and walks back to the kitchen.

McEban hears the old man talking on the phone but cannot make out the words. He bends to flush the toilet and slides down the wall and settles in the corner behind the door and doesn't try to get back to his feet.

Gunnar steps into the doorway. "That was Bennett," he says. He doesn't look behind the door. He stands in front of the sink and speaks to McEban's reflection in the medicine-cabinet mirror. "He said he's found his wife a little ways outside Valentine."

"Was that all he said?"

"He said you shouldn't worry about him. He said he was sorry he got you shot. He asked if you were one-armed or two."

"How far is the drive to Valentine?" McEban asks.

"About a hundred and forty miles."

✳

He tried to get to his feet, and when his left foot struck the ground there seemed to be none of it there, just the splintering pain, and he spun away and sat hard and felt like he was still falling. His stomach came into his throat and he vomited, and his ears rang.

He opened his mouth and the wind filled him, and for a moment his head cleared. He crossed his left foot over his right knee. He gripped the heel of the boot and pulled and screamed and stopped pulling and looked around until he realized it was his own scream he'd heard. He gripped the boot again and pulled harder. The pain spiked up his leg clear to his gut, and then the boot came off and everything felt better than it had.

"How bad are you hurt?" Bennett called.

He looked away from the foot to Bennett and said, "My foot's broke," but the wind sliced the words into the swirl of snow and he had to shout again, "My foot's broke all to hell."

He felt hot and weak and like he might have to shit. He shouted, "Is my horse alright?"

"He's fine," Bennett said. He knelt behind McEban and hugged him around his chest and stood all at once. He dragged McEban away from the bottom of the hill, and steadied himself at the creekbank and took a deep breath. He squatted and hefted the weight altogether up in his arms and slid them both down onto the apron of stones beside the channel of ice and struggled to his feet again. McEban was up in his arms and Bennett staggered up the creek until he found an overhanging cutbank out of the wind.

He lowered McEban to the stones and helped him crawl in under the overhang and stumbled out into the dizzying white mess and came back with his arms filled with spruce boughs he'd beaten away from a tree. He leaned the boughs up against the cutbank to make them some sort of shelter and crawled in.

"Did you catch my horse?" McEban asked.

"We aren't going anywhere in this storm."

"Did you catch him?"

"He got by me."

"But he was walking?"

"He was running."

"What about yours?" McEban asked.

"He's tied to an aspen just above us."

There was the smell of broken evergreen, the faint musk of frozen soil. McEban laid his head back and stared up into the tangle of shredded roots that hung out of the undercut ground.

"You better have a look at my foot," he said.

"Right now?"

"You better look while we still have the light."

Bennett bit into the fingertips of his gloves and pulled them away from his hands and unbuckled the waiststrap of his chaps and unsnapped them from his legs. He rolled the chaps into a pillow for McEban.

"You cold?" he asked.

"I'm hot."

"You're hot?"

"Yes, I am," McEban said. "I feel like I'm burning up."

Bennett crawled to the broken foot and worked his pocket knife out of his jeans. The wind still howled and the snow fell against the pine boughs, and it sounded like something was digging its way to them. Something that had a long way to go.

"How's it look?" McEban asked.

"The sock's soaked with blood."

"Cut it off."

"I mean to."

Bennett lifted the elastic away from the ankle and eased the blade under it and sliced right down to the toe and sat back from the foot with the bloody sock in his lap.

"Did you get it off?" McEban asked.

"It's off."

"Are you going to tell me?"

"The bones are broken through," Bennett said.

"Where?"

"The top and bottom both. They've snapped and broken right through." Bennett pulled off his slicker and spread it over McEban's chest.

"I don't need it," McEban said. "I'm still hot."

"Your teeth are chattering."

"I can't help what my teeth are doing. The rest of me's hot."

"Just leave the slicker where it is," Bennett said. He got out of his jacket and shirt and peeled off his long underwear top and put the shirt and jacket back on again. "I'll be right back."

When he got back in under the slant of spruce boughs he wrung the last of the creekwater out of the undershirt and kicked a half-dozen head-size stones away from the frozen ground. He ringed the broken foot with the stones and knelt over the ring and gently tucked the wet cloth around the foot.

"Does this hurt?" he asked.

"What are you doing?" McEban raised his head from the rolled chaps.

"I'm trying to keep the bone-ends from drying out, but I'm worried your foot might get frostbit."

"I wouldn't mind if it froze solid. Is it still snowing?"

"Like it just remembered how," Bennett said.

❋

Gunnar lifts a gray-faced golden retriever onto the Formica-topped kitchen table. He takes up a pair of needle-nosed pliers and hooks an arm around the dog's neck and goes to work pulling the porcupine quills from its mouth and muzzle, a single quill at a time. The dog quivers and whines and Woody crawls under McEban's bed, and stays there, nosed into the far corner.

"Somebody want to give me a hand?" Gunnar asks.

The dog's owner moves to the table and rubs the retriever's ears, whispering, "There's my sweet boy. Yes, that's a brave dog," and Paul steps to Gunnar's side and works his hands into the ridge of thick fur along the dog's chest and smoothes its underbelly.

McEban sits in the soft chair by his bed. "Are there any physicists in Valentine?" he asks.

Gunnar looks at McEban over the tops of his glasses. He holds a bloody quill up in the pliers. "Physicists?"

"Kind of a bulked-up mathematician," McEban explains.

"I know what a goddamn physicist is. I'm just trying to remember if I heard that Stephen Hawking had plans to winter in Nebraska."

"There's the Renquist boy," the dog's owner says.

They all look at the woman.

"Adam Renquist got his doctorate in physics from Northwestern," she says. "He's raising sheep a couple miles south of Valentine on his folks' place. Out on Highway 20. He used to work in Denver but moved back when his folks retired to some old-people's compound outside of Phoenix."

"I need a better grip on this orange son of a bitch," Gunnar says. "He's got one broken off in the roof of his mouth."

The woman hugs her dog up against her breasts and sings, "There's my brave boy," and the dog moans, and then Gunnar has the last quill out. He sets the dog on the floor, where it sits begging until he brings a biscuit from his pocket and hands it down.

"It's a comfort to have neighbors with a trade," the woman says. She snaps a leash to her dog's collar, and turns to McEban. "You the guy chasing his wife across the West?"

"I'm the guy with the guy."

She cocks her head and studies McEban's face as though there are quills that have never been pulled out. "I suppose there's more than one way to serve the Lord," she says.

I'm cold now," McEban said.

Bennett nodded and lifted the slicker away and wriggled in against McEban's side. He bent his knees back so his legs wouldn't jostle the ruined foot. His mouth was just an inch from McEban's ear.

"Is that better?" he whispered.

"It probably will be. I can't hear the wind anymore."

"It let up," Bennett said. "The snow's just falling straight down."

They were quiet for a moment in the dense, wet silence.

"I shouldn't have put that horse up the slope," McEban said.

"I know it."

"You think he went back to the buildings?"

"Yes, I do."

McEban nodded. They could hear his hair scrape against the rolled chaps. "Do you love her?"

"Like fire," Bennett said.

McEban turned his head. "I'm warming up now," he said. There was enough light left that he could see Bennett blink. And Bennett's smile.

"I throw off a lot of heat," Bennett said.

McEban smiled too.

"Are you scared?" Bennett asked.

"A little bit. You?"

"Yeah."

"Thanks for acting like you're not," McEban said.

R ita stands with McEban on the screened porch off the kitchen. The sky has cleared and a halfhearted chinook has swept in from the southwest. They watch Paul sweep the inch of melting slush out of the back of Bennett's pickup and Woody take his place against the toolbox. Gunnar leads Aruba around the corner of the house and loads him in the trailer. The ground is dark with melted snow. In the shadows remain clods of grainy ice-crystal, shrunken to humps and rounded angles.

Rita leans into the doorjamb at the top of the steps and closes her eyes and sniffs at the warming air.

"The weather's changing," she says.

"We'll be fine as long as this wind holds."

"It finally smells like fall."

McEban eases his arm out of the sling draped around his neck and lifts the arm away from his side. The pain spikes up through his neck and sparks along his jawline.

"I'm going to need you to drive," he says.

Rita nods. She stares absently toward the river and holds an opened hand against the slight swell of her abdomen. She is not aware of where she rests the hand.

"What's it like to be pregnant?" he asks.

She drops the hand to her side. "Rodney tell you?"

"He said he'll help out with the costs when he gets out of school."

"I'm able to help myself." She smiles toward the river. "I like not having my period."

"You never hear about that being a major selling point."

She turns back to McEban. "I wish Alma would tell me whether it's a boy or a girl."

"Have you asked her?"

"I ask her every day." She places her hand high against her abdomen again and spreads her fingers. "The really bad news is I haven't got any sort of excuse for my bitchiness now. I haven't had day one of morning sickness." She looks down and scuffs at the porchboards with the heel of her shoe. "I'm worried I'll be a shitty mother."

"You'll probably be fine."

"I don't think being loving is something that comes naturally," she says. "Anyway, not for me."

"I'd help if you want," he tells her, and when she just stares at him, adds, "I can be good help."

She smiles and he digs the rose-colored stone out of his jeans and holds it up in the light. It flashes dull as a pearl. He thinks of his father's hands on its surface, and his grandmother's, and his own younger hands, oiling it with the scent of family.

"Why don't you give this to Paul when you get a chance?" he asks.

She cocks her head before the offered stone and holds out her hand. He lays the stone on her palm.

"Tell him he can keep it in his pouch with the rest of his treasures."

"If you want him to have it you should give it to him yourself."

"It's for both of you," he tells her. "You'll get the gift of the look on his face when he knows it's his."

He thought he must have fallen asleep because when he opened his eyes it was flatly black. He could feel Bennett still against him, could feel Bennett's even breath against his cheek.

"Are you awake?" he asked.

"I am," Bennett whispered.

"Is it still snowing?"

"I was afraid to check. You got to sleep and I didn't want to jar you awake."

"Why don't you check?" McEban asked. "And when you're up make sure there's nothing chewing on my foot. It feels like there is."

Bennett sat up in the dark. "Is it that bad?"

"It's real bad."

Bennett thumbed a lighter into flame and scooted on his butt out from under the spruce boughs and then right back in and snapped the lighter closed.

"It's quit," he said. "But there's a good two feet on the ground."

"Did you look at my foot?"

"There wasn't anything chewing on it."

"I hope your horse is still there."

"I hope so, too."

McEban got up on an elbow and the pain shot up his leg, and he knew his hands were shaking even though it was too dark to see them. He felt the tears run down his cheeks and he was breathing through his mouth.

"I'm crying," he said.

"I already did," Bennett told him. "While you had your nap."

Rita drives them through the small towns of Hay Springs, Clinton, Gordon, Merriman, and Kilgore. The towns advertise themselves from miles away, with the sunstruck flare of their grain elevators and water towers.

And in between the towns the early October light falls bronzed and buttery on the endless sweep of grazeland, on the fenced pastures of mown hay, on the descending ridges of cedar and pine.

There is an occasional planted windbreak, the leaves gone yellow and red and rust, and a house and shop and toolshed and outbuildings squared in its lee, and everywhere there are cattle. Cream-colored cows, beige, red, black, spotted cows.

Rita shifts on the seat behind the wheel. "Did you know there are more cows in Cherry County, Nebraska, than the whole state of Wyoming?"

"Then we ought to be able to find an affordable steak in Valentine," he says.

"I want pizza," says Paul.

The boy sits at the edge of the truckseat with his hand laid out on the dash. The rose-colored stone rocks in his cupped palm. "Did you buy this for me?"

"I found it," says McEban. "When I was a boy. I built a rock tumbler and put it in and it came out like that."

"Are there more stones like this one?"

"I guess there are. But that's the only one I ever found that color."

The boy sits back in the seat and holds the stone in his lap. He looks up at McEban. He looks concerned.

"Wouldn't you rather give it to Bennett?" he asks.

"I'd rather you had it."

"Has Bennett seen it?"

"Sure he has."

"When?"

"When we were boys."

"Anybody else?"

"My mom and dad and grandmother. And a man named Ansel."

"Is that everybody?"

"Now you and Rita."

Paul nods and pops the stone in his mouth and shifts it from cheek to cheek with his tongue. He breathes through his nose, and smiles around the bulge of the stone, and spits it back into his hand, freshly wetted and sparkling in the sunlight.

"What do you think would've happened if I'd've swallowed it?" he asks.

"I think you'd've lost your appetite for pizza," McEban says.

"You wouldn't have been mad?"

"I wouldn't have been mad."

"Do you think it would have come out?"

"First thing tomorrow morning, I imagine."

Paul brings the stone up inches from his nose and squeezes his eyes into slits.

"It looks like it belongs in a dream," he says. "Don't you think it does?"

McEban nods and Rita gears them down into Valentine and parks along the curb by the Pizza Hut, and they take a booth under a street-side window.

A blocky teenager sets plastic water glasses and silverware and paper napkins on the table and shifts her weight back solidly onto the heels of her red tennis shoes. She hums while they study their menus.

McEban looks at the nametag pinned to her shirtfront.

"I guess a deluxe," he says. "With everything but anchovies."

"And extra pepperoni," Paul says, and looks to McEban.

"You want a pop with that extra pepperoni?" he asks the boy.

"I'd like a Coke. A medium, please."

"Just tell Maxine, then," McEban says.

"Max," the waitress corrects.

McEban looks at her nametag again.

"I like Max better than Maxine," she says.

"I'll stick with water," says McEban.

Rita folds her menu. "I'll have the salad bar. And a glass of milk."

Max writes their orders on her pad and McEban sips his water and stares out at the truck and trailer. "Is Alma around?" he asks.

"In the booth here next to me," Rita says.

"Could you ask her about Bailey? If he's feeling okay?"

"Alma says he's feeling just fine."

McEban watches a truck and trailer park across the street. He watches Ansel step out of the truck and walk to the tongue of Bennett's trailer and crank the tongue away from the ballhitch. He watches the old man drive Bennett's truck to the corner and leave it idling, and unhook the ranch truck from its trailer.

"Do you know that man?" Paul asks.

"Yes, I do."

"Is he the old man who listens to Beethoven?" Rita asks.

McEban stands out of the booth. "He listens to Mahler too," he says. "I'll be right back."

Ansel backs the ranch truck under Bennett's trailerhitch and drops the safety chain over the ball and whistles Woody into the bed of the new rig. He tips his hat back from his face and smiles as McEban approaches.

"You getting something to eat?" he asks.

"A pizza," McEban tells him.

"Pizza sounds good."

"It looked good on the menu."

"What happened to your arm?" Ansel asks.

"I got shot."

"I can't remember you ever did that before."

"I got in the middle of an armed shoplift."

Ansel steps onto the sidewalk. "I had to go clear to France to get shot," he says. "If I'd've known I could have done it at home I could've missed a whole war."

"You come down here to bring me home?"

Ansel points his chin to the trailer across the street. "I came down here to sell cows," he says. "I had six open heifers in the trailer just there."

"You get tired of the truck you were driving?"

Ansel lifts his hat away from his head and scratches his head and reseats the hat. "I thought you might like to drive something that didn't have a bullet hole in it. It catches the eye."

McEban looks back to the Pizza Hut. The windows glare white and blue.

"Bennett in there?" Ansel asks.

"No, he's not."

A Highway Patrol cruiser passes in the street and McEban steps his slung arm against the truck's side panel, and Ansel moves in front of him and nods to the trooper and the trooper nods back. They watch the car until it turns the corner at the light.

"Thank you," McEban says.

"I don't guess anyone's looking for an old man," Ansel says.

The wind lifts the streetdust and the people out on the sidewalk tuck their heads against the grit. McEban looks at the ranch trailer.

"Were those the only open cows we had?"

"Just the six," Ansel says.

McEban nods and humps his back into the lifting wind, and the cop cruises past again and he doesn't bother to step his shot arm away.

"I might bring some people home with me," he says.

"What kind of people?"

"A woman and a boy. The woman's pregnant."

Ansel pulls a pouch of Red Man from his shirt pocket and gathers out a wad and works the wad into his cheek. "Is this for permanent?"

"Probably just for the winter. Maybe not even for that. I'm not sure they'll come."

"Are you in love?"

"It's not like that," McEban says.

Ansel nods and pulls a string of tobacco from his mouth and snaps it away. "Is the boy big enough to be some help?"

"He's plenty big enough."

Ansel spits into the street. "It's your house."

"I know it's my house. You give up smoking?"

"Just giving my lungs a rest," Ansel says. The pickup door stands open and he leans in against the edge of the seat.

"I don't know what else to talk about," McEban says.

"You need anything out of your rig?"

"There's a few things in the toolbox."

Ansel pushes away from the seat and they walk across the street to the tailgate of Bennett's truck, and McEban steps onto the bumper and into the bed. He hands down his duffel and Rita's backpack and a bedroll and Ansel stacks them by the tire, and McEban steps out of the truckbed. He shoulders his duffel on his good arm and Ansel brings the rest. They load the gear in the ranch truck and Ansel spits against the curb. McEban stares down at his boots. "I saw Gunnar," he says. "He sewed up my arm. Maybe you'll want to stop and see him on your way home."

"Is he sick?"

McEban levels his head. "He looked fit to me."

"Then I guess I'll just go home. Gunnar and I catch up on the phone every Christmas, and lately on the Fourth of July."

"I thought he might've called you," McEban says. "I thought that was why you drove all the way down here to sell cows."

Ansel wipes his mouth on the back of his forearm. "Gunnar got worried for you," he says. "He's no good when he worries. He called because he couldn't stand the worry."

McEban looks down at his boots. "Maybe I ought to get off the street before that cop wants another look at me. Thanks for trading out these trucks."

Ansel nods. "Gunnar's family," he says. "The man doesn't need me to stop by and tell him I love him. It's not something he'd forget."

"I guess I'm just feeling old," McEban says.

"Hell, I'm the one that's old," Ansel tells him. "You're just done being young."

Bennett threw the spruce boughs back and scrabbled up the creek-bank and slid down, and went up and down three more times to trench out the snow. The last time down he kicked a series of shelving footholds for himself, so he might not fall when he carried McEban out.

He rolled the rocks away from McEban's foot and lifted the wet underwear away and struck the lighter into flame.

"How's it look?" McEban asked. He was panting and couldn't quit.

"It looks just like it did before. I'm going to wrap it up."

"Do it fast."

Bennett pocketed the lighter and gently sacked the undershirt around the foot, gathering the bottom and neck at McEban's ankle, and tying it together with the sleeves.

McEban began to whine, and was still whining, up high in his chest and thought he might need to scream. Bennett took him by the hands and pulled him up onto his good foot, and steadied him where he hopped. He caught his balance and settled.

"You ready?" Bennett asked.

McEban nodded. He wasn't sure Bennett could see him nod, but Bennett turned and crouched and reached back and hefted him up piggyback, and then hefted him higher. McEban circled his arms over Bennett's shoulders and gripped his right elbow with his left hand.

A quarter moon had come up in the gauzy sky and the snowcover gathered the weak light and they stood for just a moment blinking out at the soft, gray world, and then Bennett took just one step up the creekbank, and the next, and the one after that, slowly, and when he got to the top, turned down the creek, shuffling ahead through the thigh-deep snow.

"Where's your horse?" McEban asked.

"There was just the bridle reins where I had him tied."

"Why didn't you tell me?"

"Because I wasn't sure I could even get you up away from the creek." Bennett moved ahead steadily, huffing, and when McEban's weight settled lower against his hips, he stopped and hefted his friend up higher on his back.

"Are you sure you can do this?" McEban asked.

"I'm sure."

"If you get tired I could stand down until you catch your breath."

"I'm not going to get tired," Bennett said. "How's your foot feel?"

"It feels better than when I was lying down. How come you have a lighter with you?"

"I borrowed it from my dad."

"Do you have cigarettes too?"

"My mom says smoking keeps her thin," Bennett said.

"You aren't that fat."

"Yes, I am that fat." Bennett stopped and leaned his forehead into an aspen trunk to rest, McEban straddling his hips.

"Things aren't ever going to be the same. Are they?" McEban asked.

"You're going to be a gimp. That's for certain."

"That's not what I meant."

Bennett was breathing in huffs. "I know that's not what you meant," he said, and then, "No, things aren't going to be the same. Not for me, or you, or her either."

✳

They drive southeast out of Valentine and the sky has dulled and the wind picked up steady out of the west.

McEban looks at Rita, at the side of her smooth face. She downshifts past a row of mailboxes along the edge of Highway 20 and Paul reads aloud the name "Renquist" stenciled on the side of a box, and Rita gets the truck stopped without jackknifing the trailer and backs up even with the mailboxes.

"Where to now?" she asks.

"I guess there," says McEban, meaning the dirt-and-gravel track that curves away to the northeast.

She nods and turns onto the road and a mile out into the sandhills the wind blows harder still. The light talc the truck raises sweeps ahead of them and they put up their windows and open the floor vents.

"What are you going to do after we find Bennett?" she asks.

"I'm going back home," says McEban.

"To Wyoming?"

McEban fills himself up with the overwarm air and holds it high in his chest. "You could come if you want," he says. "I've got rooms I don't use. I wouldn't bother you if you came."

She looks down at Paul. "What do you think?"

"Are there horses?" the boy asks.

"There's a dozen of them," says McEban.

Paul nods and brings his heels up against the seatedge.

"Do you have MTV?" Rita asks.

"I'm not sure I can get whatever that is," McEban says. "Maybe if I bought a satellite dish I could."

"I'm just messing with you, Barnum," she says. "Is there a town near where you live?"

"Ishawooa," he says and her cheeks lift into her eyes. She looks back down to the boy. The boy smiles too.

"Why is 'Ishawooa' funny?" McEban asks.

"It's not," she says but she cannot relax her smile.

"It sure seems like it's funny." He looks back and forth at their grinning faces.

"It's what my grandfather used to call the BIA agent," she says. "It's a Shoshone word."

The boy bends his smile into his lap.

"A bartender told me it means to lie down against something un-comfortable," McEban says.

Rita pulls a handkerchief from her skirt pocket and wipes her eyes and holds the handkerchief in front of her mouth. "I don't want you to see me laughing," she says.

"But I can see that you are. I can hear you laughing."

"I don't want you to see me this happy." She wipes her eyes again and asks her brother to pinch her leg to ruin her smile. When he does, she says, "It doesn't mean lying down next to anything. It means not telling the truth. It means 'lying prick.'"

"Bullshit."

She asks Paul to pinch harder. "It's pronounced with a 'j' or a 'g' sound after the first 'a,'" she says. "Harder," she tells the boy, and then, "There's an accent over the last 'a.' Ishajwooá."

McEban leans into the armrest. "You're telling me I went to high school in Lying Prick, Wyoming?"

"Where'd you think you grew up?"

McEban opens his mouth to answer and Paul says, "There it is," and points ahead to Gunnar's red Subaru wagon parked just off the chalk-white road. Rita pulls in behind the car and kills the engine and the wind rocks the truck. She's still smiling but she's put her handkerchief away.

The car sits at the edge of an oval of sand where the grassland has worn away from the surrounding hills.

"You sure it's Gunnar's?" McEban asks.

"It's the right color and the right bumper sticker," she says.

The bumper sticker reads: NATIVE AMERICANS HAD LOUSY IMMIGRATION LAWS.

McEban steps out of the truck and looks in through the car windows and comes back and stands by the truck.

"Is Bennett's rifle in the car?" she asks.

McEban shakes his head. "How do you suppose a town got named 'Ishawooa'?"

"How would I know?" She looks past his shoulder. The sandhills rise and fall away behind him. "Maybe some white guy asked some Shoshone guy where he was and the Shoshone smiled at him and said, 'Ishajwooá.'"

He tests his arm and winces. "That's probably what happened."

"I'll think about your offer." She looks down at Paul. "We'll both think about it."

McEban nods and looks to the west. "I better go find Bennett."

"I think I won't," Rita tells him. "I think I'll stay right here." She pulls the truckdoor shut, and McEban walks to the back of the truck and tells Woody to stay.

Bennett stopped only twice to lean into a tree to catch his breath and he never put McEban down. Not once.

And then they heard the horse before they saw it and Bennett called out, and a flashlight beam shone in his face, and Ansel spurred the horse right to them and stepped down into the deep snow.

"How bad are you hurt?" Ansel played the flashlight down McEban's leg and they all stared for a moment at the blood-soaked undershirt knotted at the end of the leg.

"I'm going to need to go to the hospital right away," McEban told him. "Did my horse come in?"

"Yours and Bennett's both. I had to wait until the snow let up before I could get out after you. I rode up on the bench first and didn't find you."

"How far are we from the buildings?" Bennett asked.

"Probably two hundred yards is all," Ansel said.

"I want to take him the whole way."

Ansel shone the flashlight into Bennett's face. "I can put him on this horse."

"I want him to take me," McEban said.

Ansel shifted the light to McEban's face and then turned it off. They stood for a moment letting their eyes adjust. And then they heard the stirrup leather squeal when Ansel stood up on his horse.

"Shuffle along where I broke the trail," Ansel said.

"I will," Bennett told him.

"I'll have the pickup chained up by the time you're there."

They heard the horse dig in and the muffled hoofstrikes and Bennett stood just holding him.

"I told you I could do this," he said.

McEban crosses the road and down through the borrow ditch and seats his hat against the wind and bows his head. The wind is hot and stiff and lifts the grasshoppers out of the seedtops, and they rain against his thighs and die broken in the grass.

He finds Bennett just thirty yards on the other side of the crest of the first big hill to the west. He lies belly-down, lifted up on his elbows, pointing the rifle toward a stand of buildings arranged across a spring-fed slough at the hill's bottom.

McEban squints into the wind. The slough is choked with cattails and on the flat beyond there's a small blue house and a barn and a row of weathered lambing sheds. Cottonwoods grow along the irrigation ditches and rattle in the wind, and from this distance look to be just slants of yellowed steam escaped from fissures in a newly cracked earth. A tractor and swather and baler are parked against the leeside of the barn.

A man and two black-and-white border collies work a couple hundred ewes and this year's lambs through a gate and into a holding pen.

The sheep bleat and turn away in drifts and the dogs mold them back through the gate, and when the last of them are through a woman walks the gate closed and stands up on the fence next to the man.

The sun catches in the woman's hair, and it flashes red as flame.

McEban walks down the slope and sits in the thick grass by Bennett's side. He doesn't take his eyes from Gretchen. He hopes she won't look their way and wonder why two men sit in her pastureland, watching in this wind.

"It's a nice little place," Bennett says. "Don't you think it's a nice little place?"

The rifle is still up in his hands. He hasn't taken his eye from the scope. His voice is phlegmy and choked.

"You crying?" McEban asks.

"Not so much anymore."

"You do me a favor?"

"I will if I'm able."

Beyond the man and the woman and the sheep the sky is massed black and gray and purple, and before it, stabbed into the earth, just the blunt and broken end of a rainbow. As though some comet has smashed there into the earth and left the bright evidence of its effort.

"Look at me," McEban says.

"Is that all?"

"Just put the rifle down and look at me."

Bennett lowers the rifle into the grass and turns to McEban. His face is swollen and yellow and red and in places gone dark as eggplant. The skin has split above his eyebrows and his eyes are blackened and glazed and run with blood, and he dabs at them with a kerchief he holds wadded in his hand. He swipes at the smear of snot that runs from his nose.

"What do you think the chances are of getting snakebit this late in the year?" Bennett asks and pushes his chest away from the matted grass and pulls out the limp body of the rattler. "It's this goddamn warm weather," he says. "I crawled right on the little fucker. He tried to squirm away, but then he got confused."

He tosses the dead snake ahead of him, down the slope, and McEban blinks at the set of fang marks at the top of Bennett's nose.

"We've got to get you to town right now."

Bennett chokes and coughs, and hacks up a gob of venom-stained spittle. He tries to smile, but his lips won't pull away from his teeth.

"I guess I should've been to town three hours ago."

He rolls onto his back and McEban lifts him up against his thighs and holds him there.

"It might not be too late," he says. "You don't know that it's too late."

"You think I could stand the amputation?" Bennett asks, and laughs and coughs, and when he stops, the slaver that runs from his mouth is spotted with blood. "I never did put any shells in this rifle."

"I never thought you did."

"I just wanted you to know."

The wind has turned sharp and the light is damped from the air. McEban looks to the west. The horizon is bruised as Bennett's face and roiling and risen into an entablature of night-stained cloud.

"There's the way winter comes," Bennett says.

"Goddamn you."

Bennett takes an envelope from his shirt pocket. It's folded in half. "This was in Valentine." He hands it to McEban. "I think she said all she had to say to me."

The envelope is addressed to McEban and unopened. He tears the end off and lifts the paper out and it snaps in the wind. He holds it against Bennett's shoulder and reads:

> Dear Barnum,
>
> If I could have carried our son to term I would have named him Bennett. Wouldn't that have been fine? Besides me you are now the only person who knows this, or needs to. May God forgive us all.
>
> Love,
> Gretchen

They hear a sound on the wind and look up the slope, and there is Paul at the top of the hill. He sits alone in the grass and the wind snatches at his hair and blouses his shirt.

"That's a good boy," Bennett says.

"Yes, he is. He's first-rate."

Bennett rolls his head toward the buildings and sheep and dogs. "You aren't going down there to bother her, are you?"

"No, I'm not."

"You want to tell me what the letter said?"

McEban folds the letter into Bennett's shirt pocket and rests his hand there, against the pocket. "It says she loved you best."

Bennett nods and settles against McEban and closes his eyes. His mouth hangs open and his tongue is thickened in his mouth.

"You could have come into town," McEban says. "You had time to come in."

"I meant to," Bennett says. "Just as soon as I got tired of looking at her."

McEban hugs Bennett to him until his back aches, and then he stands and slings the rifle strap. He squats and gets Bennett up in his arms and stands leaning into the hillside. He can feel the stitches tear in his shoulder and the welcome jag of pain, and when he gets close enough so the boy can see what he has, Paul runs ahead and drops the tailgate and puts Woody in the cab.

"Is he dead?" the boy whispers.

"Just a little bit ago," McEban tells him.

They skid the body onto the truckbed and McEban gets in with it and the wind tears at him, and he sits there until it's dark and the snow has started to fall.

Rita and Paul wait in the cab. They run the heater and the boy kneels on the seat, watching through the back window.

When the storm has pressed all the light from the sky and McEban cannot feel his hands or feet he staggers against the wind and gets over the side panel and into the cab.

Rita turns on the domelight and after a few minutes in the heat his face runs wet with the melted snow, and she pulls an arm out of her jacket and wipes his face with the empty sleeve.

"I'm sorry," she says. "Alma says he's okay. She says his people were waiting for him."

McEban nods and wonders if his memory is accurate enough to construct who he might now be. He wonders if he would exist if his mind was lost, or if it would matter. If he is kept alive only in the memories of his dead.

"Do you believe it?" he asks.

"Yes, I do," she says. "It's exactly what I believe."

"I'm his people too."

"You're bleeding," she says.

He looks down at his shoulder and she rips his shirt away and makes a bandage of some sacking she finds behind the truckseat and binds the wound, and turns off the domelight.

"You want to sit out here all night?" she asks.

He looks at her, stares at her, and then at the boy. Paul blinks slowly and smiles and bows his head. He curls down against McEban's hip, and McEban smoothes the boy's hair, feeling him shift and settle under the comfort of his hand.

"We better get the body to town," McEban says.

"And then what?" Rita asks.

"And then it'll be tomorrow and I'll trailer Gretchen's horse back out here and tell her she's a widow. If you'll ride with me we can get Gunnar's car while we're here."

"What about the law?" she asks.

"I'll check tomorrow to see if they want me." He looks through the back window but there is only the swirl of snow in the night. "He'll need a memorial," he says. "I'll take him home for that."

Rita starts the truck. In the headlights the prairiescape comes crystalline and rippling in against them. She dims the lights.

"Will you come with me?" he asks.

She turns to him. Her hair catches green and red in the dashlights.

"How about right now we get in out of this weather." She eases the truck out onto the drifting two-track. The tires bite and squeal against the snow. "Maybe I'll come for a while, Barnum," she says. "Maybe just until the baby's born."

In the dream the candle's flame stirs the room. Her body drifts and begins to sink. She is sinking away from him and the candlelight wavers and sucks as water does. Like that. He feels her falling and tightens his grip. His hand gripping hers. And then with both hands. He shuts his eyes.

He hears the horses outside rear and strike at their leads and squeal, and stand shifting, quivering in the night—the pale and the dark alike. They lower their heads and snort at the ground, and stand listening to the promise of water beneath them. A stream run underground. All of it. Fish and foam and all.

And then it is her voice he hears. Clearly. Softly.

"It is a boy," she whispers. She smiles but does not open her eyes. "Tell my sister it's a boy," she whispers. "In her belly it's a boy."

The words rise against his face, his tongue. They taste of salt. And they taste of mercy.

Acknowledgments

When I became lost in this book it was my wife, Virginia, who walked me home, who cared for these words. I am grateful for the blessing of her. I am indebted to Dawn Marano, my once editor and always friend, and Laura Shepherd, for carrying *Rivers* east. Maggy Rozycki Hiltner and Annette Wenda own my considerable thanks; I'm grateful to Donna Gershten, for the example of her fine writing and the gift of her laughter; my brother, Richard, for his quiet and thoughtful review of the manuscript; Kent Haruf, for his friendship, guidance, and the inspiration of his fierce music; Nancy Stauffer, whose care and good advice I hope never to be without; Julie Grau, for her embrace of, and belief in, these pages.

About the Author

MARK SPRAGG is the author of the memoir *Where Rivers Change Direction*, winner of the 2000 Mountains and Plains Bookseller Award. He lives in Wyoming.